# Unearth The Tides

# ALSO BY ALISSA J. ZAVALIANOS

---

*The Earth-Treader*
*The Wishing Seed*
*Endlewood*

SHORT STORIES
*From the Mountains to the Valley*

COMING SOON
*Aliferous*

# Unearth the Tides

## Alissa J. Zavalianos

Scripture quotation taken from the New International Version of the Bible



Printed in the United States of America

Cover by Miblart
Map by Alissa J. Zavalianos
Edited by Caitlin Miller
Proofreading by Micaiah Keough
Interior Artwork from Canva

ISBN 979-8-9881439-1-8 (paperback)
ISBN 979-8-9881439-0-1 (hardcover)
ISBN 978-1-7361371-9-2 (ebook)

# Unearth the Tides

"Fans of adventure, redemption, and Jules Verne will enjoy *Unearth the Tides*, and the depth its characters reach in this imaginative and wholesome retelling."

— NOVA MCBEE, award winning
author of the *CALCULATED* Series

"Do you hear the gulls calling to you? Do you smell the salty spray of the sea crashing at your feet? A classic story retold in a heart-pounding, soul-soaring fantasy as hypnotic and enthralling as the ocean deep where it is set, Unearth the Tides is nothing short of an invitation to embark upon one of the most magical and mysterious adventures of your life. All you need to do is walk up the gangplank and set sail upon the Wasteful Tides. Only one question remains: Are you ready to be swept away into worlds unknown and uncover the secrets that lie beyond the water's edge?"

— CHELSEA BOBULSKI, author of
*THE WOOD, REMEMBER ME,* and
*ALL I WANT FOR CHRISTMAS* Series

"Perfect for young hearts who desire a new adventure and old souls who long for the familiarity of the classics, *Unearth the Tides* is told with nautical flair and wit, subtly weaving in Scripture alongside a splash of mystery with memorable characters, wholesome romance, and Zavalianos' signature cozy atmosphere. All aboard! This is a voyage you won't want to miss!"

— ERIN PHILLIPS, author of *A CROWN
OF CHAINS* and *A BOND OF BRIARS*

"Zavalianos is a storytelling master with her extraordinary ability to create stories that beg to be both savored and devoured. *Unearth the Tides* is a heartfelt adventure and a fantastic twist on a well-loved classic. Zavalianos puts her signature touch on this magical piece, gently but unwaveringly pointing readers to God and sharing powerful truths within her beautifully written words."

— ERICA DANSEREAU, author of
*COME FORTH AS GOLD*

"*Unearth the Tides* will sweep you off your literary feet and transport you to a world you'll never want to leave. With elements of mystery, a cast of characters who hold your heart, and thrilling adventure coupled with a heartwarming romance, Zavalianos' retelling is magical, intriguing, and attention-holding. Reminiscent of Amanda Dykes and Joanna Ruth Meyer's master storytelling, *Unearth the Tides* is not to be missed!"

— CAITLIN MILLER, author of
*THE MEMORIES WE PAINTED* and
*OUR YELLOW TAPE LETTERS*

"Equal parts dangerous intrigue and delightful adventure, this cozy fantasy hides more secrets than it has any right to. Alissa Zavalianos brings a fresh take to Jules Verne's classic, interweaving the story with soul-touching truths and themes of mercy and forgiveness."

— JANE MAREE, writer and director
of the *THE NEBULOUS SAGA*

"Alissa's newest adventure story is another win in her repertoire. Told from the point of view of a man on the run, readers will joyfully come aboard for the page-turning plot twists, characters with suspicious backstories, an unexpected love interest, and a message of mercy. Alissa has the gift of crafting stories that stay with the reader long after the last page has turned."

— JORDAN TAYLOR NILAN, author
of *MARZIPAN'S FIRST CHRISTMAS*

"I saw the enigmatic individual as essentially pitiless and cruel, as he was forced to be. I felt him as being beyond the pale of humanity, insensible to feelings of pity, the remorseless enemy of his fellow beings, against whom he must have sworn an undying hatred."

— Jules Verne, *20,000 Leagues Under the Sea*

THE HERRING SEA
NESKA
KETHNAR
STRAITS OF KETHNAR
THE WASTEFUL TIDES
VASTIA
N
W E
S
EDGEFOLD
GREYMIST
CASTLE FARRADOR
BRAKA
FYRANDELL
LAMMERSMITH

# Table of Contents

# $\mathcal{P}$ROLOGUE

## A Legend

"$\mathcal{B}$eware the Wasteful Tides should the Crimson Death take you."

My mother's words filled our small kitchen, making all the hairs on my arms stand on end. I'd heard the stories many times, but they always had the same effect. They terrified me, but I couldn't wait to hear them again.

"That's how the lore of the green waters always begins and ends." She smiled, but somehow, she looked sad. "And with that, my sweet Huxley, it's time for bed."

"Bed? But the sun is still in the sky!" I whined. "If Father were home, he'd let me stay up longer."

"If he were home," she laughed, "he'd tell you to listen to your mother."

I sighed. She was right. My father was a royal guard in the castle—a role I was being trained for. Obedience was a strict code for Royal Guards. He guarded Prince Albertus, and someday, I hoped I'd guard one of the princes, too.

But tonight, I just wanted to stay up late.

I gripped the chair's cushioned arm as if it would prolong the inevitable trek to bed, watching the candlelight flicker against the walls. It writhed like tentacles, reminding me of the stories.

"Do you think there's really something out there, Mum?" I asked the same question I always did whenever she talked about the Wasteful Tides.

I didn't like the idea of an unknown creature haunting the sea. Since before I learned how to walk, I'd been told the stories. But the Edgefold beacon was always lit; it'd illuminate the beast if it ever came close. Surely Mr. Bates would send it running if that were the case.

Besides, ships docked in the harbor every couple of weeks, coming and going from Braka's ports. So, the waters couldn't be *that* dangerous.

"I think it's always best not to let our imaginations get away from us, especially when we're twelve and should be in bed." My mother winked, ushering me to my cot.

I heaved a defeated exhale, dragging my feet across the wooden floor.

Once beneath the cotton folds of my comforter, my head hardly on the pillow, I attempted one more question. "When will you tell me the stories again?"

My mother laughed, smoothing back the hair from my face before kissing my forehead. "Tomorrow, Huxley. When Father's home."

I frowned, then nodded. I loved it best when we were all together anyway.

As she left me to fall asleep, my mind drifted back to the Crimson Death. The legend felt real enough to be true. Enough to haunt my dreams on the nights it was freshest.

A shudder coursed through my body as my mother's words thumped inside my chest.

*"Beware the Wasteful Tides, Huxley, should the Crimson Death take you."*

I pulled the covers up around my neck, unaware that would be the last time I'd ever hear the story from her lips again.

BEWARE THE

WASTEFUL TIDES

SHOULD THE

CRIMSON DEATH

TAKE YOU

# ONE

## Treason

*Sixteen Years Later*

Garbled sounds, like wheezing or choking, echoed along the corridor, standing out against the usual noises of Castle Farrador's keep. It was enough to rouse me from my stupor. I cracked open heavy eyelids and rubbed my pate where a large bump above my left temple throbbed—fire-hot to the touch.

Apprehension rose in my gut, threatening to take hold. I shouldn't be on the ground; a guard's eyes and ears should always be keen.

*What happened?*

I heard it again. More choking. Gasping. Struggling.

Shifting my body, I reached for the sword at my waist as it knocked against my thigh. I leaned forward, listening. My fingers twitched on the hilt, the triple-time tempo of my heart beating in sync with the pulsing dizziness behind my eyes. Feeling my heart hammering in my chest reminded me of the need to breathe, to curb the rising panic.

A violent scream shook the halls. The queen's? The shrill cry stretched across the stone floor and snaked up my ankles, my legs, my middle, before rattling my bones.

I clenched my jaw, wondering where the other guards were. *Are we under siege? How long has the prince been unguarded?*

Pushing to a stand, I stumbled forward. The room spun, but I shook it off and started running down the hallway.

On the walls, pictures of familiar faces rushed past me in the opposite direction. Of the king's three sons—Albertus Gerard Barrington III, Clark Guthrie Barrington, and Tristan Albertus Barrington—and his wife and himself. Other paintings depicted a warrior slaying a monstrous beast at sea: a crimson creature rumored to haunt the very waters at Braka's doorstep.

I kept running, and the familiar images blurred together in a swath of color, my vision losing focus once again. The only face that stood out clearly was that of the second son with his amber eyes and blond hair—the rarest of combinations.

He was the new heir apparent. The hope of Braka. My charge.

*I must find Prince Clark. My life depends on it. Maybe his, too.*

A turn here. Another there. A few doorways on my left and right. Nothing.

*Where is he?*

My head pounded like a hammer to an anvil. But it was the sound bellowing behind me which sent shivers up my spine.

"Stop him!" a man shouted.

*Stop who?*

I recognized the voice; it was as familiar as the prince's. But this one rang with a different tone. Rageful like a tempest. Unrelenting. The king's—His Majesty Albertus Gerard Barrington II.

"Seize that blackguard!" he shouted again.

*Blackguard?*

My stomach dropped. I needed to find Prince Clark. Assume my position.

"How he runs from his guilt! Murderer!" The king's accusation hung in the air like a dagger. But over *who* was the question.

A glance over my shoulder showed five of my fellow men-in-arms, their pursuit hot on my heels.

*Why in the blast are they chasing me?*

King Barrington was a few paces behind them, clacking along with his cane, his red robes contrasting with the paleness of his gray hair. His outstretched arm pointed in my direction.

I couldn't ignore the way his final accusation rattled inside my chest.

*Murderer. Me? He can't mean me.*

There was no time to reason it out. The weapons pointed at my back showed just how far my reasoning would take me…

I had no death wish.

I bit back a groan. For all my years of service in Castle Farrador, I couldn't remember the keep's corridors stretching this long. I descended a flight of stairs and rounded a corner, my presence disrupting the flickering torches along the walls.

Heavy footfalls echoed behind me. They were gaining.

I fled the remainder of the keep and entered the outdoor

battlements along the curtain wall, sucking fresh air into my lungs. The deciduous boundary in the distance stood green against the backdrop of a darkening sky, the trees a welcome sight from all the gray stone of the castle. What I needed was an exit, but at this time of day, I knew the portcullis was down and there was no way I could escape freely. If only I had thought to use one of the secret passageways I'd stumbled upon as a child, escaping from a hidden door to the outside.

Now it was too late; no use back-tracking.

I rushed toward a turret, pushing open the door and descending another flight of stairs. My heart pounded against my ribs, adrenaline keeping me going.

Everything was spinning, and my head begged for relief, but the knot in my chest loosened a fraction when I saw a large window. I hoisted myself onto its ledge, positioning my body just so.

I paused only long enough to look down, swallowing hard.

*Am I insane?*

Icy pressure sliced through my right shoulder. I'd just been stabbed; the cool of the metal suddenly turned blazing hot. Red and black overtook the greenery of the outdoors as my vision clouded over.

*Yes. Yes, I am.*

I forced myself to jump, gravity pulling my body down like a grindstone before the hands of men who had treated me as a comrade and now as a criminal could clamp down on me and drag me away from my only means of escape.

What I wouldn't give for a moat to catch my fall. But what Castle Farrador lacked in water defense, it doubled up with an extra gate. Little use that would serve me now.

I landed with a heavy thud upon a bed of grass and granite, my left leg breaking my fall. Pain shot up the appendage with a violence I was all too familiar with since joining the ranks of a royal guard and soldier.

*Broken.*

I groaned, vomiting into the blades of grass. The taste of blood mixed with that of my emptied dinner, and it took everything in me not to heave again. I wiped my sleeve across my mouth.

Laughter rained down from the fortified walls, the derisive tone igniting a bitterness that burned inside my core. If they wanted me dead, why not kill me outright? I was also a lefty. Not much stabbing my right arm would do, unless they hoped the fall would kill me instead.

I raked my gaze over the castle wall and tracked the few yards I'd plunged to the earth. I paused when I saw my comrade, Hugh, standing in the window, his sword tip stained with blood. My blood. A moment of remorse passed over his features, and it was then that I had my answer. He believed me a traitor, but his mercy in sparing my life was based upon years of friendship. A friendship that had apparently just run its course; all traces of brotherhood were gone.

My hand instinctively moved to my chest, the organ inside almost hurting worse than my shoulder and my leg.

The king staggered forward, looking down on my discarded body. He sneered. "Still alive, Huxley? That drop should have killed you!"

That was something I knew all too well.

"We Gannons are made of tougher stuff than this." I grimaced, leaning forward on my good knee. I silently cursed my aching body. I needed to make heads or tails of this. To find out what was going on… "Your Majesty—"

"Silence!" he barked, his scowl deepening. "Not another word from you. I won't have Clark's killer poison *me* too, though it be with just his words."

*Clark's killer? The prince is dead?* The news sent bile to my throat. It couldn't be. Not…not Clark. Please. "This is absurd!" My lungs burned, and my left hand found my sword once more.

"I said not another word!" the king yelled, motioning with his finger as two guards pushed forward with bows.

*Confound it. They're going to shoot me.*

I gritted my teeth, forcing my beaten body to a stand. My leg howled under the added pressure, and my head throbbed like a severed artery. Everything in me wanted to stop moving, to succumb to the pain in my limbs and my heart. But the blood seeping through my shirt needed staunching; there was only so much time before I bled out entirely.

My fingers reached for my own bow, only grasping at air.

*Blast.* I'd left it in the keep.

An arrow cut through the wind and landed at my feet. Good thing its owner was a poor shot; another inch, and my leg would have been rendered broken *and* impaled. Useless.

Only a simpkin—a fool—would stand here and take this sort of death.

I turned and ran, or rather limped, like a madman. There was no use in pleading my case at this point.

Arrows continued to whoosh past my head, narrowly missing

my body.

I dodged them, zigzagging my retreat.

"You'll pay for this, Huxley. We'll track you down until the day you die. And by my own hand, I swear it on my son's grave!" the king roared from his tower, his voice growing distant behind me. "Don't even think about seeking asylum in Vastia..."

Too confused to linger, I focused instead on trying to remain alive. A king never did his own dirty work, especially not one at Barrington's age.

I limp-ran down the hillside, clenching my jaw against the pain; it was safe to say that only adrenaline steadied me at this point. I rushed past the baffled expressions of guards not yet informed of my "crime" before exiting the exterior gates surrounding the castle. I knew that if duty allowed it, they would have sought after my health, but as it was, I was thankful a guard was never supposed to leave his post.

I was not welcome here. I'd never be welcome again.

A mixture of fury and disbelief burned inside me. None of this was right. None of this made sense. Everything in me wanted to turn back around and demand answers. To see for myself the validity of Barrington's accusation—and if true, to be there for Prince Clark's funeral. As his bodyguard, his confidant, his friend.

My eyes stung, but the tears threatening to gather wouldn't fall. The only option I had now was to keep going. But where to? Barrington wouldn't rest until I was dead. Dead for a crime I never committed.

My gaze locked on the horizon and the stretch of blue that glistened in the faint light of the waning sun. A knot twisted in the pit of my stomach.

*Is this some cruel fate?*

I pressed on despite the hesitancy coursing through my veins. With each step forward, my resolve grew. I had little choice.

Barrington wouldn't pursue me for long—not in the course I was taking.

It was time I got better acquainted with the Wasteful Tides.

# Two

## Old Friends

My boots scraped against the wooden planks of the wharf while the smell of fish assaulted my nostrils. The sun had now gone abed, the moon illuminating Braka in an otherworldly glow.

It was of little consequence; I worked best under the cover of darkness.

I hobbled up one of the wharfs and squinted into the night, noticing a sign nailed to a nearby post. In crude, weathered letters, I barely made out the words *BEWARE THE WASTEFUL TIDES SHOULD THE CRIMSON DEATH TAKE YOU.*

I shuddered at the warning as a wave of nostalgia fought to take hold. The stories had frightened me as a child, but I still remembered fondly the warmth of my mother's voice, her hand smoothing the hair from off my forehead.

She was taken too soon.

I swallowed back the growing lump in my throat and focused my attention elsewhere.

No ships lined the docks; there hadn't been for some time. Braka used to be a tremendous country, with booming ports here in Edgefold and the adjacent port to the east in Greymist. But that was many moons ago.

Before the resurgence of myth.

Like most countries abutting a body of water, speculations often arose of what lurked in its depths. And for Braka, the legend told of a horrific monster terrorizing the Wasteful Tides. There were supposed sightings of this beast, of its tail or arm or fleshy hide—all of which were chronicled by Brakan historians throughout generations.

But it was all hearsay and speculation, nothing to be taken seriously. That was, not until ten years ago, soon after Crown Prince Albertus' death.

At first, many of our native plants and herbs began disappearing from Braka's shores. And soon after, people began disappearing, too; though whether by force or other means, it remained unknown. This included parts of King Barrington's fleet—ships that never returned home—and those that did were beyond salvaging, their timbers used for new houses rather than trade. Because of this, major imports from other countries stopped coming by means of water altogether.

Another indicator was an incident seven years ago when Barrington's harpist was seen offshore, playing his instrument along the shallow waters of the inlet for the king's yearly festival. He'd been playing a jaunty tune only to slip, injure himself, and suddenly disappear, his cry and a dissonant chord all he left behind before being sucked below the Wasteful Tides.

We all waited for him to resurface—some of us even dove into the waters to find him—but were left to one sad reality: he had vanished for good.

There had been little to no music since. At least, not the kind worth listening to.

The incident was enough to spring Braka into a panic, especially the king. The annals were kept under lock and key within Barrington's library, only for his use or the eyes of the elite to pore over with fear and trepidation. To ensure safety. To maintain the peace. To make Braka avoid the waters at all costs.

Hence, the fishing ports were always deserted and the beacons shut down.

Now we relied on carriages and horseback for our food and livelihood, from neighboring Vastia and the countries beyond. Which meant it could take weeks, even months, for sustenance to reach our doorsteps, leaving most of us hungry. Unless, of course, you were Barrington with a storehouse filled to overflowing.

A king's horde boasted a respite for his kin and served as a mockery for his people. Should the villagers ever find out, it would be the biggest scandal in Brakan history. Though, many were already suspicious. I was an insider; and thanks to Prince Clark, I knew most of what happened within the walls of the castle, but it wouldn't be long before others did, too. Barrington wasn't the worst of kings; in fact, he was incredibly loyal, but his fear knew no bounds. And if I knew anything, it was that fear created a coward.

I limped forward, the moon now hidden behind a stretch of

clouds. A cool breeze raised the hairs on my arms, reminding me I was still alive and would remain so as long as I got off Braka.

Barrington's men were probably hot on my trail.

It wasn't so much fear which motivated my steps forward, but my wounds. Movement kept my vision from tunneling into an endless stream of black, and a rogue branch I'd snapped off a tree kept me steady on my feet.

All of a sudden, a hand came down on my damaged shoulder, and the laceration smarted like no other.

My nerves pulsed. *I'm too late. They've found me.*

Instinctively, I dropped the tree branch and reached for my sword, biting back the groan threatening to betray any weakness.

*Best to end this soon. I'm already a dead man.*

Unsheathing my weapon, I twisted under my captor's hold and freed my arm. I ground my teeth and wheeled back around, ignoring the pain shooting up my leg. In turn, I grasped my attacker by the shoulder and directed my sword at his throat.

He raised his hands in surrender, his eyes wide in the moonlight. "H-Hux?" He swallowed hard, his Adam's apple bobbing just before the metal tip. "It's me! You wouldn't skewer your best mate, would you?"

My eyes registered the shadows dancing across a familiar face, one I hadn't seen in far too long. "Monty Bates?" I shouldn't have sounded so surprised to see him here. I should have expected it, but at this hour? I studied him, noticing the swath of brown hair on his head and curling around his ears, not to mention the auburn and gray that dotted his beard. Though shorter than me by a handful of inches, he was only two years my senior, but he looked older than thirty. And in this lighting, his usually green irises appeared as coal. "What do you think you're doing, nearly scaring the snot out of us both?"

"I didn't mean anything by it, I swear. You know I live by the docks. I run the night shift," Monty sputtered, his hands splayed about his head like a scarecrow, his eyes on the sword.

I wasn't daft. I knew Monty had worked here ever since he was a child, that he'd inherited his post after his father's passing and his mother's declining health. He was the oldest of four, so naturally, lighting the beacon fell into his care.

It was only that the years all melded together, and the memories had faded. Not to mention my head was still muddled from earlier.

"You're telling me you're still keeping watch?" I arched a brow.

"Someone's gotta keep the beacon running—"

"Edgefold hasn't seen a boat in years, Bates." My gaze traveled upward to the towering beacon on the nearby hill, posted at the furthest point of the peninsula. It looked like a massive shadow against the backdrop of a darkening sky, and no light lingered beyond the pane of glass; it had remained lifeless for a decade. "Why waste your breath now?"

"Just in case. I'd defy the king's order if it meant saving a life. To warn of impending attacks, or to make sure travelers don't"—he gulped loudly—"get dashed to pieces on the rocks." He studied the piece of metal before him, its silver tip glinting in the moonlight. "Do you think you could...?" He gestured to the sword.

I followed his gaze. "Right." I lowered the weapon. "Old habit, I suppose. No offense."

"None taken," Monty said, standing straight and running a hand along the front of his throat. "Haven't had this much action in a long time, though I can't say the same for you." He did me a once over, noticing my fresh wounds. "What on Braka happened to you?"

"I'm still trying to figure that out myself." I sheathed my sword, pushing my fingers through some rogue curls on my head. This night hadn't started out well, and if I didn't get a move on, it wouldn't end well either.

"What are you doing out here anyway? It's not like you to leave the castle. Don't you have the prince to guard or something?" Monty asked, bending to grab some discarded rope by his feet.

I hobbled away and scoured the water for a ship I knew wouldn't be there, ignoring the ache his words brought. "You would think."

"Hux?"

I heard shuffling, and soon Monty's hand was on my arm, swinging me around. "Have you gone mad?"

*You have no idea.* "Not in the way you're implying."

"Everyone knows the king's getting old, that his second son is in line to claim his seat. Why are you *here* when you should be *there*?" He crossed his arms over his chest and stared me down in a full assessment. "It's not one of your nights off, is it?"

*Blast Monty Bates.* His questioning methods could earn him a role in the castle as inquisitor. Despite the few times I'd met up with him over the years, he seemed to memorize my schedule better than most; it hadn't changed much in all the time I'd been employed. Maybe he could solve this confounded mystery.

I met his gaze, grimacing. "Seems they no longer have a need for me."

Monty's eyes widened. "No longer? Have no need for *you*?" he sputtered.

"That's what I said, isn't it?" I crossed my arms over my chest to mimic his, ignoring the way my shoulder smarted against the strain.

"I don't believe it! After decades of your family guarding Barrington and his offspring, he's just decided to sack *you*, of Gannon blood, who's served and protected *his* family for years? And on a whim? Am I missing something here?" Monty's questioning was turning him into some impassioned eel, wringing his hands together and his body shaking ever so slightly.

It had always been this way. Me doing the daring and Monty doing the questioning. The back and forth, leaving Monty shaking like a leaf in the wind. Ever since we were children, playing in Braka's shallows or scheming up some sort of mischief around town, it was always Monty trying to be the voice of reason.

I didn't mind it on most occasions, but now it was beginning to grate on my nerves. Despite everything in me, I needed to get away from Braka, not make light conversation on the brink of my execution. And with each moment that passed, I felt my adrenaline failing. Soon, my wounds would catch up with me, and I'd no longer be able to stand.

"Prince Clark is dead..." Uttering those words was like being doused in frozen water. "And Barrington's pegged me as the criminal. There. You satisfied? Now, can you help me find a blasted boat so I can leave this place?" Though my tone was sharp, the pain ran deep; Clark was more friend than charge, and my heart ached at his loss. I'd failed him.

Monty stared at me as if I'd just grown a second head, but he quickly shook it off. He opened his mouth as if to ask another question, but upon seeing my hardened expression, shifted his course. "Well, that changes things, then."

Another thing about Monty: he was fiercely loyal, and for all his questioning, he never doubted my integrity. He'd abandon his ceaseless inquiries for the sake of haste. Or my disdain.

He turned around and picked up the rope he'd cast aside earlier, wrapping the rough fibers around his forearm and elbow. "You need a boat."

*Yes.* Could that be any clearer?

"But the Tides…" He looked out toward the darkened waters, his eyes wide. We all knew what was rumored to lurk below. "Where will you go?" he asked.

"To Kethnar." I'd read about the country beyond the Wasteful Tides, but I'd never been. It seemed to be the quickest place I could go where Barrington's arm couldn't reach. Kethnar, unlike the neighboring country of Vastia, resided outside of the king's sphere of influence. It was a land all to its own, yet it wasn't so far from home that I'd feel truly *lost*.

He nodded. "I'm coming with you."

"You can't do that."

"Why shouldn't I? Your life's at stake, and my job's been on the fritz for years. I'm a free man, after all."

"You won't be a free man much longer. If caught with me, you'll be charged with treason for aiding and abetting the 'enemy.'" I set my jaw.

He looked at me and shrugged. "It'll be worth it, brother."

I didn't buy it. "What about Gloria? You've loved her for years. And you're just gonna leave her behind to be a single barmaid forever?" Look at me. Now *I* was asking the questions.

Monty hesitated, his face reddening. "I've no claim to her heart if she hasn't given me hers in return."

"Ah. So you haven't even told her yet. She has no idea how you feel." I could tell the truth hit him hard with the subtle slump of his shoulders. A knot twisted in my stomach; I shouldn't have pressed the issue. "Chin up, Bates." I clapped him on the back. "You'll find your tongue, and she'll come around."

He nodded, shrugging me off. "That said, I'm getting you a boat, and I'm going with you. You look terrible as it is, and you owe me one after that verbal spar to my pride."

I opened my mouth to protest.

"And don't you dare try to stop me." Monty cut me off before I had a chance to say anything more. "We both know I'm more seaworthy than you, and you're not even fit to carry an oar."

I sighed. Maybe I wasn't resisting hard enough, but Monty was right. He knew how to maneuver a boat, and my battered body wasn't doing me any favors at the moment.

I was sure I looked as terrible as I felt, and with the adrenaline winding down, I knew it might even be more so. But talking with Monty had distracted me from the pain somewhat, and maybe his company would do me some good.

It seemed I'd be escaping Braka after all. At least, if the ocean didn't claim me first.

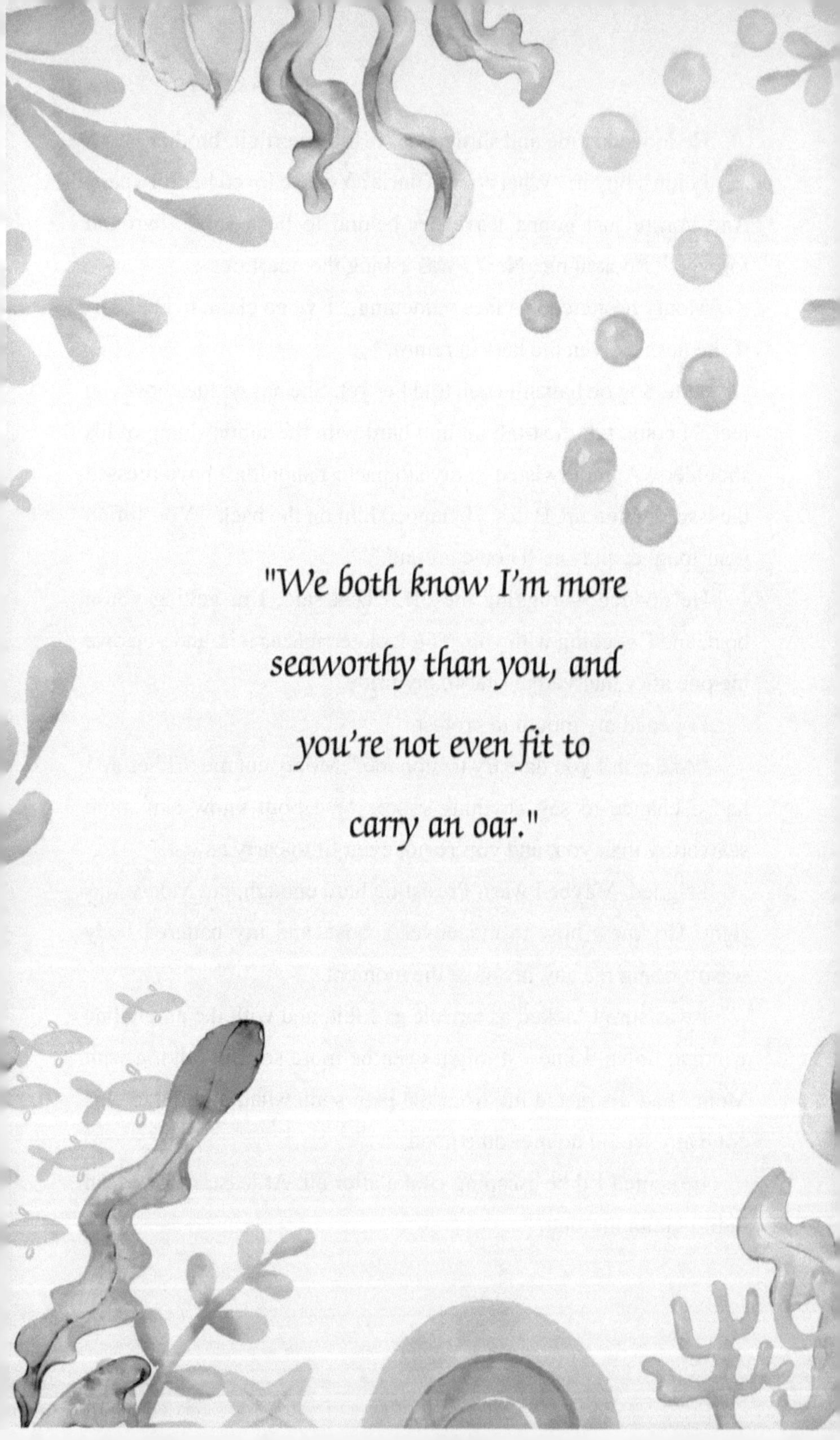

"We both know I'm more

seaworthy than you, and

you're not even fit to

carry an oar."

# Three

## The Ol' Clam Dunk

The familiar dark teal of the Tides showed brilliantly in the first lights of dawn, the sun working its magic in waking up the earth. These waters were greener than most, or so I'd heard; I'd never traveled much beyond Braka's shores.

I gripped the sides of the wooden vessel, sucking in a breath as sprays of water seeped through the bandages on my shoulder, the salt licking my wound. My head ached, and my leg throbbed something fierce, but a few pieces of discarded plywood proved a decent enough splint for the time being. My body might have been beaten, but it was nothing compared to the boat beneath my feet.

"How old did you say this thing was?" I was thankful it hadn't sprung a leak yet, but with my luck, I'd leave Braka just to sink to the bottom of the Wasteful Tides.

A pike rested in the bottom of the hull next to a pile of rope and two canteens of water. We were out in the middle of the ocean now—land too far away to be discerned even with the first light of dawn.

Monty's oar sliced through the greenish water. "'Bout fifty years old, if memory serves me right. Been in my family for generations. But she's used to the shoreline, not being way out here. Don't you remember her?"

I studied the vessel further. It was a standard fishing boat, with room for five people if seated just right. It looked too old to still be afloat, like a retired veteran of the seas.

Looking to my left, I paused. There, on the frame nearest my boots, were the initials H.K.G. III etched into the wood grains. I ran my fingers along the indentations, remembering as if it were yesterday that I had carved them.

"*The Maritimer?* But it can't be." I shook my head. "I thought she sank years ago." I'd only been on the boat a handful of times as a child, mostly to go fishing along the coast.

"She did!" Monty chuckled. "But we revived her and gave her a new name. After my family went months without a boat, my father decided to try his hand at rescuing this one. When she finally broke the surface, her belly was full of clams. She's the ol' *Clam Dunk* now." Monty stroked her starboard side as if he were petting a dog. "Suits her, doesn't it?"

"It's borderline regal." I tipped my head in mock respect.

Monty rolled his eyes. "Anyway, after her months' long baptismal, she's served our family proudly. Up until Braka shut down all our ports, that is." He pursed his lips. "Curse the Crimson Death."

My mind flashed back to my mother's stories and the pictures lining the walls of the castle's corridor, of the princes' faces—Clark's in particular sending an unbidden pang to my chest—and a warrior battling the hideous beast of the sea. *The Crimson Death.* That's what everyone called it, giving a name to something that blurred the lines of myth and reality. A name that also belonged to the disease that had killed so many Brakan civilians decades ago, including the crown prince.

As if tracing my thoughts, Monty stiffened his back and searched the water. "You don't suppose she's real, do you?"

I scratched my chin, the short hairs reminding me I was in need of a shave. "I believe she's as real as anyone who allows their imagination to run wild."

"You think she's a myth?" Something like relief sparked in Monty's eyes.

"I never said that." My mother's tales had told me otherwise.

"That the stories are true, then?"

"I've got a pretty decent imagination." I ran my tongue over my teeth, an inkling of gooseflesh prickling my warm skin. "But as to the facts, well, one can only know so much when keeping their footing on land."

Monty lifted his oar and laid it across his lap, his expression pensive. "Have you no fear of the Tides, Hux? No fear of what lurks below? If anyone could see us right now, they'd deem us madmen. Absolutely psychotic."

I shrugged. "Let them see. Maybe we'll even prove Braka wrong. There's no reason to stop living just because of some legend. Besides, this is quite nice." I leaned back and closed my eyes, trying to ignore the way my muscles ached or the way my heart pounded from being so far out at sea. It was easier to feign all was well. If not for my sake, at least for Monty's.

After narrowly escaping death from Barrington's guards—my own men-in-arms, my brothers—facing the mysterious unknowns of the ocean might prove less harrowing. I was still uneasy, but there *was* something invigorating about the cool, salty breeze whipping against your skin, snatching your breath. The way the boat rocked beneath your feet, keeping you afloat. You were a small, insignificant dot in the midst of a dark, far-reaching pool, and that…well, that notion was freeing.

I'd almost forgotten how beautiful the ocean could be, though my heart still belonged to Braka's mainland. As did my blood and loyalty.

Tightness gripped my shoulders, and I squeezed my hands into fists. It would be that way no longer.

Everything I'd worked so hard for was now gone. Stripped away. Though I hadn't poisoned Prince Clark, I'd failed to keep him safe.

*Failure.* The word resounded inside my head like a relentless gong. *Failure. Failure.*

The Gannon line of Royal Guards was ended with me, and I couldn't keep the guilt from pooling in my middle. My title was a mockery of what I once was.

Since a child, I was bred for service. Like my father and his father before him. Three generations of Gannon blood, pouring out everything we had for the Barrington name.

*"Gannon blood is meant for war. For wielding weapons. For ensuring protection. But above all, loyalty. Always loyalty. You'd*

*do well to remember it, son."*

And so I had. I'd worked tirelessly for it. I was born Huxley Krew Gannon III, an only child to Huxley and Joanie Gannon, in a little cottage within the castle grounds. There I was raised and trained, learning loyalty before learning my letters, instructed on all things "war" before assuming my full-time position as guard and soldier in Castle Farrador. It was a position I'd grown to love.

Then, one day, a flame was kindled.

My mother passed from a stroke when I was twelve, and my father, contrary to his previous word about loyalty, took to the seas some years later, joining the ranks of King Barrington's merchant fleet. I knew he was only trying to outrun his grief, and for a time, it appeared to serve him well. That was, until his ship never returned.

I never learned if he managed to assuage the ache of his broken heart. But that's the thing—a broken heart couldn't be outrun. Instead, he only managed to disappear, orphaning his only child in the process.

And pretty soon, that kindling flame began to grow from a smoldering wick into a blazing inferno, its birthing place residing deep inside my chest.

As I aged from a boy into a man, I'd learned the wisdom in hardening my heart all the while that the flame grew. It was a soldier's duty to remain strong; we couldn't afford to be broken over things lost or new hurts gained. Though, the irony of those words now throbbed around my left leg. And that internal fire could now be felt externally around my entire body, not so much due to anger as it was from my wounds.

"How long do you plan on staying in Kethnar?" Monty asked, his voice easing into my subconscious like the lapping waves.

I unclenched my fists, adjusting my position in the bow. "By the looks of it, I plan on building a house."

"Have you no hope that Barrington's tirade will blow over? What about a fair trial?"

I scoffed. "The last time I tried reasoning with him, I almost had an arrow lodged in my skull. I think I'll take my chances elsewhere." But loyalty didn't die easily. How would it truly feel to be parted from my beloved homeland?

"I can't believe it. All those years gone, just like that. Your father—"

"I know," I said. "He'd be trying to wage war from his grave. Or from wherever he is."

"Well, maybe something will change. Maybe you'll find enough evidence to clear your name."

*One can only hope.* "The answers might as well be buried at the bottom of the sea, Bates. At this point, combating the Crimson Death sounds more promising than Barrington's lunacy."

Monty chuckled wryly. "Then let's hope we meet the foul thing. Give her a piece of our minds."

With the sun midway through the sky, the force of its rays relentlessly beat down upon the *Clam Dunk*. The warmth of my skin was replaced by a burning, my forearms a bright red against the white linen of my shirt. Before setting out, I'd torn the sleeves to fashion a tourniquet of sorts for my shoulder, staunching the blood flow and shielding it from the sun. But that did little to quell the throbbing against my temples.

"How many days?" I asked, scratching the back of my head. I squinted into the horizon to see if any visible shoreline presented itself.

"What's that?" Monty asked.

"How many days 'til we reach Kethnar's shores?"

"We've gone half a day already. 'Bout two more if the wind's on our side." Monty stuck his oar into the water, and the boat tottered forward a fraction of a league. "Sure could use a break, though one glance at you says I shouldn't count on it." He laughed. "Your body's a mangled mess, Hux."

"Thanks, Captain Conspicuous."

Monty waved his arm in the air and dipped forward into a half-bow. "I live to serve."

I rolled my eyes but regretted it instantly as it sent my head spinning. Steadying myself, I bent forward, roving my hands over the makeshift splint around my leg. I couldn't tell what was broken, but I knew it wasn't my femur. It hurt, but it didn't compare to my pounding headache...nor the ribs I'd broken last spring. My Andalusian, Verdun, had thrown a shoe and then thrown me in turn. My body hit a spruce, ribs cracking beneath my weight, as my horse bent over my limp form and nibbled my hair in apology.

*Verdun.* Who would ride him in my stead? Who would feed him sugar cubes after a good brushing? By the looks of it, I wouldn't be seeing my favorite horse ever again, and that was a friendship I cherished almost as much as Prince Clark's. The loss burned keenly.

In fact, everything burned at the moment. What I'd give to have this appendage properly set. Or some blessed ice.

Something hit me square in the chest instead. A glance at my shirt revealed a red dot, the stain resembling something of another wound. But the thought gave way to a mushy-looking orb, a beach plum native to the shores of Braka, now resting in my lap.

"Thought you could use some nourishment. Keep up your strength and all that." Monty nodded, biting into a beach plum of his own, the red juice dribbling down his chin.

*Leave it to Monty to come prepared.*

I lifted the fruit to my lips and sank my teeth into its skin, my tastebuds dancing at its sweetness. "I haven't had one of these in years." Its taste brought me back to the fruit cobblers my mother used to bake when I was a child; my father and I downed three of them a week, much to her chagrin.

Another ache—another burning—assaulted my chest, reminding me just how much I'd lost.

Monty flashed a smile. "Barrington's table boasts of wealthier substance, I suppose. Though no better, I'd add."

"Fair enough." Beach plums didn't necessarily line the stomachs of the elite; they were deemed a poor man's fare. But after tasting such sweetness, I wondered why. Kings should be satisfied to eat such a fruit, and one so readily available for the taking—*the Maker's gift to man*—seeing as it was one of the few plants that hadn't disappeared with the Crimson Death.

I took another bite, and the juice dribbled down my chin. I didn't bother swiping it away. "How many more of these have you got left?"

Monty turned and slid a burlap bag from around him to the middle of the boat, positioning it before me. Inside, I could already see a few more orbs of shiny red smiling toward the sun, their presence a welcome sight amidst the vastness of an endless sea.

"I'd give us two more days, enough to take us to Kethnar's shores."

"And what of the return journey home?" I asked, licking the remaining plum juice from my fingers.

"Ah well, all journeys happen in their own time. I'll see you settled in Kethnar and then make my way back home. Simple as that," Monty said. "And with more beach plums, of course."

"Of course." I chuckled, reaching into the burlap bag to eat my second plum. I brought the fruit to my lips when something thwacked against the *Clam Dunk*'s hull, sending the boat rocking in the amassing waves. The burlap sack tipped and plums scattered, rolling about our feet, the pike clattering beside them in a song of protest.

I gripped the sides of the vessel, my own plum dropping into the murky depths, disappearing amidst the churning surf.

I could only pray that Monty and I didn't succumb to the same fate, that its descent wasn't a cruel foreshadowing of what was to come.

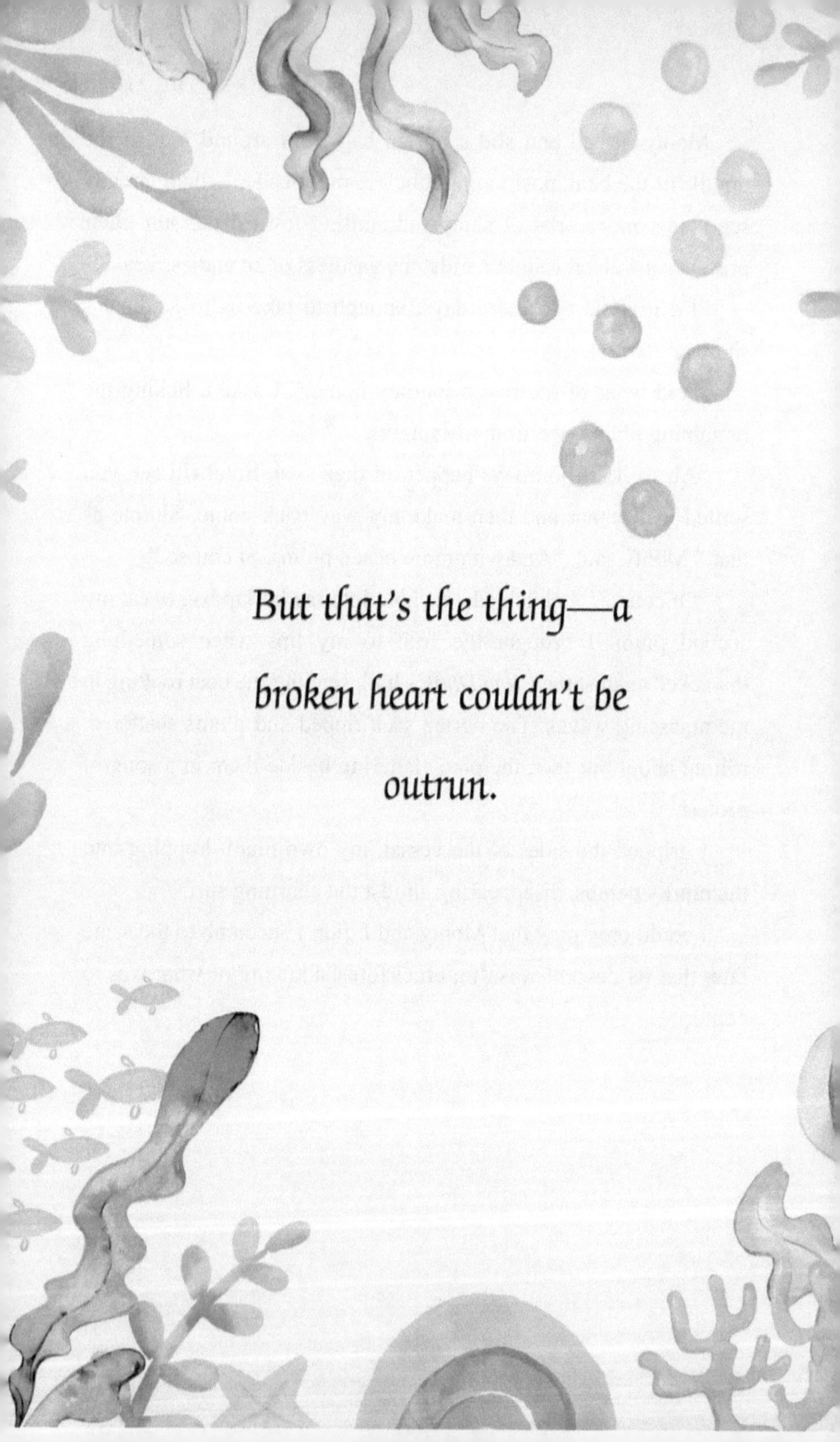

But that's the thing—a

broken heart couldn't be

outrun.

# FOUR

## Maelstrom!

My heart pounded against my ribs, and I could feel the blood rush to all my wounds, making them throb wickedly.

"What in the blasted depths was that?" Monty asked, his eyes wide. His hands gripped the wooden oar so tightly that his knuckles had turned a ghostly white.

"I have no idea." A shiver climbed my spine and settled about my neck. My hand gripped the sword strapped by my waist.

"Do you think we hit a reef?"

I shook my head. "Not many reefs would be out at these depths." Monty knew better than to ask that question, but fear did strange things to logic.

"A rock, then?"

I scanned the waters surrounding the *Clam Dunk*, hoping to catch sight of something—anything—that might give us any indication as to what hit us. But the waves had slowed, and there was no sighting of a rock nor any movement from below. Instead, I saw parts of my own reflection—short-cropped, dark, curly hair and shadowed eyes staring back, the blue of my irises pools of liquid midnight.

"Do you think…" Monty trailed off, fidgeting with the folds of his shirt.

His unfinished question needed no explanation; I already knew what he was thinking.

"Perhaps, though I can't be sure." My pulse said otherwise.

It was no secret that strange things had occurred in the Wasteful Tides. But the Crimson Death?

The line separating fact from fiction suddenly seemed rather blurred. Was there even a line to begin with?

With each oar stroke, I felt the distance grow keenly; I'd never get to go back. It had been a full day since our departure from Braka's shores. Since our run-in with an unknown force. And my head pounded now more than ever, eased only slightly by the emptying of my stomach every couple of leagues.

On a more positive note, no damage was done to our hull, or else we'd have sprung a leak by now. We succeeded in returning all the beach plums to their rightful spots, and my hand hadn't strayed to my hip for some time. Though, the cool metal of my sword was my confidence.

It was almost as if the incident had never happened. I was beginning to feel hopeful that my feet would touch Kethnarian soil after all, that my departure from my esteemed homeland wouldn't result in my imminent death.

Today, with the spotted clouds covering the sun in intervals, the journey was more bearable, reminding me once again of the ocean's beauty. The briny sea tickled my nose, and I could feel the wind lodged in my chest from having been out on the water longer than the few hours I was used to. It was invigorating, though my body was more than ready to step foot on land.

My leg was stiff, I most likely had a fever, and I feared my arm had grown septic, the limb nearly unusable in its numbness. The last thing I wanted was to undergo forced amputation…

"Should be there in another day or so, maybe less," Monty said, his oar making the telltale splash against the tide, moving the boat forward. "Do you think we'll have any more obstacles?"

Ever since the slam to our hull, Monty had been leery of what lurked below the surface. I could tell that every time he put the oar in the water he was wondering if it would get snatched from his hands. And his shifty eyes said more than that, too—that he regretted ever challenging the beast in the first place. Monty had no piece, or peace, of his mind to give.

I couldn't say I blamed him.

"Let's hope not." And I meant it. I didn't think my body could handle any more action at this point.

I looked at Monty, his mouth open as if ready to ask another question, but then his expression shifted from interest to fear. The whites of his eyes claimed the majority of his sockets.

"Wh-what's that?" He placed the oar on his lap, pointing to somewhere over my shoulder.

I turned in my seat, settling my gaze in the direction he was referring. A shiver crept up my spine.

There, in the water, was a smooth-looking stone, just barely cresting the lip of the Tides. It was wide and of a striped, brownish-red nature, spanning the length of at least four yards. And as our boat drifted closer, I noticed the glossy surface of its formation was as slick as rain on a paver.

I looked back at Monty, his white knuckles reclaiming their hold on the oar with renewed vigor.

I returned my gaze to the rock, but all I saw was the endless stretch of the ocean, extending in all directions at once. The slick landmass had disappeared. Gone.

Was I seeing things? Had it merely been a trick of the light?

Monty groaned. "Strange things be happening in the Wasteful Tides as of late, Hux. I don't know about you, but I'm starting to feel the effects." His shoulders shook, and his skin took on a sickly, green pallor. "If it's that beasty, I want out!"

"Bates, you said it yourself—we're almost to Kethnar. A little longer and we'll touch land." I said the words more to assure myself.

Rocks didn't tend to float one minute and then sink the next. If there *was* something living in the Wasteful Tides as big as that "rock," we were in for a rude awakening.

"That's if we don't die fir—" Monty hardly finished his sentence when a violent rumble shook the waters, rattling the wooden craft.

Suddenly, bubbles sprung up all around us, and the water began swirling in a circular motion, forming a funneling shape only a few paces away. Slowly but surely, we were being pulled into the ocean's movements as it tossed the *Clam Dunk* in a chaotic dance, first one way and then another, as the vessel fought to steady itself amidst the surf.

"What's going on?" Monty yelled, holding onto the boat for dear life.

Our boat rocked almost horizontally, the beach plums tumbling out of their burlap home and disappearing in the whitecaps. I lunged for the pike before it had a chance to follow suit, but I couldn't say the same for our canteens of water or the rope. Though, something told me that we'd need any weapon we could get our hands on.

I scoured the ocean, bubbles popping up at increased intervals and the speed of the Tides swirling about us in an intense, circular motion. Our craft mimicked its rotation, but this time at a faster rate than before, the vessel dropping deep enough into the vortex that the surface of the water was above us.

My heart leaped to my throat. I'd read about this in books, about seafaring adventures gone wrong. We were in the midst of a nameless, faceless storm, where the only way out was to go down, if we were to get out at all…

I swallowed the bile rising in my throat, gripping my weapons and the sides of the *Clam Dunk* like they were my lifelines.

"We're in a maelstrom, Bates!" I hollered above the churning sea, the waves crashing over our craft and thoroughly drenching our clothes. Drops of salt water pelted my skin, and no amount of blinking kept the sting from my eyes. The boat was merely a flotation device now, doing little to protect us from the elements.

All of a sudden, I heard a deep, unearthly groan bellowing up from somewhere in the depths. Out of nowhere, two red, tentacle-like arms burst out of the middle of the maelstrom and latched onto our boat, dragging us down even farther.

Even if we wanted to try our hand at outrunning this storm, it was too late now. We were being sucked into the murky deep by a creature who sought our doom.

I looked at Monty. His skin had shifted from green to stark white.

"Hux?" he yelled, the walls of the ocean growing higher the farther down we were dragged.

There was so much said in just the sound of my name. *What's happening? Will we survive? Is this the Crimson Death? I should've let you come out here alone. What if we hadn't come here at all? What of Gloria? I'll kill you if we both die!*

I met his gaze, nodding once to assure him I understood. That I was here, and I wouldn't let him die alone. I wouldn't let fear claim him without me there, too.

I promised.

Water crashed against the port and starboard sides, filling the hull with bucket-loads of water. Suddenly, the planks squeaked and snapped, splintering apart and sending Monty and I to separate ends of the broken vessel. The monstrous tentacles still held onto what was left of the craft.

I abandoned the pike to ensure my grip on the discarded wood, my muscles screaming in protest. Anything to keep me afloat a little longer, from meeting the depths too soon.

"Hold on, Monty!" I yelled back, gritting my teeth and straining every muscle for all it was worth. "Hold on!"

I sucked in a breath as a wave plunged me under, feeling the cool liquid pool in my ears and still the chaos with muted silence. I kicked with my good leg to keep from delving deeper, the promise of oxygen only a moment away. When my head broke the surface, the world was thundering once again, and I spit the briny water out of my mouth with lungs rejoicing.

But all too soon.

A rogue plank hit a wave and jetted backwards, beaming me off the temple. My head spun, my hands loosening their hold.

All I remembered was falling, drifting off to sleep amidst the swirling chaos of an empty vow.

I wouldn't let fear

claim him without me

there, too.

# FIVE

## The Crimson Death

*Am I dreaming? Is this what death feels like?*

My vision swam with images of running through hallways, of a king's anger over a dead son, of a boat once filled with clams and now trapped at sea, of monstrous tentacles latching onto the broken remains of a wooden craft, of the cries of one scared beyond imagination. Of my head pounding, muscles screaming, and water pouring down my throat and staving off any form of life.

And yet there was oxygen in my lungs. If breathing was any indicator, I was still alive.

But now I felt something new. Coarse fibers beneath my fingertips, something soft cradling my head, a warmth on my shoulder, and suddenly, a pinch, rendering all my nerves on fire.

My eyes flew open, my breathing heavy.

*Where am I?*

The room was dark, the ceiling made of wooden panels not

unlike the *Clam Dunk*'s. A tallow candle burned somewhere along the wall, casting flickering shadows around the small, empty space. And all the while, I felt an intense pressure about my ears as if my head was being squeezed by some unknown force.

A look to my left revealed a figure bent over my shoulder, examining it closely. The smell of spices, like oregano or rosemary, tickled my nose, and as I craned my neck farther, I saw a thick poultice being applied to the wound by a weathered hand stained with dyes.

"Just some yarrow, don't you worry." His sudden speech took me by surprise. "You've had a mild case of sepsis, so it's a good thing I got to you when I did." He smoothed the substance deeper into the cut, and I grimaced, biting my tongue. "Should have you right as rain in no time."

The voice…the accent… I couldn't place either, but they belonged to someone far older—I could tell that much. There was a maturity behind his words as if he had years of experience in saying them, in trying them on his tongue.

I opened my mouth to speak, but all I could taste was mint and something strangely earthy. I licked my lips and swallowed, trying to bring moisture back to the parched places.

"Ah, yes, that would be the sage," the man said. "Should help with the spread of infection. A cure-all, really."

I nodded, my head feeling as if I'd been enveloped by some thick, fiery fog. I scanned the room once more, taking in my surroundings. There wasn't anyone else besides me and this odd man.

The muscles in my chest tightened. *Monty.*

Pushing to a seated position, I finally noticed the cot beneath me—or rather the webs of fishing nets covered by a rough sort of blanket. I tried to get up only to be stopped short by my splint snagging on something sharp hidden beneath the folds of the netting and a hand steadying my shoulder.

"None of that, now. Your friend is safe." He pushed me back down so that my head hit the pillow.

It took me a moment to register the man's words. *Your friend is safe.* Monty was alive.

I breathed a sigh of relief and allowed my weary limbs to relax into the coarse fabric beneath me. My head throbbed violently, clouding over with muddled thoughts once more.

Everything hurt, my leg barking like a wily spaniel. The appendage felt swollen, radiating an intense heat that rivaled the pain. I attempted to massage the affected area.

"I reset the bone; your tibia was severely dislocated, but not broken like you probably assumed. Nothing a little plantain can't fix, but leave it be," the man said, pushing me back down again, and suddenly I caught a whiff of something else, like fresh grass, and it seemed to be coming from the man directly. "The swelling is normal; it will go down with time."

I abandoned my task and succumbed to his will, no longer having the strength to fight it. The room was already spinning.

"You need your rest. You'd do well to close your eyes."

All at once, the man's words made sense.

*Close your eyes.*

There was no use in fighting a command my body desperately needed.

I heard the soft rumblings of unintelligible words drifting in and out of my slumber. Whispers. They were too far away to be discerned, yet heavy footsteps brought them nearer.

*Am I dreaming?*

"Tend to him, will you?"

Even in my half-daze, I recognized the voice belonging to the man from earlier. I wanted to open my eyes and see who he was talking to, but they felt as heavy as lead, my forehead as hot as iron tongs.

"He's been burning up for days. I've only just stopped the infection from spreading, but that doesn't mean his body has recovered. The Crimson Death won't take him, I swear my life on it."

I felt myself stop breathing, or at least, a hitch caught in my lungs. *The Crimson Death?*

A stretch of silence met his words, and after a few padded footfalls, I felt something cool press against my eyes. The burning heat diminished under the sweet scent of something citrusy, and I turned my head, leaning into the cloth—anything to keep the cool pressed against my temples a little longer.

"Try not to move." A gentle voice stilled my movements. It was so unlike the other, this one both light and feminine.

I listened against my will, allowing her ministrations to ease away the burning fever clanging against my skull.

My mind wavered between reality and dreams, first urging me

to get up and demand where I was before clouding over once more, succumbing to the hand of immobility.

"You'll get well soon. Just be still."

Despite the assurance of her voice, I doubted her words; behind these lidded eyes lingered visions of death, writhing tentacles, and cries of anguish amidst a violent, churning sea.

Spinning, spinning, spinning into an endless black abyss.

I awoke slowly, a yawn escaping my parched lips. Pushing to a seated position, I leaned back against the wall behind me, a lightness about my head that I hadn't felt for some time, a clarity that wasn't there before.

I lifted my thumbs to massage my eyes, feeling crust caked into their corners; the effort it took to move at all surprised me. Wiping at them, I felt the clammy skin beneath, pausing when my hands strayed to my cheeks and then my chin. I couldn't ignore the thick bristles twining through my fingers. I may as well have been Verdun's rear end, my growing whiskers rivaling that of my horse's tail. If only I had a straight edge to trim them down.

My hand suddenly stilled. But with hair this grown...

*How long has it been? Where am I?*

A quick survey of the room reminded me that I'd been here before, or at least, I'd seen it in my dreams. Somewhere in my muddled memory, I recalled a burning candle and shadows dancing across an unfamiliar face, hands tending to my shoulder.

Which reminded me...

A glance at the appendage revealed a green-colored bandage, and upon closer examination, I recognized it as seaweed. I ran my thumb over the affected area, feeling its slimy slickness, the smell of brine undercutting the sage and rue already swirling about the small space. It was tender to the touch, but the ache didn't feel as deep.

I heard seagulls calling and waves lapping nearby, and my gaze was drawn to the circular window I hadn't noticed earlier. Outside looked strangely green, and a muted beam of sunlight filtered in through the pane of glass, inviting my legs to move.

I swung them over the bed and stood, nearly collapsing had I not thrust my left side up against the adjacent wall. The contact sent the small space rattling, but I ignored it, hugging the wall as I moved to the promise of the outdoors. To catch a glimpse would be enough to ground me in reality, to let me know where I was.

If I've had any luck, I'd made it to Kethnar and was in some hovel along the shore.

The window proved of little use upon first examination. It was clouded over, too foggy to see through. I lifted the hem of my shirt to wipe at the condensation, stopping when I didn't recognize the material. I fingered the fabric between my forefinger and thumb, the sage green cloth soft to the touch. Somewhere in my sleep-induced sickness, I must have received a new shirt.

Shrugging, I proceeded in my course. A swipe at the window revealed something curious—a pane of glass speckled with water, drops defying the laws of gravity and traveling from the bottom of the pane upwards every few seconds.

Was it raining? I doubted it; I didn't hear any hitting the roof, and last I recalled, rain came *down,* not up.

Another swipe revealed even more water droplets, some trickling in rivulets, others splashing helter-skelter, only to be replaced anew with another wave of water. One last swipe cleared the pane entirely, and my heart dropped to my stomach.

A stretch of endless green ocean and then blue sky danced beyond the casement, and all at once, I felt the rising and falling movement beneath my feet, rendering my already weakened knees unstable.

There was no land in sight.

Suddenly, all my senses were wired.

*What's going on?*

"Good to see you're finally awake. You sleep like the dead."

I jumped, my pulse quickening of its own accord. I turned at the familiar voice, taking in the profile of the man who had tended to my health earlier, standing in the doorway, a tattered cloth draped over one shoulder. He had dark brown hair down to his shoulders and hazel eyes that glinted knowingly. He leaned slightly on his left leg, and he rubbed his thumb over his wrist as if out of habit, to the point that I could make out a slight indentation in the skin. He was both young and old, as if he'd weathered more storms than years, housing decades of secrets, or stories, within his bones.

There was something curious about him, in his manner of speaking and looks, that seemed to spark a memory from the past.

I shook the feeling away. There was no memory here, wherever *here* might be.

"Who are you? What is this place?" I asked, bracing myself with one hand against the wall. I felt like Monty, peppering the man with questions—a child who could barely stand on his own two feet. Speaking of Monty… "Where's my friend?"

"Two weeks in a fevered state produces a slew of questions. I don't blame you for it; I'd do the same myself," the man said.

I blinked at him. Had he just said two weeks?

"Your friend is safe. He's been kept in another room while your fever passed, doing some healing of his own, thanks to my apprentice. A long gash on his right leg required him to remain bedridden for a time." The man paused. "And as to what this place is…well, once I tell you, you won't be able to leave." *Not like you'll have a choice anyway,* I thought I caught him mumble.

Was this man insane? I took a step forward, using every ounce of strength to remain standing. "Come again?" I couldn't keep the challenge from my voice. "What do you mean I 'won't be able to leave'? What sort of place is this?"

"Curiosity gets the better of them, I suppose. It always does," the man said this more to himself than to me. He walked a little into the room, and the familiar scent of grass danced around my nose.

My hand reached toward my hip out of habit, shocked to find the sword missing; it must have been swallowed by the Tides; either that or removed from my person and stowed away somewhere. I stamped down the dread creeping into my arm and fingers, ignoring the itch to grip the hilt. My only weapon now was courage…and my fists.

"Do you really wish to know your whereabouts?" Something in his question sounded like a challenge.

"I beg you not to delay." I could handle the truth, whatever it might be. I'd fight my way out of this place if I had to.

"Full of vigor, I see. The Crimson Death spared you well." He chuckled. "As to your question, an airtight craft serves many a purpose beneath the raging Tides. One, namely, of anonymity."

I forgot about my sword, struck by the man's strange words; he was madder than I thought. "I'm not sure I understand."

He sighed. "You're aboard a vessel of my own making. I took two weathered hulls, flipped them so the gunwale trims are banded together, and then reconstructed the inside. So you see, you're not in one boat, but two, and you'll find it quite accommodating." He paused, watching me carefully as if to gauge my response. "As to it being airtight, well, the resin, ash, and sap—a waterproof concoction—are what keep this vessel from coming apart, allowing it to submerge and rise at my command. The *Neptucadis*, as it were. Top speed of fifty knots. I move about the Tides faster than you would your own home. Though currently, we are simply floating, or bobbing, if you will."

My head was swimming. "But how is that possible? There's no machinery capable of such things, no means of—"

"Ah, but you forget. The ocean is teeming with life, some of most peculiar size and form. Creativity was not spared in the making of the sea beasts, I assure you. And one just so happens to tote around my vessel, doing my bidding."

*Sea beasts? Bidding?*

"You're in here for the long haul now. I suggest you get comfortable," the captain said.

Suddenly it all clicked into place.

The slam to the hull, disturbing the beach plums.

The monstrous bellow from the depths.

The red tentacles latching onto the *Clam Dunk*'s remains.

The fevered dreams of a sea monster.

I swallowed, feeling a rush of fire climbing my throat.

I might have fought and defeated one Crimson Death, but the sea monster still remained. And I'd done more than find it.

I was inside it.

# Six

## Sinking Secrets

*No. That can't be right.*

I shook my head, pacing the small space of my infirmary; it was a slow process regaining my strength and range of motion. My leg was sore, but at least I could walk.

*Not inside. Strapped.* Like luggage to a mule. The strange man had said so himself. And a glance out the porthole only confirmed this. Though I couldn't see the beast which carried us, it seemed as if we were attached somewhere on its side.

The thought settled little. My strides could have created a rut in the rough-hewn floorboards by now with all my attempts at reason.

After the strange man left to attend to "tasks on board," he told me I'd be free to move about the vessel, to explore it at my leisure. But it wasn't as welcoming as it seemed; I was no better than a prisoner here. I escaped execution only to be trapped, inevitably and for all eternity, at the bottom of the sea.

My one consolation was looking out the porthole and still seeing the sunshine streaming through it. We hadn't submerged yet, but my hope was teetering with every rise and fall of the bobbing craft.

Fate was cruel if fate be anything at all.

To make matters more frustrating, there was something recognizable about the man, but his familiarity escaped me.

All he left me with were these perplexing words: *"I am nothing to you but Captain Aldo, and all on board are nothing to me but my passengers."* The way he said it, though, felt more like a rehearsed speech than a warning. And I knew he was an apothecary of sorts, as elusive as the sea itself.

A riddle just waiting to be solved, though not by me.

All my thoughts were bent toward one thing: escape.

Which reminded me—*Monty!*

Abandoning my ceaseless ponderings, I took to the adjoining hallway and cautiously poked my head out around the doorframe.

It was empty. The corridor was darker than my sun-filled bed chamber, lit instead by small candles, burning on holders along the walls. They cast an eerie glow around the narrow space, and I couldn't help wondering what might happen should the flame catch on the wood.

Something told me that it wasn't likely, that this unknown apothecary had more than tricks up his sleeve. This airtight vessel seemed like a hard nut to crack, but I'd find my way.

A guard always did.

I slink-limped down the hallway; fortunately, most of the doors were open a crack, allowing me to sneak glances inside them. One room revealed a table—two lobster traps pushed together with a piece of driftwood lying on top. Around it were chairs made from oversized sea stones that looked to have been hauled in from the dark depths. I assumed that was where Captain Aldo took his repast.

Another room revealed sparse shelves of food, a storehouse in need of restocking. Though my stomach longed to be filled, to peruse what was available, I had a mission first. I turned and kept going.

Suddenly, a spark of light glinted in the corner of my eye, stopping me from going any further. Curiosity besting caution, I paused at the door from which it was coming and pushed it in, revealing a staggering sight. I stepped over the threshold as if I'd entered hallowed ground, forgetting my previous task. A quick survey of the small space revealed weapons of every make: pikes, swords, longbows, axes, broadswords, throwing knives, maces, shields... It could rival Farrador's armory in spades.

"Where did all these come from?" I breathed out, awe lacing every word.

I walked deeper into the room, running my hand over a pauldron lying limp on a table. I couldn't ignore the green tarnish on the metal nor the subtle details hammered into its curves. I moved onto a sword, its hilt engraved with a faded crest: a destrier—the largest, heaviest warhorse in history—with vacant eyes, treading over fire and thorns... It was a symbol that all must surrender before the king.

My hand found the rest of the weapons, testing their weight and assessing their make. Most of the armaments looked waterlogged and forgotten, as if they had been salvaged from the sea and kept here as tokens of what once was. And if the grime and rust were any indicators, it appeared they'd been lying here for years.

There was memory built into this room, in the sense of touch, and my skin was alight with a familiarity I never thought I'd find— and *here*, of all places. This strange space felt like coming home.

It was a truth I knew in my marrow, sight unnecessary to confirm. Aside from a few pieces here and there, everything was Brakan made.

It made sense, to a degree. The Crimson Death had haunted the Tides for years, so of course it would take some of its souvenirs.

But that still begged the question warring in my mind ever since I'd stepped foot into the room.

"Why so many?" I said it more to myself than anything. What would a mysterious apothecary need *all* these weapons for?

Then a thought struck. *My sword!* Would it be here, too?

Another turn about the room proved it wasn't, but it disclosed something curious instead—something small enough to be overlooked yet too arresting to go unnoticed.

A gilded handle of sorts poked its head out from underneath a broadsword, a brass so rich it almost looked gold. I pried it loose from its makeshift cage, peeling back the supple cloth covering the rest of its body. Unveiling the object, I rotated it about in my hand, the refracting light glinting off the intricately detailed alloy. The same golden material stretched up the handle and branched off in two directions, forming a rounded arch before meeting once more at the top. In its middle lay a pane of glass, much like the portholes in each room, but this one was spotless and clear like a frozen lake.

"It's nothing but a looking glass." But as I said that, something seemed to shift on the mirror's face, darkening the glass in some swirling cloud.

Was it a trick of the light? I blinked, rubbing my eyes.

"Hux?"

I jumped at the sound of my name, my fingers loosening their hold on the gilded handle and sending it clattering to the ground. The impact was accompanied by a shattering cacophony, shards of glass scattering everywhere.

*Blast.*

I turned and found Monty standing in the doorway, his hands held up in mock surrender and his teeth set in an uncomfortable grimace. "Was that my fault?" he asked.

Relief flooded through me at finally seeing my friend, easing some of the guilt burning inside my chest. The broken shards scattered about my feet seemed paltry in light of everything else. "I should have been more careful."

"What was it?"

"Something of great value, no doubt." Another voice joined the fray, snarling. Appearing out of nowhere, the mysterious Captain Aldo stepped around Monty and entered the room, the familiar scent of freshly cut grass following him. Bending to pick up the mirror, he reached inside his pocket and extracted a cloth, snapping it once in the air before gathering the broken shards. He paused, glancing up. "If you two don't mind."

I nodded, his message as clear as the once unbroken glass itself. Something told me it wasn't any ordinary mirror. "We were just leaving." But before doing so, I accidentally stepped on a shard near the doorway, its crunch resounding beneath my foot.

"I'm sure." Captain Aldo gave a knowing look, waiting for us to move.

There was no use in lingering. I shook my boot and left the room, hoping Monty followed. In doing so, I caught the mumbled words of the mysterious apothecary in passing.

"Should've locked the door. A secret's not worth keeping if…"

Monty closed the door behind us, shutting out the remainder of Captain Aldo's speech. He turned and looked me over as if assessing my body for injuries.

"Good to see you on your feet, Hux."

"I could say the same about you." I was grateful to see Monty, and after nearly escaping death no less. But my mind was reeling.

I longed for an exit out of this place, and I couldn't stop thinking about the strange Captain Aldo, the now broken looking glass, and the fact that I had no idea where we were. Not to mention everything that happened prior to leaving Braka.

"You want to see my scar?" Monty didn't wait for my answer and lifted the hem of his pants to his mid-thigh, revealing a long gash that traversed the full length of his leg. It was red and ghastly, but I'd seen worse.

That was always the case when it came to these things. I'd seen and been dealt a lot when it came to injuries, but there was always an ever-moving threshold that implied *it could always be worse.* And in most cases, that was true.

"Nasty, that." I tipped my head at the wound, watching a sly smile spread across Monty's face.

"Aye, but you've been dealt a worse blow, I've no doubt. Miss Reid told me so herself."

I blinked, taken aback. "Miss Reid?" The last name struck me as familiar.

"You know." He leaned in, making sure no one was listening and brought his voice to a whisper. "Willa. The blonde with the freckles. She's a beauty, don't get me wrong, but how she manages to get freckles in a place like this is beside me." Monty chuckled, gesturing to the dark corridor.

*A place like this.* There was no sun, aside from the occasional light streaming in through the portholes. That was, until Captain Aldo's sea beast decided to take a plunge to the depths.

"I have no idea who you're talking about." I crossed my arms over my chest, the strain pulling at my wounded shoulder.

"She tended to your fever these past two weeks. I got worried; you were burning up like a bonfire. So she promised to keep me posted on your progress." Monty grew serious. "I didn't think you'd make it, Hux. What with all this talk of the Crimson Death… That sea beast wasn't named after some lousy sickness, and you know it."

I nodded, wracking my brain for any images of a blonde-haired girl with freckles, but any that came to mind were those of urchins who belonged on the mainland of Braka.

"She has the voice of an angel, too. Much like Gloria's back home. Right soothed me, it did." Monty sighed as if the memory alone was enough to make his pains go away.

*Her voice.*

Then I remembered. The cool cloth dipped with citrus scents. The sweet assurance of a gentle lilt. It must be the woman Monty was talking about.

But a woman's presence on board hardly mattered. Time was of the essence, and with Captain Aldo's harrowing words of this vessel submerging at his command, something told me we didn't have much left before it dipped below the surface for who knew how long.

"I'm sure this will 'right soothe' you, too. Come, Bates. We've some things to discuss." Relief at seeing my friend was soon replaced with newfound urgency as I grabbed hold of his shoulder and dragged him back to my abandoned chamber, the small room a welcome presence amidst the uncertainty of our future.

Once inside the space, Monty brushed me off before I shut the door and made for the porthole, the assurance of sunlight my saving grace.

"What's gotten into you, Hux? From the moment I saw you in that room, you've had a wild look about you—I can see it in your eyes! Have you gone, you know..." He pointed to his head and rotated his index finger in a circular motion.

I almost had to laugh. Monty looked calm and collected for once, while I appeared to have gone off the deep end.

"I've not lost my mind, if that's what you're asking," I replied, breathing in the sight of sunshine still cresting over the rolling tide.

"Then what's going on?"

I turned and faced him, irritation rising. "Do you not understand the direness of our circumstances, Monty? Have you any idea where we are?"

"Well, my guess is we're on the ocean, I can tell you that much. I'd know the feeling of a boat anywhere—"

"Have you not taken it upon yourself to look outside?" I

snapped, not keeping the low growl from my voice.

Monty looked taken aback. "My room boasted no view." He limped to the pane of glass and followed my line of sight, his eyes wide. He gasped. "Mercy! We're being swallowed by the sea! Look, the waves are lapping over us! And there—we're now below the horizon!" It was true; with each downward motion of the vessel, the waves claimed us whole. "What are you not telling me, Hux?" He turned and gripped my shirt, his hands starting to tremble. "We're not stowed away in some pirate's brig, are we?"

"A brig?" I felt my eyes narrow at his question. "No, we aren't some pirate's bounty, Monty. We're aboard a submersible vessel. The blasted *Neptucadis*, named after some childish fairy tale." I could hardly believe what I was saying.

"A submersible vessel?" he asked. "What in Braka's name is that?"

"Many things, apparently. It means we sink below the surface per the captains' will, to depths I can only guess at. But that's not even the worst part." I ran a hand over my face.

Monty swallowed hard, and for once, he didn't ask a question. He didn't need to.

"We're aboard Braka's bane. The terror of the Tides. You see, Bates, we've found the Crimson Death. Captain Aldo has trained the sea beast to do his will, and we're on it!"

Monty's face turned as pale as a sheet of linen. His limbs began to shake, and I could tell he wished he'd never come with me at all. "Are you certain?"

I nodded. The captain didn't have to name this creature for me to know. And though it was still a hypothesis, the evidence spoke for itself.

As if struck by a sudden thought, Monty said, "Then let's just ask the captain if he can drop us off at Kethnar. He's bound to let us free."

"I wouldn't count on it. The captain's been decent enough to help us, but we're as good as prisoners here." The admission made my fists clench.

"Prisoners?" Monty raised a brow.

I nodded. "He said we can't leave. We'll have to break ourselves out if we're ever to be free. I just need more time to devise a plan."

"And how are we going to do that?"

"As long as the beast remains at the surface, we have time. If it decides to sink, well, let's just say we'll have to hold our breath."

As if on cue, a rumbling shook the vessel, rattling the wooden beams of the walls and floorboards. A monstrous cry rent the waters, and the gentle bobbing of the tides was replaced by a strange sucking sound.

I braced myself against the wall, my leg and shoulder barking at the strain.

Monty tumbled to the ground, his eyes wide. "What's going on?" he cried.

A look out the porthole confirmed my greatest fear, my stomach sinking like the vessel itself. The sunshine was now replaced in full by a deep, murky blue, and any traces of the world above—they were gone.

*We're too late.*

"Time to hold your breath, Bates." I swallowed hard. "We're

going under."

All my thoughts were

bent toward one thing:

escape.

# Seven

## Polishing Silver

The pressure around the vessel intensified. My ears popped, noises and voices a distant echo one moment and crystal clear the next. The drastic altitude change was dizzying. Suffice it to say, the makings of a headache were settling in.

"Where are we going?" Monty asked, getting up from the floor. He met me at the porthole once more, now looking out into the dark depths. "I've only traveled atop the seas, not beneath them! What do we do now?"

I clapped my friend on the shoulder and tried my hand at steadying him. I felt his fear; it lodged somewhere in my throat like a suffocating knot, but we needed our wits about us if we were to make it out of here alive.

"Now? We wait. That's all we can do." I said the words but didn't feel their assurance. They were more a raft keeping us afloat rather than a sturdy ship.

"To wait in a place like this…" Monty shuddered. "Hux, it makes me wish you'd never shown me that window in the first place." He groaned, shrugging me off, and limped to the makeshift cot I'd abandoned earlier.

"Ignorance is bliss, as they say. Would you rather be kept in the dark, then?"

"I'm beginning to think I'd much prefer it. I can't imagine walking about this place much longer." He avoided my gaze.

"We have little choice now. In fact, the more 'walking about this place' the better. We need to know every inch of this vessel if we're to escape it. And you'd do well not to abandon a brother in the task."

"Abandon?" He snapped his head up. "Do you think so little of me, Hux? After all these years?"

"On the contrary. I think so highly of your ability to question yourself into a panic. All I ask is that you steel your nerves and trust me." I crossed my arms over my chest, waiting.

Monty shook his head, placing it in his hands. Then he snorted, a slow disbelieving chuckle following. "I can't believe we're doing this."

Another thing about Monty: once his nerves passed, he came to grips with his fate, whatever it might be. It was as if the chokehold of death loosened its bony fingers from around his neck enough to bring clarity to his once-anxious mind. And then he'd laugh as if there was nothing else left to do.

"I trust you, Hux. Always have, always will. But if we die down here, you know I'll kill you."

"That's the spirit!" I cracked a smile, clapping him on the back.

"But first things first—we have to see what kind of beast we're dealing with here."

The wooden beams of the submerged vessel creaked and groaned the further down we dropped as if crying out in mockery, *"Wouldn't you like to know? You can't escape!"*

I shook off the uneasy feeling and rolled my shoulders back.

It was time to get more information.

We moved about the sinking craft, hands on the walls, careful not to disrupt the fiery sconces lighting our path. It was significantly darker now that the sunshine no longer filtered in through the panes and lit the hallway. An otherworldly stillness enveloped me, and I could tell Monty felt it, too.

We had already covered all our tracks from my bedroom to his, poking our heads inside more rooms and trying the handle on the armory again, only to find it locked. I figured Captain Aldo didn't want us nosing around in there after what I did.

Even though this vessel felt small, I had a hunch it boasted more than met the eye.

As we neared the end of the corridor, Monty let out a sigh. "Looks like this is the end of it. Again."

He started turning around but stopped when he ran into my outstretched arm.

"Not quite." Squinting into the darkness, I made out strange shadows behind a set of barrels, deeper and boxier in their making. I walked closer, and a crude set of stairs revealed itself, barely distinguishable in the flickering torchlight. Hope rose in my chest. "Looks like we're going up."

"Up? That's promising, right?" Monty said, trailing after me.

I suppressed the urge to snort. Yes, a few feet higher and somehow the prospect made the leagues separating us from the surface feel much smaller.

I climbed the steps, putting weight on my good leg before swinging my injured one up to follow. A glance behind showed Monty was doing the same. A pair of bumbling invalids we were; the idea of escaping now was almost comical.

As we climbed higher, a faint sound, almost like scratching, reached my ears.

Finally at the top, the landing opened into another hallway, though this one was wider than the one below it. It was brighter up here, too, with additional wall candles, these ones burning at different hues—more of a yellowy gold rather than a burnt orange. How that was managed, I hadn't the slightest clue, but then again, the apothecary-turned-captain was a man of secrets.

From our vantage point, there seemed to be even more rooms lining the walls and another staircase at the far end of the hall. And the scratching sound had increased two-fold, though it was less rhythmic than before.

"We're in the belly of the beast, er—ship, rather," Monty said beside me.

We both stood there, probably looking like fish out of water, and the irony wasn't lost on me.

"Let's just hope this one isn't prone to digestion." I moved forward, my ears drawn to the mysterious scraping; it sounded like stone on metal or the scraping of mortar on rock.

"What's that awful noise?" Monty asked, his hands rubbing against his temples.

It wasn't wholly unpleasant, the sound reminding me of the smithy and many turns about the whetstone.

"We're going to find out." Tracking down the room from whence the sound came, I pushed open the door, expecting to find the mysterious apothecary. Instead, a gangly man as weathered as the sea glanced up, his eyes like pools of liquid silver.

"Cyril?" I asked, my mouth gaping.

Perhaps I was mistaken. There was indeed something familiar about him, much like Captain Aldo, but maybe I had spoken too soon. Maybe I was relying too heavily on the rumor from seven years ago, though this was surely an aged version of the man I once knew. Was it possible that he had disappeared only to end up here?

The man finally stopped staring and nodded, his gaze darting between me and Monty. "Yes, I am he." A crease worked its way into his brow as if he struggled to comprehend why we were standing in the doorway. "Do I know you?"

I took a step over the threshold, adrenaline coursing through my veins. "This must be some coincidence." Or divine intervention. "We're from Braka. You knew my parents, Huxley and Joanie Gannon. I'm their son."

Realization seemed to dawn as the man's eyes alighted in understanding. "Yes, you're the young guard, a soldier from Farrador. Well, I'll be. You look just like your father did when he was your age. How old are you now? One and twenty?"

"Almost a decade more, I'm afraid. Eight and twenty."

"My, how the young ones grow."

I nodded. "And you might remember Monty Bates. His family works the docks. He was there the day you…" Was it insensitive to bring up the past? The day Cyril vanished off Braka's shores and left the whole country in a panic?

"The day I wound up here, you mean? Yes, I do recall a likeness. Nice to see you again, Monty."

"Likewise." Monty tipped his head.

"What brings you young men out here? It's not everyday strangers come aboard." He picked up the steel wool and resumed his task of polishing, his ear still bent toward us. His fingers were long and slender but nonetheless strong, for his hands were as muscular as they were bony.

"We were making a trip to Kethnar." I didn't bother mentioning my fall from grace with Barrington nor the pain of learning of Prince Clark's death. "Then our vessel was ruthlessly attacked."

"Ah." He nodded. "The captain has a unique sense of justice."

"I think that's putting it lightly." I scoffed.

"I didn't say I agreed with his methods, for many are ill-born, but there is some goodness there. Hidden in the dark." Cyril shifted in his seat, scrubbing the silver even harder.

*It must be* really *hidden.*

I couldn't help watching his hands, the slump of his shoulders, the haggard look in his overall form. "How long have you been here? Surely, you're in need of a break," I said.

"There is still much to get done. The captain likes his instruments clean." He continued his scrubbing, the strain evident in his aged limbs.

From this angle, I could tell Cyril's fingers were calloused and red from overuse, from hours spent wiping away grime and tarnish. But there was something else there, too—a shakiness to his hands, a shaking so severe that it was remarkable he could do anything at all.

Catching my notice, he chuckled. "Not much use these things are now." He indicated his extremities, glancing up ever so slightly. "But you should have heard them in their heyday."

"Heard?" I asked before thinking. A strange word for talking about one's hands, unless they were prone to clapping.

"Don't forget. I was the royal harpist." A wistful longing lingered in his somber smile.

I silently berated myself for having forgotten that detail.

"Dreams die with age, I'm afraid, but they live on through generations. The greatest gift a father can leave behind is a legacy for their young ones to take up themselves," he said, his hands shaking even more than before. A silver spoon tumbled to the floor, clanging unceremoniously on the wooden beams by his feet. "Oh bother."

Without so much as a second thought, I closed the gap between us and picked up the fallen object, setting it down on the barrel beside him. "I believe this silver is polished enough."

Cyril looked at me before shaking his head. "I must work 'til the task is done. The captain desires clean instruments if he's to work. Clean spoons to stir the tinctures. Clean knives to cut the herbs. Clean pestles to ground the leaves. Clean forks to eat his fill. Clean—"

I placed a hand atop his, stilling his shaking limbs for a moment.

"Then let me help. Why don't you go rest? I'm sure it will do you some good."

"I can't let you do that; you shouldn't have to do an old man's job."

"It's the least we can do," I said, reaching down to help him up.

Cyril nodded again as if he saw no point in arguing and made for the door; his slow gait rivaled my gimpy leg. He paused after a few strides, turning to face us. "Just when I think all is forgotten, here in the abyss, our Maker sends reinforcements. He sends light." He smiled. "Thank you, boys." He turned and shuffled out the door, disappearing down the corridor and leaving Monty and I alone.

*"We?"* Monty turned and pinned me with a look like he couldn't believe I'd just volunteered him to polish silverware.

"Just shut up and get to work." I tossed him some iron wool and a rag before dragging over an extra crate to sit on. Together, we dipped the silver utensils into a steaming bucket of water and lathered soap over them, scrubbing hard.

It seemed an hour had passed by the time our hands, too, had turned mottled and red. My skin blistered and smarted, not to mention my shoulder burned from all the movement—a strange sensation for one who practiced with swords half the day and guarded the prince the rest of it…or *used* to guard the prince. It felt good to work, though I missed utilizing my muscles in the training arena. I'd never been in an actual battle, but I was ready to fight in one should the time ever come.

"Well, this isn't what I had in mind when you suggested we go searching for information." Monty chuckled, wiping his wet hands on a dry rag.

I agreed. My mind was still addled from the current change of affairs. "You and me bo—"

"Father?" a gentle voice called from somewhere in the hallway. "Are you still working?"

I had little time to wonder who the voice belonged to when a pale figure came hurrying into the room. In her hand was a small, gilded instrument, strung and all.

"I just learned a new song and wanted to—oh! I'm sorry." Her eyes widened, her face going a shade red. "I didn't think anyone else would be here. My father… Have you seen him?" She shifted her weight from one foot to the other.

"Cyril?" I asked, the only logical explanation. I knew he had a daughter, but I had no clue as to her age. By the looks of her, I'd guess she was in her early twenties.

She nodded.

"I have. He was relieved from duty over an hour ago. Should be resting now, I'd presume." I tilted my head, gesturing in the direction of the hallway. The anxious look on the woman's face abated a fraction. From her blonde hair and freckles, I surmised she was the lady Monty had mentioned earlier: Miss Reid.

No wonder her last name had sounded so familiar.

"Thank you. For helping him, that is. I fear he works too hard sometimes." She reached for the nape of her neck, scratching gently at a space behind her left ear.

"It was the least we could do." Monty, the boor. *Now* he was grateful for polishing the silver?

I couldn't help rolling my eyes.

Miss Reid bit her lip. "Well, I'd best be going, then." She turned to leave and paused in the doorway, looking over her shoulder in my direction. "Um…I'll come by tonight to check on both of your injuries and redress them, if that's all right with you."

"That won't be nec—" I oomphed, my side barking under Monty's quick spar to my ribs, cutting off any remaining words. I rubbed the affected area.

"We thank you, Miss Reid," Monty said.

She nodded, dipping out of the room as quickly as she came, this time with a subtle crease to her brow.

I turned and leveled my friend with my gaze. "What in the blast was that for?"

"Are you daft? That's *her*, the blonde angel I was talking about! If you had half a brain, you wouldn't tell her to leave you alone," Monty whispered as if he was afraid his voice would carry beyond the walls of the small room.

"I prefer being left alone. Always have."

Monty groaned, shaking his head. "You're impossible, Hux. I'm friends with a boneheaded clodpoll."

I snorted. "Why's that, I wonder? You still trying your hand at matchmaking, Monty Bates? *You* can't even talk to the girl you're in love with."

"Bah!" he guffawed. "That's a low blow, mate. And it's a different situation entirely. The difference is, I have intentions to and you don't. It's just like you to deem merely being in a woman's presence as 'matchmaking.' Is it that painful to simply talk to one? To spend a little time in her company and get to know her? You've been avoiding them at a distance thrice the length of your broadsword. Ever since—"

"Don't." I snapped, holding up my hand to stop him, my insides like a match to tinder. That part of my life had a steel cage built around it; I didn't need Monty's words as the key to pry open the blasted door. "I don't have time for women, Monty. Not then, and *definitely* not now." Not then, when I had a prince to protect. Not now, when I was a hunted man. Not *ever*—I shoved a random spoon in the water and scrubbed vigorously at the grime, water sloshing over the side of the barrel and onto my shoes.

I could tell Monty was staring at me; he always did that when he didn't know what to say, but I couldn't bring myself to meet his gaze.

Slowly, he sighed, releasing the tension in the room. "Suit yourself, brother. Just promise me one thing." He clapped me on the shoulder, and I flinched beneath his touch. "Don't let one woman's follies taint your opinion of the rest of them. Not all women are coldblooded." He pushed to a stand and headed to the door, his footsteps echoing along the timber floors.

*The blighted...*

"Where are you going?" I grunted. There wasn't much space to roam in this vessel—nowhere to go.

"To rest. I'm dog-tired." And with that, Monty departed, leaving me alone with my thoughts and his challenge to my resolve.

*"Not all women are coldblooded."*

The words tumbled around in my mind, but like a Brakan thicket in a heady gale, they never found a place to land. Surely there was truth to that statement, but I had never cared to test its theory.

And I still didn't now.

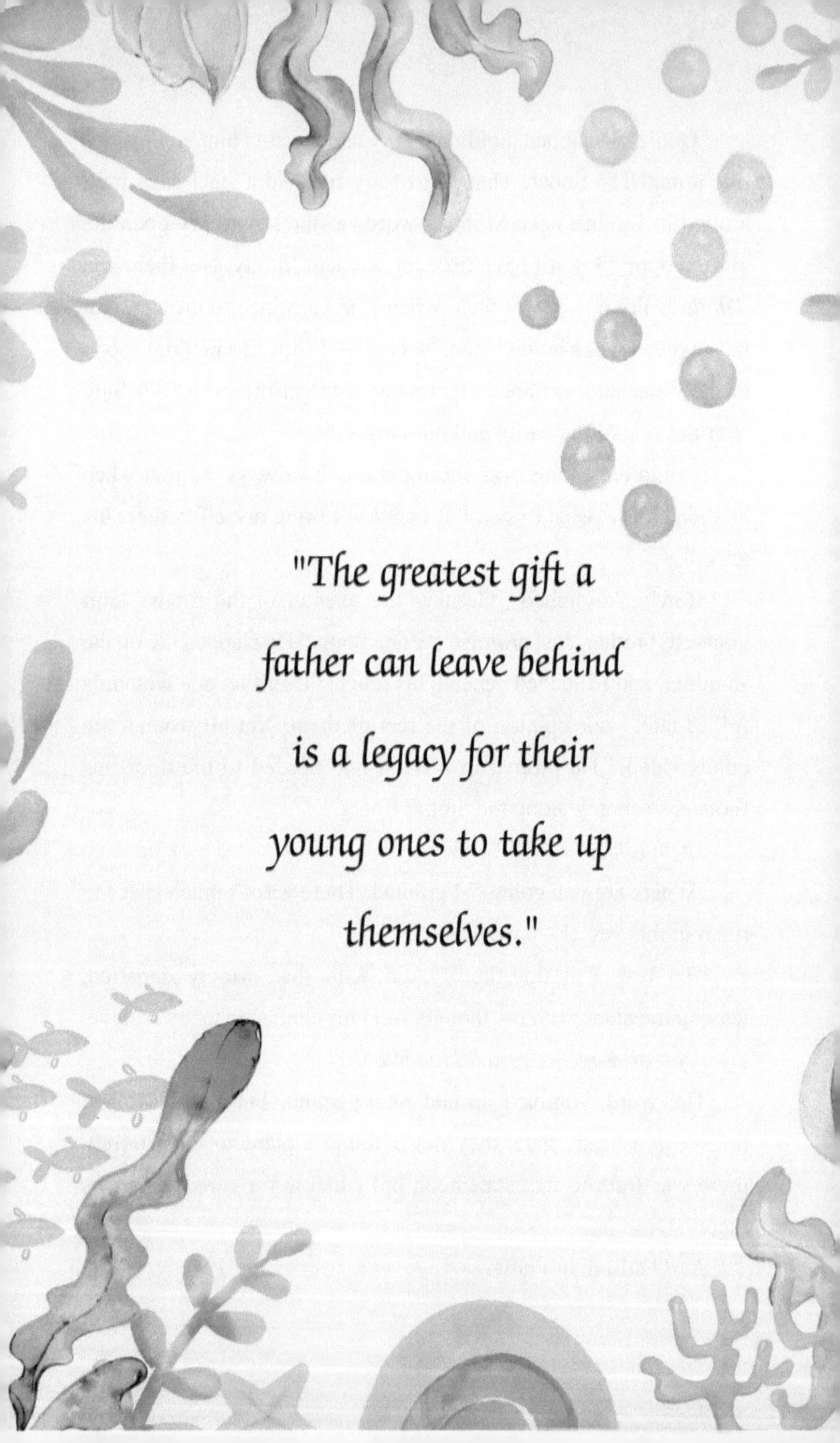

"The greatest gift a
father can leave behind
is a legacy for their
young ones to take up
themselves."

# Eight

## Cuddlefish

After Monty retired early, I scoured the rest of the second floor, not finding much to report. I peeked inside bed chambers which I assumed were Cyril and Miss Reid's but, wanting to give them their privacy, didn't bother examining them further.

Another couple of doors boasted a storehouse for herbs and what looked to be additional bunk rooms, a kitchen, a lavatory, another pantry, and a second dining parlor with a bigger table. Every room had at least one porthole. Was there a large crew on board this submerged vessel? If so, where were they?

I tried the staircase on the far end of the hall, only to find the trap door to the top floor locked in place. My assumption was Captain Aldo spent most of his time up there, but doing *what* was the question.

Until I could get my hands on a key, or even a weapon, it looked like we'd be roaming these same halls for all eternity and then some.

I shook my head.

We'd get out. We had to.

Finding nothing else to do, I kept myself busy by pacing the small interior of my bedroom, missing the weight of metal on my hip. My body itched to move, to fight, to trace the perimeter of the training field back at Farrador, to stab one of those practice dummies in its wooden stomach. All in the name of fundamentals, of course.

But that luxury was stripped from me. If I ever got free, I'd show up just to have my head served on a platter.

I paused near the porthole, running my hand over the divots in the panels beside it; a set of sixteen tallies, carved subtly into the wood, marked the two weeks we'd already been trapped at sea and the two days prior when we'd first left Braka. I took out the broken fish hook from my pocket, turning it over in my hand. It wasn't much, but it was a windfall to have found it snagged on the netting of my bed. It was enough to keep me sane.

As long as I made the marks on the walls, they could serve as my lungs and allow me to breathe for another day, even from below such depths. The Maker knew what He was doing when He made man *above* sea level.

It was hard enough to gauge the passing of time without the sun, but as a royal guard, I'd learned to count the minutes in my mind. It was a practice required of all of us.

A knock sounded on my door, and I quickly stuffed the fish hook back in my pocket. My apprehension rose along with the hairs on my neck. Had Captain Aldo finally left his throne to descend amongst his prisoners?

But what poked around the doorframe was a blonde set of locks, a wad of fresh bandages in her hand. "May I come in?" she asked, already halfway over the threshold.

"Sure." I walked to the bed and took a seat, figuring the best way to get this over with was to comply and keep my mouth shut.

Miss Reid came forward and stood before me. She was a mite of a thing; her overall height was barely taller than my sitting form. She laid her bundle down, taking out a jar of green goop from a wooden box and a silver spoon I could have sworn I had a hand in polishing earlier. She scooped out some of the salve and placed the spoon on the wooden crate beside my bed as if saving it for later.

"Needs a moment to cure," she said, obviously noticing my creased brow.

The smell of rosemary tickled my nose, and I couldn't stop myself from sneezing.

"The Maker anoint thee," she said.

The Brakan saying was like a balm, a welcome comfort amidst the foreignness of the vessel, one I hadn't known I needed.

She unwrapped the green band of seaweed from around my arm. It had grown stiff from being parched all day, flaking off with her touch. She then took the green goop on the spoon and smeared it along my cut; I sucked in a hiss at how fiercely it stung. "Just some more yarrow. Your wound is healing nicely."

Her words were so gentle, I felt as if I could breathe a little easier. Or perhaps that was only because of my tally marks on the wall.

She recapped the salve and took the fresh bandage, wrapping the linen cloth around my shoulder before pinning it in place.

"No more seaweed?" I asked, surprised at myself. The last thing I needed was to make conversation or take Monty's advice about women.

She shook her head. "The seaweed is only necessary for helping to keep infection out the first couple of weeks. The salt from the plant acts as a protective barrier against the elements. And now that you've been alert for almost twenty-four hours, I figured you could use something a bit more comfortable before you fall asleep." She smiled warmly.

I nodded. "You're from Braka." Of course she was. Her father was Farrador's harpist, so obviously she had grown up there, too. And I was more than certain our paths had crossed at least a handful of times. Why I felt the need to point out the obvious was beyond me.

Her expression shifted, dipping from joy to something more pensive. Or was it thoughtful? Not talking to women for years had left me out of practice in reading any of them.

"Was." She gathered her supplies and started putting them back in the box. She slammed the lid closed, a blush climbing her cheeks at its loud noise. "I haven't been home in years, I'm afraid. Don't even know if I can rightfully call it that now."

Her words did something strange inside me. It was as if the hope I'd felt earlier was now infused with dread. I knew it had been seven years since her father first ended up here, but what about her? The urgency to leave this place had suddenly increased ten-fold.

"How long has it been?" I asked.

She paused, rubbing her hand near her ear the same way I'd seen her do it before. "Nearly seven years, though time moves differently in the ocean, so I can never be sure."

*Seven years, too?* My muscles twitched. So very much like her father's timeline. But how? She hadn't disappeared off the coast of Braka with him.

I was tempted to ask another question but clamped my mouth shut when she spoke again.

"It's not all bad, though. Captain Aldo is kind and hospitable enough, and I've got my father on board. The fact that he's alive is more important to me than ever seeing dry land again. Though, I do miss the kiss of the sun."

*Aye. What I'd give for the sun to scorch my entire body.*

"In fact, I believe Captain Aldo wants to meet with you tomorrow. On the second floor. You and your friend…" She paused as if she'd just realized she didn't know our names.

"Huxley Gannon." I nodded. "And he's Monty Bates." Would we be introducing ourselves to everyone on this blasted contraption?

She smiled. "Right, well, the captain has something to show you, or at least, that's what he hinted to me."

I nodded again, my tongue tied. I still wanted to ask her how she had ended up here, but it was looking like that question would have to wait. Right now, there were more pressing matters to attend to.

"Well, I think it's time I checked on your friend. Sleep well." She tucked the box under her arm and walked toward the door.

"Thank you," I said to her back. I might not know how to talk to women, but my mother had always taught me how to respect them.

She smiled and left, taking her angelic presence with her.

And suddenly, a knot of apprehension weaved its way into my chest as Miss Reid's words affected me anew: *"Captain Aldo wants to meet with you tomorrow."*

I could only hope he'd garnered some sense and decided to let us go.

Sunlight danced over my eyelids in waves, warming my face. The sky poured forth a gentle rain amidst a brilliant sky, spattering my skin with its touch. These were my favorite mornings, ones that came too few and far between—sun showers atop the battlements of Farrador.

Once every three months, I got a specific night off from standing guard over the prince's bedchamber, entrusting my charge to the care of one of my comrades. A night to refuel and do as I pleased. To weasel my way through Farrador's secret passageways and end by bedding beneath the stars; I'd pass the time counting them while the distant call of the barred owl lulled me to sleep, then wake to the sun of a new morning.

Over the past few years, I noticed no one went to the top of the old keep, the pinnacle too high and the stairs too difficult to navigate in their slow deterioration. All the better for me; I hauled up some seed and planted a bed of grass to *keep* me. It was there where I lay now.

And it was made better with a light sprinkle of rain.

I rolled to my right, expecting to feel the grass beneath me, only to fall off my bed and slam my skull into something far less forgiving than my homegrown meadow.

Wood paneling.

I cracked open an eyelid, the buoyancy of my dream fading. A sinking, twisting knot settled in my middle instead.

It was as if reality had struck me anew with a cruel hand.

Prince Clark was dead. I was accused of treason. And now… *I'm trapped.* Stranded at sea. All because King Barrington had called me a traitor for something I never did; the events from that night still played over in my mind, and I couldn't make sense of them, couldn't accept that Clark was actually gone. My steady resentment for the king was growing by the second.

The only positive was that it appeared we had breached the surface of the relenting tide, if the morning light filtering in through the porthole in spurts was any indication. The sight of the sanctifying sun seemed to wash away the dread but for a moment, soon replaced with frustration that it was only a glimpse. A fleeting one at that.

I clambered to my feet and fished out the hook from my pocket, striking yet another tally mark on the wall. I paused, laying both my hands on the lip of the porthole, gripping the frame hard.

*Get yourself together, Huxley.* Shouldn't a guard be better at handling this sort of thing?

It was only my second day awake, but knowing I'd been stuck here for over two weeks challenged my sanity. *How much longer?*

I feared for Monty; in fact, the guilt ran deep, threatening to spill over. *He* had a family to care for; I only had myself.

If only he hadn't come with me. If I'd only escaped to Kethnar on my own. If only I hadn't been accused of a crime I never committed. If only Prince Clark hadn't died…

I slammed my palm into the wall, stifling a cry that threatened to break free. And then I slammed it again. My hand rested there a long time until my internal fire dulled enough to feel the coarse wood grains beneath my fingertips. "Why has this happened to me?" It came out as a whisper, a plea. I hadn't known I was crying until a single tear rolled down my chin.

My free hand skirted it away, my lungs expelling an exasperated breath.

If only one could change the course of the past to bring it to justice. To wholeness.

*Enough of this.* I pushed off from the bulkhead and rolled my neck before pulling my shoulders back. If onlys were for those who feared the future. Today was a new dawn, and whatever Captain Aldo had to say, I'd face it like a man, not some emotional fool.

Escape would come. I just had to bide my time.

I stalked out the door and retrieved Monty before climbing the stairs.

It was time to meet our fate.

"So glad you two could make it," Captain Aldo said, nodding at Monty and I.

He wore a long overcoat atop a billowy, white shirt. His hands were still stained with herbal dyes, but there was a gleam to his eyes that wasn't there before. Not to mention, I caught the lingering scent of grass, and I couldn't shake my dream from earlier.

It was strange how the sight of him ignited an unbidden ire in my chest. I didn't know the man, yet I was forced against my will to be in his proximity. If it wasn't for his hand in saving my life, I'd loathe the man entirely. And Miss Reid thought he was kind?

"Now, if you'll both follow me." He gestured with his hand, walking the length of the corridor to the set of stairs leading up to the trap door. Though he was an older man, he climbed them with the agility of a youth despite the slight hobble in his gait. At the top, he reached beneath the folds of his shirt and drew out a long chain. On its end boasted a shiny, hollowed-out skeleton key, wielded and bent into the shape of a destrier with rubies for eyes.

My eyes lingered on it, a light dawning as the hairs on my arms rose in recognition. *It's Brakan made, too.*

He inserted the device into the lock and, at the sound of an assuring click, pushed the trap open and motioned for us to follow.

I glanced at Monty, his mouth set in a grim line, but I could tell his eyes held thousands of questions. Just yesterday we were on this floor, trying our hand at finding an escape, and just yesterday, I had attempted the lock on this door, only to find that today I'd have my questions answered.

I held the railing as I ascended, noticing the motion in both our injured legs significantly improved from yesterday. At the landing, I was slapped in the face by the smell of something earthy and strong, my nose twitching like one of those hares darting about the grounds by Castle Farrador's kitchens, the place where Cook Greta dumped the days-old vegetables.

I eagerly surveyed my surroundings, soaking up as much as I

could before the moment was gone. Before the trap door swung shut on an ocean of possibilities.

My mouth went slack.

"Welcome to the control hub. The observatory, I like to call it," Captain Aldo said, walking to the center of the room with arms splayed as he slowly spun in a circle.

The sight before me seemed to defy technological odds, or at least, odds for such a craft as this. A wide panel of glass stretched along the far wall, reaching about three yards wide and one yard tall, looking out into an endless horizon of greenish-blue. Sunlight filtered in through the glass with reckless abandon, and the mere sight of the outdoors, and this much of it, squeezed my chest. Much like the porthole in my room, I ached to be on the other side.

I forced my gaze away, finding the source for all the earthy smells. Countless pots with plants varying in all shades of green surrounded the enclosure, most very close to the large window. I couldn't discern their make and kind from such a distance, but something in their leafy stalks and scents reminded me of Braka's shores. Of Braka's native plants.

*Is this some sort of coincidence?* I felt as if I already knew the answer.

A more thorough survey of the room revealed a few bedrooms on the adjacent wall, and my heart nearly beat a triple-time tempo when I spotted a spiral stair leading up to some sort of hatch above. My fingers joined in with the beat of my chest, twitching at my hip as if willing my sword to appear.

It was the feeling of hope. Of freedom. A way out.

"What do you think?" Captain Aldo asked, snapping my

attention back to him

I swallowed, not wanting to give suspicion toward my thoughts. "It's a nice room."

"I guess you could say that." He chuckled, crossing his arms, and turned to stare out the window. "Just wait." He curled his lower lip and whistled through his teeth, a high-pitched noise that echoed throughout the room.

As if in response, something moved outside, churning the waves right below the window's base. And suddenly, a large tentacle escaped from the water and suctioned itself against the glass.

"Mercy! What in the blast is that?" Monty shouted, his hands starting their telltale wriggling. "Some sort of giant squid?" His eyes widened, and I could tell he was reliving the episode from a few weeks back when we plunged to our doom and ended up here.

His apprehension echoed my own, my muscles remembering that moment as if it were yesterday.

"Not a giant squid. A giant cephalopod—a marine mollusk of unsuspecting intellect—or as you Brakans call it, the Crimson Death. She's a sentient lass."

All suspicions were confirmed, then. We really *had* found the alleged beast that haunted the Tides. Braka's bane.

"An octopus?" I asked.

"Nay, a cuttlefish."

"Cuddlefish? As in cuddly?" Monty's tone said it all. How could a sea beast hold such a name?

"Cu-*tt*-lefish. As in she will cut you should you make the wrong move." Captain Aldo smirked. "But no matter. Under my control, this forty-five-foot creature is virtually harmless. A quarter cup of valerian root and a tablespoon of the poppy flower works wonders on her eight arms and two tentacles. Though, she'd much prefer if I just fed her catmint; makes her hyper."

"Why have you brought us here?" My eyes wandered back over to the potted plants and to the hatch in the ceiling. In order to keep these plants alive, they needed sunlight. The thought brought some comfort; that meant we wouldn't be submerged for weeks on end.

"Ah, yes. Seeing as you two are healing nicely, we're going to go on a little excursion tomorrow. You see, we've landed in the Straits of Kethnar just this morning. Tomorrow, we'll be in the Herring Sea, and it's there I have something to show you."

*An excursion?* That sounded promising.

Captain Aldo moved to a wooden chair in the center of the room and brushed his coat back before sitting down.

In his movements, I saw the broken looking glass sticking out of his pocket, its gilded frame taunting me. The smoking glass was never far from my thoughts, though it seemed I'd never discover its secrets. What would have happened had I not dropped it? And why would the captain choose to keep the busted-up instrument on his person?

"That will be all," he said, facing out toward the sea, his gaze latched on the giant tentacle still suctioned to the glass.

*That's it?* Forget the mirror. I fought the urge to approach him and shake him by his collar.

"Can't you tell us more about this excursion?" I asked. "What's in the Herring Sea?"

He waved his hand in the air, not bothering to turn around. "And spoil the surprise? No, no. Wait but a day, for then the jars will be lit. And if you prefer illuminated spaces over dark ones, your curiosity will be sated." He whistled again, and the large tentacle unstuck itself from the glass and disappeared in the waves. "Now, if you'll excuse me…"

*Illuminated places?* This man spoke in riddles more than water was in the sea.

A war raged inside me within those few seconds as I glanced between Captain Aldo and the hatch. Should I make a run for it? Tell Monty to follow?

Something warned me to bide my time and wait for the excursion, no matter how much the flame in my middle flared. To escape now would only end in bringing us back here, most likely locked in our chambers.

And if all else failed, I needed to figure out a way to steal Captain Aldo's skeleton key, for by the looks of it, it could unlock any door. But something told me there was a secret within his looking glass that warranted answers, too. If not, why carry it on his person?

Until tomorrow.

Retracing the steps back to the second floor was almost more painful than getting stabbed in the shoulder. It would be another day of roaming these halls and doing nothing about it.

"Monty," I whispered to him once we were out of earshot.

He looked askance at me.

"Did you notice anything about the captain's key?" I asked.

He paused, running a thumb under his chin. "No, can't say I did. I was too busy staring at that blasted tentacle suctioned to the glass.

What about it?"

"It's Brakan for sure, but that's not what's odd." On my rounds with Prince Clark, I'd gone to the surrounding countryside, throughout all of Edgefold and Greymist and even the distant farming village of Fyrandell, and no merchants sold anything of its kind, for there was no such place that boasted the insignia of the king.

"This key…" I turned its image over again in my mind, recalling the unique shape of a war horse molded into the metal—Farrador's symbol—and the rubies, the same color red as the flag which bore the crest, for its eyes. "It came from within Farrador itself. I'd bet my life on it." Only those entrusted in the king's service were given such a trinket.

But how a strange apothecary-turned-captain who lived on the Tides came by something such as this… For some reason, I had a feeling the looking glass held the answers.

# Nine

## Books Tell No Lies

The next morning, I opened my eyes to darkness. A candle burning low in its holder on the wall was the only light my chamber boasted. So unlike yesterday with its morning light filtering through the porthole.

The sight was near suffocating, but the promise of an excursion was my confidence.

Today, I *would* taste fresh air. Today, I *would* find a way for Monty and me to be free. If not, I'd consign myself to solving the riddle of the king's key and the strange mirror.

When we got to the second floor, Captain Aldo was nowhere to be seen. It was only Miss Reid, gesturing for us to follow her. She led us into the dining parlor, where Cyril and two other men were already seated around a driftwood table.

Monty and I each took a seat, sharing a look that read: *Who are these people? Other prisoners of the captain's?* Something about their appearances looked foreign.

"Morning, Huxley. Monty. I trust you slept well?" Cyril greeted us, lifting a shaky mug toward his lips. He took a long sip of what smelled like herbal tea. The men beside him didn't acknowledge us and continued to chat quietly between themselves.

"I always sleep better *on* the water, not *in* it, if you catch my drift," Monty said like a true sailor, one who missed the wind in his sails and the caress of the sun.

"And you?" I asked, not bothering to give my two cents. Sleep never came easy to a soldier plagued with memories.

"Well, this body isn't getting any younger, but I've grown accustomed to the fishing nets. Could always be worse." Cyril slurped more of his drink, a smile on his lips.

I nodded. The fishing nets were not the most comfortable thing for a bed, but it beat sleeping on the cold floor.

Miss Reid entered the room and approached the table with a set of clean plates in one hand and a tray of food in the other. It was laden with slabs of salmon, tuna, fish eggs, dried seaweed, and oysters. Seafood, to be sure, but that was not what my stomach could handle this morning—nor ever, really.

The two unnamed men each took some fish onto their plates, and Cyril took a couple of oysters before squeezing his daughter's hand affectionately, a gesture that demonstrated his gratitude. Her smile boasted two dimples, a fullness to it that I hadn't seen prior— the power of a parent's assurance, I supposed.

It used to affect me like that once, too. When my mother was alive and my father hadn't gone missing.

"Breakfast?" Miss Reid asked. She'd finally made her way over to us.

Monty nodded. "Thank you, Miss Reid." He took the offered food and put some on his empty plate. He turned to me, the salmon already stuffed in his mouth. "Nothing like some raw fish to settle the nerves, huh?"

I could think of plenty better options to settle nerves. Like a medium rare steak and a side of poached *chicken* eggs. Or a stuffed duck doused in a horseradish glaze. Or…

Miss Reid looked at me, and I shook my head.

"I'll pass."

She nodded, but I noticed a subtle crease in her brow. Was it disappointment? She left the room before I could discern it further.

Monty leaned in and whispered, his breath smelling distinctly of the sea. "So, what's the plan today, Hux?"

"I'm still trying to figure it out."

"Well, that sounds promising." Monty's hands shook while he devoured his fish, but at least he was eating. Anything to keep his mind from thinking the worst.

Something I'd failed to do.

"It really depends on *what* this excursion is. I think once we set foot on land, we make a run for it."

Monty's limbs stilled slightly. "I like the sound of that."

*Me too.*

Miss Reid came back into the room, placing something on the plate in front of me. I looked down and saw that the something was charred, like a lump of coal. What on Braka…?

"It's a sweet roll," she said.

I couldn't take my eyes off the awful thing.

"I made them fresh this morning, with what little stores we have left… I may have gotten a touch too close to the flame." She ducked her head, a familiar blush climbing her neck.

*A touch?* This bun was more like the brave young men in the Great Book who were thrown in the fiery furnace, only this roll didn't receive divine intervention. I could think of a thousand other words to describe it other than *sweet.*

I glanced at her face, noticing the expectant look in her eyes. I never realized how blue-green they were until now. She was eager to please; anyone could see that. It did something strange to my chest, as if my actions had the power to break her.

I picked up the offending food item and brought it to my mouth. I'd eaten some strange things during my training years, but being a guard in a wealthy king's court, I'd grown spoiled.

I sank my teeth into the roll, being careful to steel my expression. The charred bits hit my tongue first, breaking off into ash. I ignored the need to retch and desperately chewed, searching for any edible parts amidst the incineration.

There, just barely, I could make out the yeast and flour. A little butter may have helped, but anything good was soon overpowered once more by the coal. I somehow got the char past my esophagus, nearly choking as I swallowed back the bile climbing up my throat. I refused to fold, meeting her gaze once more and only nodded, unable to get a word out.

A slight crease formed between her brows, but she was kind enough not to ask the dreaded question I knew was playing on her lips: *What do you think?* She just smiled and turned to leave the room.

My shoulders relaxed as I expelled a long breath. The roll tasted awful, but at least she'd been sincere; I couldn't fault her for that.

One of the men from across the table started to laugh. "You've lasted longer than most," he said, the subtle lilt to his words betraying that he was foreign. "Miss Reid's sweet rolls nearly did me in the last time she offered me one."

His friend chuckled beside him. "It's true. You've got taste buds of steel. I had to climb the hatch and disgorge into the ocean just to be rid of the awful thing." His accent was the same, and I suddenly realized they were both from Kethnar, my initial destination.

*How did they end up* here?

Cyril shrugged. "I love my Wilhelmina, but she didn't inherit her mother's cooking, I'm afraid."

"That bad, huh?" Monty asked.

"We just stick with the fish. Not much damage you can do to something that can be eaten raw, now is there?" Cyril replied. "But you learn to live with what you have when visits to the mainland are sparse."

My ears perked up at that. "What do—?"

"Good morning, everyone," Captain Aldo interrupted, stepping over the threshold.

I groaned under my breath at my missed chance of learning some valuable information. It would have to wait until later.

The captain's ensemble boasted a burgundy shirt, but it was his overcoat, or over-outfit rather, which stole the show. He was decked from head to toe in some strange-looking, grayish suit. From where I was sitting, it appeared to have a glossy sheen, almost as if it were…

"Blubberduds are first up on the agenda today," he said casually, tossing identical suits to Monty and me.

I caught mine, hearing Monty's whispered *"What in the blast are blubberduds?"* behind me.

I stifled a snort, the same question running through my head.

"Ondru and Niam." He gestured to the two other men sitting at the table. "You'll man the upper deck in the old gunwale like usual. Easy access to the hatch should we need rapid reentry."

*Rapid reentry?* Why all of this work just to step foot on land?

"Captain Aldo, surely this is a bit excessive. You want us to wear"—I held up the blubber-suit, the material both slick and pliable in my grasp—"these things for a land excursion? There's bound to be a better disguise…" I stopped talking when he burst out in a loud guffaw.

Captain Aldo had doubled over; even his shoulders looked as if they were chuckling.

"Did I amuse you, Captain?" I licked my teeth, not bothering to hide my rising irritation.

"Land excursion? Did he just say *land* excursion?" he addressed the others in the room, his delight as clear as day.

No one answered.

He looked at me. "What a jest! I didn't know I needed that this morning." He wiped at his eyes and flung away the fake tears. "A good laugh is always good for the bones; medicine for the soul and all that."

I stood from my place at the table, placing the blubberdud on top of my plate. "It wasn't a joke, Captain."

Captain Aldo's smile turned down, disappearing altogether. The tone in the room shifted. "No?" He straightened, assessing me more fully, before taking a few strides in my direction. He stopped when he was only a couple paces away. "Then let me make it perfectly clear." All humor vanished from his eyes, and I could feel his hot breath against my face. "No one steps foot on the mainland, not even myself, unless they have proven themselves faithful crewmembers of the *Neptucadis*. And that, my friend, takes years. Many, *many* years."

I swallowed the unaccounted-for lump in my throat, one born not so much from his implication but from his cold use of the word *friend*. Nothing felt more vexing than to be given the title by someone who truly did not embody the meaning of the word.

"Any more questions?" he asked, his stare challenging me to buckle.

My ire breached snarkiness in that moment; he didn't know the resolve of a weather-beaten soldier. I bit my tongue instead and stared back, unblinking.

We remained this way for the count of ten finger-taps against my leg when the captain suddenly averted his gaze and cleared his throat.

"That's it, then." Captain Aldo stepped back and nodded to the room at large. "We meet at the observatory at noon. The room will be unlocked. Be sure to come prepared." He turned on his heel and left the dining parlor, a weighty silence hanging in his wake.

I heard Monty release a shaky breath behind me, and it seemed everyone finally found their lungs again. "Is he usually that—"

"Difficult?" Ondru, or Niam, cut in.

"I was gonna say cryptic." Monty laughed.

*Infuriating. The man is infuriating.* "What's wrong with him?" I asked. He had more secrets than I could count, and his erratic behavior wasn't doing him any favors.

"I'd wager many things, but you learn to accept it when living at his mercy," Cyril said. "And the secrets? Well, they only grow deeper and wider the longer you stick around, much like this ocean."

"More like deeper and more deranged," I amended under my breath. None of this was helping. There was no hope to be found on this day. Not anymore.

Cyril pushed up from his seat and walked to my side, placing a shaky hand on my shoulder. "Be that as it may, the captain is owed my gratitude. For saving my life and his kindness to my Wilhelmina. He may be of the imperious sort, but deep down, he has a heart of compassion." He paused to sip his tea. "A true testament of character is how one treats those who are weaker than they are, Huxley. Maybe it's only a matter of unearthing that side of him more." Cyril patted my shoulder and walked out of the room, a lilting tune, like birdsong, whistling from his lips while water sloshed out of his teacup.

*Unearthing.* Yes, if only it was that easy.

It was noontime, the hour of our expedition. Monty and I were already in the observatory, him gawking over the various plants and me surveying anything and everything worth noting. Captain Aldo was talking with Ondru and Niam near the hatch, and Cyril was nowhere to be found. My guess was that he wasn't needed for this sort of thing; his shaky hands were too much of a liability.

I poked my head inside one of the adjoining rooms and was shocked to see piles upon piles of books. There were so many—they almost entirely lined the walls, forming little towering clusters here and there—that I almost didn't see the table in the center of the room nor the small chair just beside it.

*The captain's library?* Where would he have acquired so many tomes?

I looked over my shoulder, and seeing Captain Aldo still engaged in conversation with the others, stepped over the threshold. Once inside, I peered closer at the titles, marveling at their gold embossing:

*An Apothecary's Journey*
*From Seed to Flower*
*Sage, a Cure-All*
*Herbal Remedies to Ease the Weary Soul*
*A to Z: An Apothecary's Guide to, Well... Apothecarying*

Nothing surprising there. He was an apothecary after all. I was curious who else had access to such a library, though; had Miss Reid read any of these? She was surely knowledgeable enough.

I moved deeper into the room, noticing the color of the books were of a darker hue. I read some titles:

*Herbal Remedies for the Vengeful*
*Poisonous Plants & How to Diffuse Your Enemies*

*Ten Uses for Wolfsbane*
*Herbs for the Wayward Heart*
*Truth Serums & Other Herbal Spells*

The tone of these were different. Much different. Wicked, even. Was it normal for an apothecary to have such a vast collection, even ones that were…of a darker nature? Cyril had said Captain Aldo had a heart of compassion—and I begged to differ—but did that exclude his poor taste in literature?

Secrets were piling up. The eerie feeling that I was on the cusp of discovery crept up the back of my neck.

Or maybe it was the fact that I was being watched.

A throat cleared behind me.

I nearly jumped out of my skin but forced my body to relax, not showing any sign I'd been alerted to fear. I stood to my full height and turned, making eye contact with Monty—not Captain Aldo as I'd expected.

I heaved a sigh of relief.

"Sorry. Didn't want to sneak up on you, brother," Monty said. "But it's time we got ready to go. According to the captain, we just made it to the Herring Sea."

# TEN

## The Harrowing of the Herring Sea

The wind whipped against my face, the feeling sorely welcome. I never thought my next breath of fresh air would be from atop a floating monster, the Crimson Death of all things, and out in the middle of the ocean.

It was true. No land was in sight, but that didn't matter to the captain. In fact, he seemed to revel in it, this floating vessel amidst an endless stretch of blue.

We were in the Herring Sea—a body of water I'd never seen before and a far cry from Braka's green Wasteful Tides—past Kethnar entirely, and reaching toward the surrounding countries, most of which I'd only ever studied on maps or read about in books.

I knew somewhere beyond the leagues of blue there were legendary kingdoms—the kinds you read about in fairy tales, but I had no wish to go there. I'd heard plenty of rumors from local merchants or other guards who'd gone on voyages for the king, about those storied lands being rife with magic, of talking animals and people who understood them—*Earth-Treaders*, they were called…

And though I knew the like was sure to travel to Braka, if it hadn't already, I wished not to be a part of it. I longed only for a peaceable existence, a life on the mainland. Preferably in Braka, but I would settle for across the Wasteful Tides in the land of Kethnar.

Why in the blast were we in the Herring Sea?

"Isn't it invigorating?" Captain Aldo said, breathing deeply of the briny air. His nostrils flared wide, sniffing.

Monty stood beside me, a look of pleasure on his face as he, too, began sniffing the air.

We were bobbing in the soft waves, the heavy sun beating down on us. If not for the blubberduds on our skin, I'd be soaking in the sunshine instead of slowly roasting beneath a layer of seal flesh.

"Here." Without even looking, Captain Aldo extended his hand in our direction, his gaze still locked on the waves.

I glanced down, noticing something green with yellow flowers sticking out from his palm.

Monty and I pulled the sprigs loose. "I don't suppose we're to simply stare at it," I said, twirling the plant in my fingers.

"You're to chew it, wise tongue." If it wasn't for the slight smirk of the captain's mouth, I'd have thought him truly miffed.

"Then what is it exactly?" Another one of the captain's herbal remedies, most likely.

"Mullein. Helps with respiratory function; should aid in your breathing as we descend."

*Descend.*

It's not like I had expected a different outcome once the captain crushed my dreams of stepping foot on land. But after basking in the brilliant sunshine of the new day, the last thing I wanted to do was travel to an abyss devoid of the very thing.

One glance at my friend revealed he felt similarly, a question on the tip of his tongue.

"And how…" Monty gulped. "How long will we be down there, Captain?" he asked beside me, his mouth set in a grim line.

"Ah, until the task is done. You'll see." Captain Aldo snapped his fingers, and suddenly Niam and Ondru were beside us.

In a matter of minutes, we had large glass jars strapped over our heads, the bases of which were secured beneath the folds of blubber at our necks. Out from the glass jars ran a tube that wound long and wily back through the hatch of the submersible vessel.

"Fresh oxygen feeds through this here." Captain Aldo tugged on the tube, his voice only slightly muffled from the glass. "Ensures we don't die and all that." He winked.

My jaw ticked to the side. This excursion was enough of a death sentence as it was.

"Why us, Captain? What could possibly be at the bottom of this ocean?" Monty asked.

Captain Aldo paused, a somber expression etched into the lines of his face. "Well, my fine gentleman, the sea is charitable. And when you've had much taken from you, it's nice to take something back. You'll see."

His words struck a chord; I wanted to take *everything* I'd lost back. But his was another cryptic answer. Another thing to add to the list of growing mysteries.

"Niam. Ondru. Be sure to watch the levels. You know Jollie's stores fluctuate; she can only produce so much at a time."

The two men nodded and disappeared within the hatch.

"Oh, and I almost forgot." Captain Aldo reached into a crate and pulled out three burlap sacks. He handed one to each of us. "You'll be needing these."

The question *What for?* was on the tip of my tongue, but it was just as soon squelched when the captain shouted, "We're off."

A rough hand pushed me into the water, and I steeled myself against the brazen cold.

The first thing I noticed was the pressure. It was cool around the blubber, and aside from my hands, it surprisingly didn't reach the rest of my skin. What a strange sensation to be trapped in a seal's outer flesh and descend to the depths like you were the creature itself.

Captain Aldo was beside me, a spark of eagerness in his eyes.

Each of us had jars strapped to our chests with glow worms, or rather bioluminescent fungus gnats, taken out of sea caves somewhere in the northwest. Regardless of their exact location, there were enough to permeate the darkness and send halos of muted blue-green around each of us.

The color reminded me of Miss Reid's cyan eyes.

I shook my head; now was *not* the time to be thinking of such things. Or ever.

Captain Aldo had said the light lasted as long as the larvae were immature. Once they reached adulthood, their properties changed.

I could only hope that their properties didn't decide to change when we were at the bottom of the sea.

"Who's Jollie?" I asked, my voice sounding strange to my ears, suffocated by a wall of glass and water. I wondered if anyone could even understand me and if it was worth voicing my question at all.

Captain Aldo looked my way, pointing up. He didn't say anything, but his gesture was enough.

Jollie was the cuttlefish. The sea beast. The Crimson Death.

I followed his finger and nearly gasped at the sight. Seeing the underbelly of the alleged monster was nothing short of alarming. Thick tentacles hung from off its body, nearly colliding with us in our descent. Its girth and size alone were enough to rival a small island—or country, for that matter.

The *Neptucadis*, though somewhat roomy for an underwater home, now appeared inconsequential as it lay bound to her side with ropes and straps, looking more like a barnacle on a whale than a vessel that carried seven people.

My gratitude for the captain's "hold" on the animal increased a mere fraction, but that's all I allowed him. I still didn't appreciate the fact that I was a hostage, now in open water with the creature bobbing above my head and the rest of me descending like a millstone.

I glanced at Monty, his eyes wide in the fuzzy, blue-green light. He had a million questions etched into the creases on his face, and it was only a matter of time before he began to spew them all like a volley of arrows. And it was only a matter of seconds before the guilt crept back in for having my friend join me on this ridiculous expedition in the first place.

The halo of light throbbed around us, vibrating along with the pulse of the sea. It was dark beyond where the illumination couldn't reach, and what swam in that inky black was enough to keep my eyes fixed on the jar of glowing gnats in front of me.

I counted them. How often they blinked their lights, suddenly to have one go out and another take its turn. It was like a dance, the blinking cerulean amidst a sea of blue, only I'd never heard of a dance that was responsible for the lives of three men.

Down, down, down we went.

I wondered if the abyss would swallow us whole. All my training on the battlefield never prepared me for this, a sort of soul-sucking endeavor that left the lungs wishing for oxygen. Was it possible to die of claustrophobia?

I chewed more furiously on the mullein, feeling my nerves settle and lungs expand a touch. At least the captain had enough foresight to give us the herb.

Suddenly, I felt a tug on my shoulder. Normally I'd brush it off, but seeing as we were in the midst of a dark, unknown chasm, all senses kicked on high alert, my heart pounding in my ears.

I wheeled around, only to find Monty's hand pulling me back, his eyes wider than I'd ever seen them. A garbled sound came from his glass dome. It sounded like "Big trout!" but was probably something else. "Look out!" more likely.

And just in time, too. I nearly collided with a wooden beam, standing like a sunken sentinel in front of me. But what it guarded was left to be determined. A tattered canvas swayed gently from a rod running perpendicular to the beam, its movements a softer billowing beneath the waves than one would see on land.

I followed the length of the pole down to its base, and my heart nearly stopped. A long, wooden platform stretched to my left and right, resting atop what looked to be a splintered hull. It was all clear now, all of our glow gnats helping to illuminate the entirety of the scene before us.

A shipwreck. And from the looks of the decaying boards, it happened a long time ago. But to whom did the ship belong?

I scoured the waterlogged vessel before me, scrutinizing it for all it was worth. For any signs of identification.

There, caught in a tangle of seaweed and a broken mast, was a red flag, knotted and twisted by the current. I swam to it, plying the fabric loose enough to catch a glimpse, to uncover but a portion of this mystery.

A canvas, with too many holes to count, stared back at me. My throat grew thick, my breaths coming in quicker, faster, heavier as I stared at the material in my hands. An embroidered destrier treading over a thicket of thorns and tongues of fire stared back, the golden thread as familiar as my name.

I knew this flag. I'd spent the past twenty-eight years of my life staring at them from the highest pinnacles of Farrador, snapping in the ever-changing wind. A welcome sight to all who revered the Crown and a warning to those who wished it harm. Farrador wasn't one to be trifled with…

Unless you were this ship.

With the flag in tow, I swam down, apprehension rising in my chest. If this ship was what I thought it was, then the name painted along its exterior would either confirm or deny my suspicions.

The letters were hard to decipher at first, what with the seaweed and barnacles intervening, but even so, the chipped and faded paint spoke volumes: MFB *Glad Tidings.*

I swallowed hard, my mind jumping back years in time to when I was only a lad of sixteen and Barrington was rounding up men to join his fleet.

*"You'll deposit it all safely!"* Barrington boomed, his boots thumping along the Edgefold docks, inspecting each ship as it was loaded with Brakan goods. *"And bring the best of the best back to us, no doubt!"*

Merchants laughed and cheered, humoring the decree of the king. Others stepped up in line, showing their credentials and proving their "sea legs" by balancing on a narrow plank the length of five broadswords. It seemed there was no shortage of men for the Merchant Fleet of Braka.

I stood nearby, Monty and my father by my side, when suddenly, I felt a hand leave my shoulder. Glancing up, I saw my father walking toward the king, a determination in his step.

I caught the hurried conversation between them. A heavy feeling grew in my stomach.

*"You sure you want to do this, Huxley?"* King Barrington asked.

My father nodded. *"Every ship needs the services of a royal guard on board, what with the ebbing of the Tides. And Braka's merchant fleet is no exception."*

King Barrington clapped him on the back. *"Ever the hero, Huxley. But you know I'd prefer to keep you here. Who will lead my men? Guard Albertus?"*

My father pressed. *"The crown prince has many allies, as do all your sons. It wouldn't be for long. Just enough to…"* His words choked on a swallow. *"Please, Your Majesty. I thought we had an agreement."*

King Barrington studied him for a long time, regarding the slump of his shoulders and the gaunt lines on his face which spoke more volumes than words ever could. *"You're certain, then?"*

My father nodded.

The king sighed. *"So it will be. Your leave is granted for a short while, but then it's back to Farrador. I can't afford to be missing my best soldier for long."* He clapped his hand on my father's shoulder and motioned to the ship nearest to him. *"She'll be your new charge."*

Before I knew what was happening, my father stood in front of me, his hand heavy on my head. *"It's time I get going, son. Even merchants and tradesmen need protection. But in time, the* Glad Tidings *will bear me home."*

He ruffled my hair and slung a bag over his shoulder, a bag I hadn't seen him carrying earlier. So much had changed within those few minutes, and now Monty and I stared after his retreating form. But it didn't last long.

*"Father!"*

I ran after him, but King Barrington grabbed me by the collar of my shirt, holding me back.

*"One Gannon is enough, son. You'll grow in your father's stead."*

And I had, but nothing could prepare me for just how real those words would become; the very Tides that had once stolen my father had now become his tomb.

Suddenly, it was as if I was orphaned all over again, but this time, a sickening feeling threatened to clog my throat, my insides churning with familiar fire.

*My father. Drowned. At the bottom of the sea.*

*How?*

But I didn't have time to process it further.

Captain Aldo motioned for us to follow him, and I had little choice but to comply if I didn't want to be stranded and receive the same fate as my namesake.

# ELEVEN

## The Turning of the Tide

Once back inside the *Neptucadis*, Captain Aldo gestured to the room with all the books. "Unload it in there, lads. Our bounty isn't light."

After following the glow worms in the murky depths, it had finally made sense why we'd been given burlap sacks. He'd fashioned us with weapons for plundering.

"We're as good as pirates, Hux," Monty said in my ear as if reading my thoughts.

The captain overheard.

"Ah, but pirates would imply, well, *pirating*. It isn't stealing when what's gotten was no longer in someone's possession." Captain Aldo smirked, moving us along. "By all rights, it's mine."

Something in his tone shook me, and seeing the greed kindling in his eyes only drove the point deeper. *What had really sunken that ship?*

The legend of the Crimson Death had been around for years, but it reemerged about the time part of Barrington's Fleet went missing, the MFB *Glad Tidings* being one of them. Was it merely coincidence, or had Captain Aldo made his little cuttlefish do his dastardly bidding?

The thought soured my lunch, stoking the flames in my core.

We all shuffled into the library and emptied our sacks, coins splattering off the wooden table and scattering onto the floor.

My pulse quickened. I'd already seen the inscription hammered into the metal, but upon seeing it double thrice over from our combined hordes, my jaw ticked to the side.

"These are the king's denarious and pfennig," I said, my tone surprisingly even.

"And?" Captain Aldo lifted a brow, already counting off the silver coins and setting them in neat stacks.

"They don't belong here. They belong back in Farrador."

Captain Aldo's hand stopped moving, and his lips pursed as if he'd just tasted something unsavory. "And why would a *king*, who has everything, need more?"

I ground my teeth. Had he no heart? "It's not the *king* who needs it."

"Then humor me, would you?" Captain Aldo crossed his arms over his chest, his tone mocking.

If it had been socially appropriate, I'd have socked him in the mouth. Instead, I tried to keep my voice controlled, along with my fists. "Braka's been on the verge of poverty for years, and it's only gotten worse. With Barrington's wealth, we'd be able to afford more, give more to the people. But instead, you're inclined to take it all yourself, say for what, a few men on board who don't eat more than fish. An entirely *free* fare, mind you."

The captain's face was beet red, his mouth screwed up in a hideous fashion. "I didn't realize your allegiance was so ill-placed. But seeing as this is *my* vessel, I ask that you desist from your speech. Don't you *ever* utter that name in my presence again."

My mind reeled. Now the captain was mad at *me*?

*He* was the one who imprisoned Monty and me on this blasted contraption. Not to mention Miss Reid and Cyril.

*He* was the one who openly stole from my people.

I flexed my fingers, the muscles in my arms twitching.

And *he* was the one who most likely shipwrecked the *Glad Tidings,* killing my father.

"Your selfishness is embarrassing," I spat.

"Get out," Captain Aldo said.

I glared at him, my vision marring red. I hated the man. Loathed his entire being.

"Now!" he barked.

My nostrils flared. Monty and I stood to leave, but before doing so, I flipped the table, sending it flying into a stack of books. Coins scattered helter-skelter around the room, their tinny sounds echoing in my head and my chest.

*To be a bigger man, son, sometimes you just need to walk away.* I suddenly recalled my father's words; they seemed so distant now, so hard to grasp in light of this consuming fire in my veins. He'd uttered them once when my spar with a fellow guard, both of us fourteen and headstrong at the time, had turned into something serious. If not for his steadying hand on my shoulder and those wise words, who knows what would have happened then. But *this* was different, wasn't it? Clearly, he hadn't met the likes of Captain Aldo.

*Sometimes you just need to walk away.* I swallowed, knowing that if I didn't leave the captain's chambers at this very moment, there'd be another fight coming. But this time, my father wouldn't be around to stop me.

For the remainder of the long week, I mostly kept to my chamber, the embers of my previous anger dying down only to flare up again at random.

During that time, we journeyed across the endless ocean. Northwest, I'd heard, but where we were now was beyond me.

Regardless, I was able to spot much from my porthole despite it being dark; apparently the captain had found a new purpose for the bioluminescent fungus gnats—to light the exterior of our strange caravan. From their glow, I saw that we'd ventured to an underwater city—spending a day or so bobbing above its ruins— and nearly jumping out of my skin upon seeing the shed membrane of a large sea snake. Thankfully, we were spared the creature's unwelcome presence, though nothing could rival Jollie's size, and fled to "safer" waters.

From there, we entered shallower places and passed by a coral reef, running into a smack of jellyfish, a large sea turtle, a small octopus, and a school of trevallies. Even in the darkness, the world was alight with color.

The spectacle lifted my spirits, but it did little to distract me from my brooding thoughts; even Monty's uncharacteristic enthusiasm wasn't the company I was up for.

Too much rolled around in my heavy head, and I needed time to sort it all out. I was mostly running on fumes at this point, too tired to do much and yet too wired to sit still. So it was back to pacing the room, absentmindedly running a hand through my overgrown beard.

I chanced a glance at the tally marks on the wall.

What was it now, three and a half weeks since I'd last shaved? What did it even matter? This place was part observation tower, part living nightmare, and no amount of hygiene would wipe away the grime this vessel accumulated.

Captain Aldo's anger still lingered fresh in my mind. Despite all his mysteriousness and supposed atrocities, his disdain for Barrington was something I was learning to understand. My terrible fall from Farrador still colored vivid, and I couldn't soon forgive the wrongful accusations pitted against me. Nor of Prince Clark's death, which smarted every time I pictured his body now ten feet under.

But *why* did Captain Aldo hate the king? Had something happened between them? And if so, what?

The questions shocked me. To feel any sympathy for the captain should be the *last* thing on my mind. It was.

And yet it would explain so much. The Brakan weapons in his armory. Part of the Merchant Fleet of Braka sunk and the unabashed stealing of the plunder. The utter vehemence upon hearing King Barrington's name spoken aloud.

Yes, I was more convinced of it than ever. Something *had* happened to cause such hatred, and I determined it was only a matter of time until I figured out what that was.

But until then, I had some work to do. There was no way I could survive in this prison with the amount of disdain flooding my body. I had to siphon it out, to accept my fate somehow, be it temporarily. Otherwise, I'd be no better than the very man who imprisoned me.

*To be a bigger man, son, sometimes you just need to walk away.* Or hold my tongue, I amended. It would take a whole lot of willpower, but something had to change if I wanted to get off this blasted boat. In order to learn Captain Aldo's secrets, I'd need to show my compliance—a guise known by every soldier.

The thought kindled my ire, but I stamped it down.

"You can do this, Huxley." It was the worst rallying speech of the ages, but it was the best I could muster. "You'll make it out alive. You *and* Monty. You won't die in this pit, not if you have any say about it."

I could be pretty persuasive when I wanted to be, so much so that maybe I could even persuade myself.

Suddenly, I was thrust forward and would have fallen on my face had the bulkhead not caught me. The *Neptucadis* came to a teetering halt and was now steadily rising upward. It didn't take long for the vessel to breach the surface if the sudden stream of light through the porthole was any indicator.

Where were we now? Still out in foreign waters or closer to home?

Heavy footsteps pounded on the floorboards above, and voices, loud and frantic, echoed down to my chamber.

"What's the problem now?" I didn't want to leave my room, but something compelled me to investigate. It looked like I'd be practicing compliance sooner rather than later.

I opened my door and entered the hallway, noticing the voices had increased their volume.

"I nearly had it about two seconds ago!" a man called out. He sounded like Ondru.

"I'll grab one of those maces from the armory. We need something to latch onto it," another man responded, who I assumed was Niam.

I was right.

Shortly after, Niam descended the staircase along the far side of the hall and came running to the door just ahead of me. He unlocked the armory and disappeared inside a moment before stepping into the hallway once more, this time with his retrieved weapon.

"What's happening?" I asked, trying not to sound too eager.

Niam balked; apparently, he hadn't seen me standing in the dim lighting of the corridor. "Loose cargo. The Straits come bearing gifts."

"Loose cargo?" How often did this happen? From the sound of it, we were near the Straits of Kethnar again.

"It's a big one. Captain's orders are to bring 'er in. Could be something worth seeing. Most of them usually are." Niam nodded and turned, fleeing the way he had come.

I followed after him, but not before I noticed the armory door stood open at a crack. It was unlocked, and I'd like to keep it that way.

Quickly, so as not to draw notice, I tore a piece of my shirt and stuck it in the door jamb, testing my trick when I gently closed the door and opened it just as easily once more. Hope threatened to break my hardened resolve.

Perhaps compliance could be attainable on this vessel after all.

I secured the door once more and took to the stairs. There wasn't a single soul on the second floor, but I still heard voices carrying in my direction. They grew louder the closer I walked to the captain's quarters.

The trap door was opened wide, and I could see people's feet walking about, their excited words pounding around in my head.

I swallowed my pride and climbed the stairs.

At the top, Monty was already there with Miss Reid and Cyril by his sides. It was a strange trio, seeing them standing there as if they were part of the crew. Correction, as if *Monty* was part of the crew. Miss Reid and her father had earned their time in spades.

Monty spotted me, and his eyes lit up. "You'll never believe it, Hux. The whole vessel is in an uproar!" He clapped a hand over my shoulder.

"Over what? A box?" For that's exactly what I imagined the cargo to be—a box floating in the ocean.

"More like a chest. I don't know, but the thing is huge. Take a look for yourself." He gestured to the large window where Niam and Ondru were now outside, using the mace and countless fishing line to reel something in.

I heard Captain Aldo barking commands from atop the deck, and I could only imagine that the amount of spittle flying from his impassioned mouth was enough to rival the sea's own waters.

I edged closer and marveled at the cargo's size. It was indeed large. Much larger than I'd assumed.

"We got it, boys! Just a little more!" the captain yelled amidst the struggle while Niam and Ondru hauled the object in.

Jollie aided them the rest of the way, and I saw Captain Aldo toss her something purple as if in appreciation. "Some catmint for my good girl." Her tentacle wrapped around the plant before it disappeared to what I guessed would be her mouth.

After what felt like an eternity, heavy footsteps pounded on the stairs, the two men descending with the monstrosity of a box and Captain Aldo bringing up the rear.

"Over there." He motioned to the glass window where I stood.

They set the box down with a thud, causing dust flurries to waft in the air. I sucked in a breath to keep from sneezing, but thankfully the urge fled by the sudden appearance of a crowbar on my right. It jabbed unceremoniously into the cargo.

Captain Aldo, though no longer a young man, boasted enough vigor to rival all of us in the room. The hunger in his eyes was evident, mimicking the greed from his previous plundering, with perspiration beading along his hairline and dribbling down his forehead. He continued to hack away at the box, shoving Niam aside when he tried to help.

"I'd like the sole honors," Captain Aldo said, wiggling the bar underneath the wood enough to splinter the lid. "Something this big must hold *something* important. Something equally as big."

I watched in rapt attention but didn't hold the same fervor as the captain. Surely this box had a history or was a portend of sorts; it must have either fallen off a ship or been cast out to sea. Its size was unnerving for it was almost spacious enough for a…

The sound of splintering wood interrupted my thoughts as the lid broke clean off. Gasps sounded all around the room, but it was Ondru's voice which sliced through the sudden tension. "A body!" He sucked in a breath, and I could feel Monty grow rigid beside me.

I took a step closer.

Gooseflesh climbed my neck, threatening to suffocate me whole, and I almost collapsed to my knees. Was this some sort of sick joke, taunting me in my failure? This wasn't just any body, for the likeness was striking—the very same. But how could it be? And all the way out here?

The greed in Captain Aldo's eyes diminished at once and was replaced with an urgency I had yet to see from him. "Quickly! He needs aid!" he yelled, motioning for Niam and Ondru to lift him out of the box.

*Aid?* A glimmer of hope fought to take hold, but surely he was already dead!

"Captain—"

"Make yourself useful, Huxley, and grab some cloth from downstairs," he barked.

I was taken aback by this sudden change. He'd never addressed me by my given name, not until this moment.

"I got it, Hux," Monty said, exiting the room before I had a chance. I assumed his weak constitution couldn't handle a dead body.

"I'll make sure he knows where to look." Cyril followed after him.

"Willa, fetch my chest of herbs from my chambers. Mix a tincture of maca and echinacea. And don't forget the hawthorn and

118

rue," he said. "Quickly now!"

Miss Reid, who was once at my side, now darted into the room adjacent to the library. When she emerged, she handed the box to the captain and hastily moved toward the plants lining the walls.

With Monty and Cyril gone, I was left with nothing but my own awkward hands grasping for something to do. I couldn't just stand there.

"Miss Reid, do you need assistance?" I walked toward her, noticing the pinch between her brows as she knelt before a pot.

She looked up at me. "You don't happen to have a blade, do you?"

A blade? No, any weapons were stripped off my person before I first stepped foot inside this villainous contraption. And the one I did have, the fishhook, was currently resting on the porthole's ledge in my bedchamber.

Though, the idea of the unlocked armory downstairs eased that blow slightly.

"I'm afraid I don't."

I watched as she bit her lip and attacked the plant, twisting this way and that, trying to unearth the entire planter. It was a struggle against woman and leaves, and it didn't look like Miss Reid would be the victor.

I knelt and grabbed her wrists, and she stared back at me with widened eyes. "What are you doing?" I asked.

She looked from my hands to my face, her cheeks reddening. "I—" She cleared her throat. "Maca calls for the root."

Understanding dawning, I slipped my hands off her wrists and placed them around the base of a stalk. I sucked in a breath and gave a solid pull before the root surrendered its fight, emerging whole.

I held it out to her and nodded.

She gaped at me but closed her mouth and took the proffered plant. "I loosened it, you know."

If the situation wasn't so dire, I would have laughed. Sweet Miss Reid had some backbone after all, and it was borderline endearing. If I was into that sort of thing, that is.

She gathered the rest of what she needed and ground everything in a mortar, the smell of butterscotch swirling about the air. It was a pleasant smell, if not for the presence of death in the room.

There was no way he was still alive, no matter how many scenarios played out in my mind to prove otherwise. All hope was already lost.

"Bring it here, Willa," Captain Aldo commanded.

Miss Reid handed over the tincture and after a few more chest compressions, Captain Aldo administered the medicine, spooning it into the man's cracked lips.

From my point of view, it didn't look like he was breathing. His skin, now less blue in pallor, still looked off, and his blond hair lay greased across the front of his forehead, his regality stripped away in spades.

"Ladies and gentleman—" Captain Aldo cleared his throat. "This could be the turning of the tide."

"Captain?" Ondru asked, his brow furrowed like I knew mine was at this moment.

"Who is he, Captain?" Niam questioned.

Of course, they wouldn't recognize the man. They had no need to.

Monty and Cyril came up the stairs, returning to my side. Monty gave Captain Aldo the cloths and peered at the palish figure lying on the ground. The way his eyes widened and his mouth gaped like a fish, it was evident he hadn't seen the body up close until now.

"Is that…?" His voice shook.

"Aye." Captain Aldo nodded. "I'm afraid so. It's the prince."

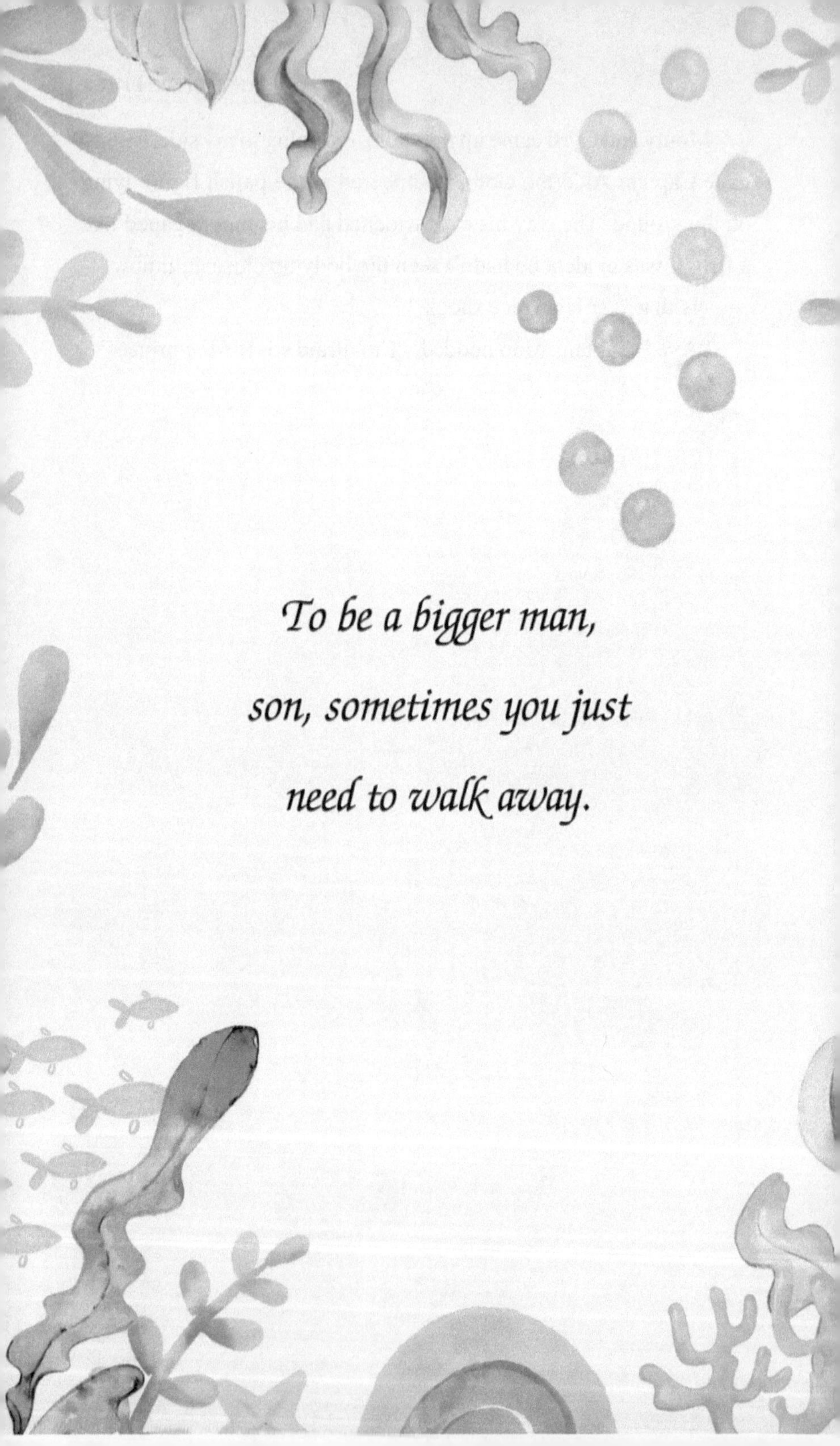

To be a bigger man,

son, sometimes you just

need to walk away.

# TWELVE

## Melodies in the Night

"Prince?" Monty was the first to utter a word after the shocking announcement. "You don't mean…"

I already knew it to be true, but now that it was spoken aloud, there was no more room for doubt. But how? As much as hope surged within me, there was no way on the Maker's green earth that Prince Clark was still alive. Statistically speaking, it wasn't probable.

And how had he ended up all the way out here? Everyone knew the royal family buried their own in the crypt within Farrador's walls. It wasn't customary to send them out to sea like fish bait.

"What prince, Captain?" Ondru asked, his brow still furrowed.

"From Braka. The dreaded castle of Farrador." Captain Aldo muttered the words through gritted teeth while pressing a damp cloth against the prince's forehead.

"But he's not…! He can't be…" Monty sputtered, trying to

vocalize the same doubts I had running through my own mind.

I'd been exiled, charged, and ruined because of my supposed hand in dealing out death to Clark. And the captain was tending to him like he was in some sick ward, not recently dislodged from his coffin.

Hope warred with reason.

"Poisoned? Yes. Wolfsbane and mad dog have a knack for that. He's been given more than one ever should have in their lifetime, but even so, it was administered foolishly."

"Mad dog?" Monty asked.

"Skullcap. Often harmless, but not in this high dosage."

"So he's…" Monty swallowed, and my own mouth felt like a desert.

"Alive." The captain's singular word answered the unfinished question, and it was enough to spur my heart rate into a marathon. "But only just. He's in a coma."

I didn't know much about comas, but I knew enough. They held promise. The potential for a brighter future. I finally let myself feel the relief I'd been staving off, for hope was now a safe passage to cross.

A little selfishly, I couldn't help thinking that if I somehow managed to get out of this blasted prison with Monty and the prince in tow, would King Barrington welcome me back to Farrador? He'd be as shocked as I was to see that his son still lived! Maybe it would even be enough to clear my name, resume my job as Prince Clark's guard. Have my normal life returned to me.

"Yes, for now. He'll need lots of rest and care." Captain Aldo snapped his fingers. "Ondru and Niam, you'll move him to a room on the bottom floor. Willa, you'll attend to his needs."

All three of them started moving in response to his orders while Captain Aldo went about his business.

"How, Captain?" I finally managed to find my tongue. There was still so much I couldn't wrap my mind around.

He furrowed his brow. "Moving a man isn't that difficult, Huxley."

I shook my head, swallowing my irritation. "You misunderstand me. How is it the prince still lives?" In all my calculations, nothing added up. This defied the impossible.

"Well, I'd imagine whoever poisoned him thought he was dead. They didn't finish the job, if that's what you're asking."

"But he was 'killed' over three weeks ago now…"

Captain Aldo suddenly stopped moving. He faced me fully, narrowing his eyes. "You mean to tell me the prince has been stuck inside a cargo box for over three weeks on the brink of his deathbed?"

"You don't think it's possible?"

He pursed his lips. "I never said that. With the amount of skullcap he'd digested, it'd be enough to slow anyone's heart rate for weeks to the point of a comatose state. I've seen it done before." He looked at me a little closer now, pausing. "I'm curious, though… How did you know the prince had died?" He crossed his arms.

There was still so much I didn't understand, and the last thing I wanted to do was bring the captain into my confidence, but wishes were for children. I'd learned to grow up a long time ago.

"I was there."

Captain Aldo studied me. His unwavering gaze was unnerving

as he pored over my countenance. It seemed a myriad of possibilities paraded before his eyes, his demeanor shifting ever so slightly with the raise of a brow, or the pursing of a lip, or the twitching of a hand. Finally, a look of understanding and resolve settled around him.

"Ah. You're that *Gannon* boy." The way he said my last name implied his distaste for my lost position. Or was it pity? "From that family of Royal Guards. I thought your surname sounded familiar."

I nodded.

"I see it now. It's a surprise I didn't before. Yes, you look much like your old man. Whatever happened to him, I wonder?" His tone suddenly turned somber.

Something about this conversation struck me as familiar. Hadn't I just had one with Cyril only last week? It seemed the *Neptucadis* held us all hostage enough to unearth our secrets, but I still couldn't place my finger on the captain. Who was *he?* If Captain Aldo was from Braka, why didn't he have the accent? He had recognized the prince, but still, there was no placing where he belonged.

"You knew my father?" My jaw ticked to the side. I was still processing the idea that it was the captain himself who very well had him killed.

"Aye." Captain Aldo didn't smile but looked as if he was lost in thought. "I knew many men once upon a time." Kneeling, he finished gathering his herbs and closed the wooden box only to hand it over to Miss Reid.

He didn't say anything more, and I found my frustration mounting despite my earlier goal of practicing compliance and holding my tongue.

"Is that it, then?" I wanted to be more than done with this enigmatic captain. If it was in my power, I would have thrust him against a wall at sword point and demanded an explanation. Not to hurt the man, but to finally get some bloody answers. Especially where it concerned my father.

The silence stretched instead, him seemingly unaware of my vengeful thoughts.

I wasn't ready to walk away just yet, and from the clearing of the captain's throat, neither was he.

He lifted his head, and when I saw the expression on his face, I felt the blood drain from mine. The look in his eyes was one that I knew would haunt me for years to come. I couldn't place my finger on it except that it felt like the sun shining on a castle ruin; the light unveiling all the cracked places where the foundation should have been secure. Much like it was unveiling all the cracked pieces of a broken man beneath a hardened exterior.

Suddenly, my hatred for him cracked, too—unexpected sympathy, the mortar for the holes.

"Not all men can be heroes, Huxley."

They were the quietest, sincerest words I'd ever heard him speak. And I knew they held more pain and truth than I'd ever dare to understand.

With a final glance at the prince being carried out of the room, the captain got up and ran a hand over his face. He looked wearier and more worn than I'd ever seen him.

"And it matters not how hard one tries."

The departing words of the captain troubled me as much as his facial expression, the scene playing over and over in my head. When I closed my eyes, all I saw were his and their dark, haunting look. It was enough to unsettle even the most valiant of men.

I tossed around on my makeshift bed, feeling the wiry netting beneath me. I couldn't get comfortable. Couldn't shake my growing uneasiness and the betraying questions rolling around in my mind.

I still didn't like the man, but was it possible my hatred was misplaced?

Could my opinion of him truly be upended within the span of a singular conversation?

Lifting my hands to place them behind my head, I stared at the wooden beams of the ceiling, wishing instead for a blanket of grass at my back and a swath of stars up above. I heaved a sigh. Sleep wouldn't come easy this night.

Maybe there was some truth to Cyril's claim. The captain could be both nefarious *and* compassionate; I'd seen it for myself.

But did that make him a good man?

I tried closing my eyes again, but the unease only grew. It still didn't explain what had happened to my father.

I needed to go for a walk. Stretch my legs. Get out of this blasted cell where any dreams were given to nightmares.

I pushed up from the bed and opened the door, cracking it open to a dimly lit hallway. All was quiet, except…a gentle plucking of notes sounded somewhere to my left. I strained my ears to listen further and thought I heard a lilting voice amidst the strings.

I allowed my feet to guide me, walking down the hallway until I came to the door where the music was loudest. It stood open a sliver, and I peered inside, noting the sleeping form of the prince within.

The words of the song came clearer now, though they were gently sung, and their tune twisted a hollow space inside my chest.

*My heart has been claimed by the sea*
*For it's there her arms have found me*
*Her beauty unmatched*
*Her soul like a flame*
*And it's where I live wild and free.*

*Not so much free as it is wild.* But the words still struck me.

Without even seeing her, I knew the voice to be Miss Reid's. It was angelic, much like Monty had said, but even more so in song. It was both gentle and mesmerizing, and without so much as a second thought, I found myself pushing open the door, standing in its frame like an awkward child past his bedtime.

Miss Reid ceased her playing and jumped. "Oh! Mr. Gannon." She quickly stood and curtsied, the hue of her cheeks deepening in the waning torchlight. "I didn't think anyone else was up."

"Neither did I," I said. We stared at each other for a few seconds.

Then she motioned to another chair before she sat back down. "Please, come in."

I walked across the room, sitting down to survey the entirety of the enclosure. It was sparsely furnished, but unlike my small chamber, this room boasted two portholes, not one. Finally, my gaze rested on the sleeping form of the prince, lying on a bed of fishing nets and what looked like a quilt. He had lost his bluish pallor entirely, and though his skin was still pale, he seemed to hold more promise with the rising and falling of his chest. It was a sprig of hope.

*Good.* This was good. If he survived, we all could go home.

"I hope my playing wasn't too loud." Miss Reid broke the silence. "I'd hate to wake you."

I shook my head. "If I could wake to this more often, I'd be a happier man." It was true. Since Cyril was taken from Braka all those years ago, Farrador had been sorely lacking in music. It'd been a while since I'd last heard the plucky notes of something beautiful. "In truth, I couldn't sleep."

"No?" She furrowed her brow. "How come?"

"I seem to have a lot on my mind these days."

She nodded. "That is something I can understand."

"You too?" I leaned back and put my hands behind my head.

"A woman's mind is always on the run, Mr. Gannon. It never ceases depending on the time of day."

"Then men and women are more alike than I'd thought." For my own thoughts were like a carriage wheel, perpetually turning.

She laughed, and I noted a slight dimple in her left cheek.

"Is there anything I can help you with? Women are also good listeners, and it's the least I can do since you helped me with the maca root earlier."

I smirked. "Oh, you mean the one you helped loosen?"

Her smile spread wide, and she tugged her harp closer. "I'll have you know, I am not as weak and fragile as I appear."

I pretended to size her up, watching a slow blush climb her cheeks once again. "No, I daresay there's more muscle in there than I can imagine. I wouldn't cross you for the world, Miss Reid, and I'm a soldier."

A warmth spread through my middle at the ease of our conversation. It'd been so long since I'd last talked to a woman that I half feared I didn't know how to. After having had my heart broken and stepped on many years ago, I could have sworn all women were the same. But Miss Reid was proving herself to be different. An actual friend.

If only Monty saw me now. I fought the urge to roll my eyes.

"So, how's the prince?" I shifted my position and looked at the man once more, remembering when, only a month ago, things had been normal. Farrador had felt safe, and Prince Clark had been well-guarded. Over the years, we'd had ourselves some adventures, and I only hoped he'd recover soon so we could continue them; he was a visionary and an asset to the kingdom, a true-born leader. Had I known so much would change in such a short amount of time, I would have doubled my guard.

"He's doing better. I gave him some valerian root and willow bark tea; they should aid in his sleeping. And then lion's mane; the herbs he was poisoned with have the tendency to affect the memory, so Captain Aldo advised me to keep a close watch. He'll awake when he's ready."

I nodded, my mind going back to Captain Aldo's library. "You seem to know so much. About plants, that is. Have you always wanted to be an apprentice to an apothecary?"

She shrugged. "Not really. But I find I have a knack for it. I love helping people, and if it means a chance at saving a life, then that beats anything else. Life is precious and should be protected at all costs, 'from the womb to the grave,' as my mother used to say."

"Well said." I smiled. "I'm sure I would have liked your mother." I knew Cyril's wife had passed away only a couple of years after they had Willa, but the depth of that news didn't hit me until now. She and I had both lost our mothers early on. Thankfully, she still had her father.

"I can imagine the role of a guard and soldier is one filled with saving many lives. Is that true?"

Yes and no. The very man I'd been tasked with protecting, I couldn't even save. That was, not until his body wound up here. And sometimes it felt like there was no hope for the Brakan people with all the poverty that plagued them. It only drove the stake of guilt in my gut deeper and kindled the flame in my soul brighter when I was surrounded by hordes of silver and could do nothing about it.

I swallowed the truth of those words and opted for something simpler. "That's our aim."

She nodded as if in understanding, not bothering to ask further.

The *Neptucadis* swayed to the tune of our silence, the rocking of the vessel causing the torchlight on the walls to dance. It was a cavern of comfort, as if our conversation were mugs filled with vulnerability rather than heady ale. Willa looked pensive in the wavering shadows, and not for the first time, I wondered how she ended up here.

I shifted in my seat. "Can I ask you a question?" Why did that sound more formal than I intended?

She nodded, inviting me onward.

"How did you come aboard here? The rumors of Cyrils' disappearance spread far and wide across Braka, but little has been told of his daughter."

A rueful smile graced her features. "And little still will, I'm sure." There was no pity in her tone, just a resolute sort of understanding. She continued, "When my father disappeared, as you said, that was one of the darkest days of my life. He's been my everything since the day my mother passed." She clutched the neck of the small harp. "And as I watched him slip below the waves for good, a part of me did, too. But it wasn't until two days later that I finally found the courage to go after him."

"How did you manage it? Weren't you afraid?"

"Terrified!" She laughed. "But I took one of the Bate's fishing boats. Mind you, it was rather dilapidated, so I had to do some work on it first and proceeded to get caught in a tempest somewhere in the middle of the ocean. I felt all hope was lost. How was I to find my father when I was sure the Tides had taken him whole and would most certainly take me, too? But that's when the miracle happened."

"Miracle?"

"I was rescued. By Captain Aldo himself. You can imagine my utter shock when I saw my father was already here, alive and with his harp. Though, I'm afraid time spent at sea has aged him far quicker than I would like."

I nodded. It explained his shaky hands and Willa's learned harpistry because of it.

She'd risked much in coming after her father, but I had a feeling that mattered little in her opinion. She'd probably gained more than she'd lost, though I suspected she longed for land as much as I did. Her tender tenacity was admirable.

I watched her as she grew quiet, her gaze flitting from the sleeping prince to her instrument, her fingers twitching on the wood. I'd already kept her much longer than I'd meant to.

"Please, don't let me stop you." I gestured to the harp in her hands, wondering if I should leave. "I've interrupted long enough."

Willa shook her head, and even that action was gentle. "It's only…I'm worried about him." She motioned to the prince. "Music eases many ails, Mr. Gannon, especially the ones we cannot see." She then turned to me. "Whether asleep or awake, music has the power to assuage the mind. To bring it comfort. Memory. Hope. So I play my harp to bring him some, if possible."

I didn't know what to say, too stunned by the passion in her voice, especially from one so small and meek. I'd always appreciated music, but never like this. I never held it in the same reverence she seemed to.

And I felt immense gratitude on behalf of Prince Clark; he was more than worthy to be serenaded by an angel.

"And perhaps…" She leaned forward and studied me a little closer, her gaze sincere as if trying to read between the worried and exhausted lines on my face.

"Perhaps?" I breathed out the word. I wasn't one for growing uncomfortable beneath another's scrutiny, but beneath another's tenderness—especially a woman's—I felt my palms sweat and my heart pound against my ribs.

I preferred the scrutiny.

"Perhaps you could use some, too." She smiled and leaned back as if confident in her assumption.

I blinked, my mouth going dry. What had she just seen? "Some what?"

Maybe it was time for me to leave the room, but despite my discomfort, I stayed firmly planted in the chair. I couldn't have moved even if I wanted to. Maybe it wasn't discomfort at all.

"I think you could use some music to ease your weary burdens, Mr. Gannon. The Maker did give us this gift to enjoy, did He not?"

*I suppose He did.* And I wasn't accustomed to a woman seeing right through me, assessing my needs as one would an imp or a wounded pet.

Though, I found I didn't mind it as much as I would have thought.

"You are welcome to stay. I can't promise a royal performance, but I can promise sincerity, which I think works just as well."

I nodded but didn't say anything. Instead, I felt myself lean into the chair as if making ready to linger. I closed my eyes so as not to make her uncomfortable, but not before I caught her timid smile.

She began plucking the beginnings of a familiar tune before letting her voice follow, a song that transported me back to my days as a child in Castle Farrador.

*In the garden where the moonbeams glow*
*Grows the thistle amongst the hollyhocks*
*And there, awaits a maiden by the rocks*
*For sleep to claim her nice and slow.*

> *But alas! And all too soon*
> *Do the fairies come out to dance,*
> *Flitting and glowing, a wondrous trance*
> *So, she keeps watch in the light of the moon.*

I'd heard the lullaby at least a handful of times—a song that, despite the fairies making it impossible for the maiden to sleep, did quite the opposite for the listener. I remembered the words but had last heard them from her own father's lips as he sang in the prince's nursery. But I found I much preferred this version and the gentleness of the voice that accompanied it.

As Willa's sweet melody swirled around me, my already closed eyes became even heavier, and before I knew it, I drifted off into a peaceful, unencumbered slumber.

# THIRTEEN

## Hard Truths

It seemed an eternity had climbed on board with Prince Clark's arrival, the unrelenting time embodied by his physical, comatose form. It was as if the entire *Neptucadis* waited with bated breath for the moment we all hoped was coming.

And twelve days later, it did. Though not in the way I imagined.

The prince woke up, yelling—screaming, more like—and rattled the entire vessel with his raucous fit of unbridled confusion.

Willa was at his bedside in an instant, Monty and I close behind. Captain Aldo was nowhere to be found. In truth, I hadn't seen him since the night the prince came aboard.

But to my immense relief, Prince Clark's eyes were open. The man was actually alive! Though at the moment, a wild fit of hysteria overtook any sound reasoning that could be had from him.

"What's going on?" Monty asked, his brow pinched.

I watched as Willa mixed some herbs and tried administering

them to the prince but, with all the man's flailing, couldn't even get anything past his lips. Instead, his hand accidentally smacked her cheek and sent the tincture flying. It smashed on the ground, the contents spilling everywhere.

"Your Highness, you need to cooperate," Willa said, her voice gentle but obviously strained. She tried holding him down, but he was too unpredictable in his movements.

"Here. Let me." I took her place and pinned Prince Clark by his forearms, an action I'd never imagined I'd ever have to do. He kicked with his legs instead, a look of panic in his wide eyes, so I gestured to Monty, and he sat on them. Though much weakened by being bedridden for so long, Clark was strong in his hysteria but not strong enough to take on two grown men.

Willa was quick, too. She gathered everything she needed and mixed a new tincture before readministering the medicine to unwilling lips.

Prince Clark, hair slicked with sweat against his forehead, sounded like he was gurgling the liquid, some of it dribbling down his pale chin and onto his cheeks. But after Willa held his head back and placed a few more drops down his throat, he had no other choice except to swallow.

In a matter of minutes, his panic died down, and he stopped fighting. He slumped back and closed his eyes, his chest rising and falling in an even rhythm.

"What on Braka..." Monty started.

I had never seen the likes of this before, either. Slowly, I extricated myself from the prince's limp form and stood. Monty was a bit more hesitant, but he did the same.

"He's delirious. A high fever can drive even the most rational of people mad." Willa rubbed her red cheek, her voice growing hoarse. "Now that he's awake from his coma, some normal sleep should do him some good. Fluids every hour should help to bring down his fever, too."

I studied her, watching her expression as it shifted from pain to holding back tears. I was about to take a step closer, hesitating only a moment, but Monty beat me to it.

"Miss Reid, are you all right?" He asked the very question that was on the tip of my tongue.

I bit the inside of my cheek and stifled a groan. It was probably for the best.

I heard a weak reply escape her lips, her gaze moving from Monty's face to settle on mine. A question lingered there, or perhaps it was only my imagination.

I excused myself and allowed Monty to console her. I knew Prince Clark was harmless, but a blow to the face to someone so small must be painful.

But she didn't need me there to watch out for her. Monty was better at that sort of thing anyway. I was used to protecting people *before* they got hurt, not so much the comforting *after*.

My rationale was sound.

So why did my chest feel tight, and why did I have the sudden urge to punch a hole in the wall?

The remainder of the week and into the next were typical for being stranded at sea: more leagues traveled across the expansive blue. How far had Jollie taken us now? At least 10,000? 20,000? I wasn't certain of the conversion of nautical miles to the ones on land, but it sure felt long enough.

Abandoning the Straits of Kethnar, we'd struck out once more toward the Herring Sea and the waters beyond. I wasn't sure where we were headed, but I felt that Captain Aldo had a plan—and a dubious one at that.

Ever since the prince had awoken, the *Neptucadis* had, too. Monty and I went on another underwater excursion, but this time, Ondru and Niam showed us the ropes. My heart nearly stopped when a shark swam into the light of the bioluminescent fungus gnats. I'd glimpsed the great white's teeth and swallowed the image that came to mind if it happened to take a bite, and I dodged one too many close calls from a rogue swordfish, but those were stories for another day.

We'd been tasked with harvesting seaweed and mineral deposits from the ocean floor. Not to mention squid ink for medicinal purposes, which was easier to procure than I'd thought. All one had to do was get close enough to snatch the poor creature and aim its expulsion into a jar.

We did all these things without seeing anything of the captain.

What was troubling his dark mind and kept him locked away in his room for weeks on end? Ever since Prince Clark came aboard the *Neptucadis,* he hadn't been the same.

And quite frankly, neither had anyone else.

Aside from the one excursion, Monty was spending most of his free time with Willa, helping her in the aiding of Prince Clark's health and recovery. They'd take shifts in bringing down his fever, and even though she protested that she could do it on her own, she seemed thankful for the help. Relieved, even.

It made me wonder if Monty had shifted in his feelings toward Gloria. Not like it mattered.

Ondru and Niam were in a league of their own; two Kethnarian men, who often slipped into another language whenever a Brakan came around. I knew they meant well, but I didn't really know them at all.

And then there was Cyril. He seemed the only "normal" one on board, though he spent most of his days polishing silver and sleeping.

So that left me on my own. Typically, I preferred it this way, but when stuck inside a floating vessel, it had the ability to drive one mad.

I just finished scratching my forty-first tally mark on the wall, an action that usually kept me sane, but seeing them add up to a month and a half's worth of time was borderline suffocating. How had I been stuck here for so long?

The door behind me squeaked on its hinges, and I turned to find Monty standing on the threshold. A glint of humor lit his eyes.

"Thought I might find you here. Hiding away again, are we?" He walked inside and met me at the porthole.

I crossed my arms over my chest. I wasn't *hiding*. Captain Aldo was doing enough of that for the both of us. "What can I do for you, Bates?"

Monty and I were best mates. More like brothers, really. Which meant we often got on each other's nerves. And currently, he was riling mine.

"Aside from that day we got the squid ink, you've been avoiding me like the Crimson Death. It's not like you to act like this unless something's biting you, Hux."

*He's right.* I always hated it when Monty was right. "Nothing's 'biting' me. I'm just eager to get off this blasted, waterlogged vessel."

"Coming from the man who warned me about steeling *my* nerves…" Monty scoffed, glancing at my tally marks on the wall. "I don't buy it. We both know you're supposed to be the most level-headed one out of the two of us."

*Right again.* Though right now, I wasn't certain what accounted for my frustrations. There were many things that vied for my concern, namely the enigma of the captain and how to get off this bloody vessel with Prince Clark in tow. But that wasn't all.

Monty continued. "Look, I know I was worried about coming aboard. Still am, quite frankly. But finding something to do has given me purpose here, if for the time being. Maybe it'd do you some good, too. Helping Willa's been—"

"Oh, she's Willa to you now, is she?" I couldn't keep the words from stumbling out of my mouth. I bit my tongue, wishing more than anything to take them back; the metallic taste of blood was enough to remind me to keep my thoughts to myself.

A knowing glint beamed in Monty's eyes. His pensiveness faded, and he had the audacity to chuckle. "Are you ready to admit it, then?"

"Admit *what?*" I snapped.

He crossed his arms, a goofy grin plastered across his face.

"You fancy her."

His admission stunned me as much as it irritated me. "We're not children anymore, Monty. I don't have a love life that needs to be found out and dissected."

That only made him chuckle more.

"What's so funny?" I didn't intend to bark.

"I'm convinced you're half in love with her already."

"Shut up." I rolled my eyes, turning to face the porthole.

Beyond the pane lay a stretch of soft blue, indicating we were only just below the ocean's surface. From here, I could see the glimmer of the sun cascading through the water, but even that wasn't enough to lighten my mood.

Monty clapped me on the shoulder, and I did my best not to flinch.

"She's a beauty, Hux. Through and through. Reminds me of my Gloria back home."

*My Gloria.* So, Monty wasn't interested in Willa after all. For some reason that truth seemed to quiet the raging tempest that rolled in my blood. But why should I care?

"Really? I hadn't noticed." I shrugged him off and walked to the center of the room, kicking at the netting of my bed. The truth was, I *had* noticed, and *that* was the problem. A woman's beauty was usually deceptive at best, and coupled with gentleness and sincerity… It was wiser to maintain a friendship; hearts couldn't get hurt that way.

Willa and I were friends. More like childhood playmates when it came down to it; we'd both grown up with each other on Braka, whether we were aware of it or not. Besides, friendship was about all I could handle.

But since when had I started calling her "Willa" in my thoughts?

"I'll believe that when the sun turns green." Monty sighed and sat down on the bed, worming his fingers through his hair. "I don't know why you fight it so hard, mate."

"I'm a soldier, remember?"

"It's madness to deny the obvious."

"What? That I'm so deeply in love and I'm too stubborn to see it?" I mocked.

"That you still hold a grudge over what Laurel did to you."

I bristled at the sound of her name. It grated on my nerves, like an off-pitch note in a choir of songbirds. "That name should long be forgotten, Monty."

"And yet you seem to react to it as if she'd broken your heart yesterday. It's been ten years, Hux. Ten! Is your heart forever hardened by one savage woman? She was young and stupid, but I can guarantee so were you."

"I wasn't the one stringing her heart along just for sport, Monty. I wasn't the one stealing kisses only to run into the arms of another lover. I wasn't—" I slammed my palm against the wall to stop myself, my rage mounting. Blood pulsed through my veins, and I wanted nothing more than to slash at something with the sword I'd stowed away beneath my bedding. Which reminded me—I was due for another trip to the armory.

"Yes, but *you* were the one who kept her at a distance. You've always been a tough nut to crack, Hux. You don't bear your heart to many, if anyone. I'm not saying you deserved what Laurel did to you, but you do tend to push people away."

This conversation was like being in a practice ring, but instead of swords clashing together, it was words. Hard, truth-filled words.

"Oh, and you know so much," I snapped.

"I know your bark is worse than your bite." Monty shrugged, looking none the worse for wear.

Silence lingered between us, and in that space, I felt the fight leave me.

I heaved a sigh and sat down next to him. I hated to admit it, but he was right...*again*. Leaning forward, I placed my elbows on my knees and combed my hands through my hair. "I guess I'm pretty messed up."

Monty snorted. "Aren't we all? I'm a habitual overthinker. You've said it yourself; I could earn a job as Farrador's inquisitor. And yet you've stuck by me all these years.

"You're the pain in my side I can't seem to get rid of."

Monty winked. "I'll take that as a compliment." He grew quiet and began picking at the netting on the bed. "Look, Hux, I'm not telling you that the thing to do is go fall in love and that it'll cure all your ails. Confound it, no human is capable of such things. But I *am* telling you that maybe it's time to let go. Of *everything*. To forgive and allow room for the Maker to make you whole again."

I knew Monty was right. What was that now, the fifth time? He'd always been the wiser one out of the two of us. With a heart prone to questioning, there also came a deeper empathy and concern for those around him. His fears weren't all bad if they knew how to produce this result in others.

And something about his wording led me to believe he wasn't

only talking about forgiving Laurel. Naturally, I took the bait.

I swallowed the lump that had formed in my throat, feeling more vulnerable than I had in a long time. "You know, it's always bothered me about my father. Why he never came home. I've never been able to forgive him for it."

Monty didn't appear surprised by the turn in conversation, which further proved I'd been right in my assumption. He nodded and brought his gaze to the wall. "I've often wondered that, too. My family lost a valued friend that day…"

My chest constricted. "But now I think I know why he didn't return. His ship sank at the bottom of the Herring Sea. The *Glad Tidings* couldn't bear him home. And all this time, I've been angry at the wrong man." My insides flared at the thought.

Monty seemed to ponder this. "You hold Captain Aldo responsible?" He was tracking with me like an arrow to a target.

"I don't know. I can't reason out any other solution. But if he is, is it so wrong to hate the wretch? To loathe his very existence? He's already been holding us hostage for over a month now. For all it's worth, his track record isn't looking too promising."

"I don't like him much either, Hux, but I think Cyril is right. Maybe there really *is* more to him than meets the eye."

It was hard to believe, yet I couldn't help holding the man accountable for actions I wasn't sure he was responsible for in the first place.

"Have you seen any signs of him since Prince Clark arrived?" I asked.

"Only his voice, but otherwise, he's made himself invisible."

"Figures." I rubbed my beard. The thing was gnarly and

desperately in need of a shave. But to think of removing it with a straight edge would draw too much attention. Surely it would alert the crew to the unlocked armory, for how else would I have come by such a tool?

No, it was better to wait and endure the rodent on my chin.

Monty clapped me on the shoulder and stood. "I'm famished, it's nearly suppertime by the looks of it." He gestured to the darkening waters out the porthole.

I stood to follow, but there was something still niggling the back of my mind. I cleared my throat, fiddling with the fish hook in my pocket. "What made you decide to help Wil—er, Miss Reid that day anyway? You haven't left her side since." I hated how desperate I sounded. Like I was some lovesick schoolboy, insecure enough to basically beg for the truth. I consoled myself by thinking that this was for Gloria's sake; the woman *had* to have some idea of Monty's affections toward her, whether he'd spoken them aloud or not.

He smiled wryly. "It's called working in shifts, Hux, but I won't argue that point with you." He laughed. "While it *has* been good for me to have something to occupy my time, I'd be lying if I wasn't curious about your interest toward the woman." He shrugged, the gesture innocent, though I knew he was anything but. "Figured I'd stir the pot a little to test my theory. Seems I was right."

I smacked him on the backside of the head.

He just laughed harder. "Love you, too."

I rolled my eyes and proceeded to follow him out the door and upstairs to the dining room.

Monty was a nuisance, but at least I knew he had my back.

Though, I wasn't so sure about my heart. The muscle didn't feel softened to the idea of allowing another woman into it. At least, not yet.

The idea was ludicrous at best.

# FOURTEEN

## Onward and Upward

Two more days passed in similar fashion, but this time, Monty eased up on helping Willa. Instead, he hinted that I should go in his stead, but I thought that would appear odd. Surely the prince was improving, and there wasn't any need for my aid.

Though, I had poked my head into the sick ward every now and again. If only just to listen to Willa's voice and harp.

Sitting down to break our fast, Monty gnawed on some seaweed while I chewed on a piece of cod. Oh, to be rid of the crumb-catcher that was my beard; I'd picked more than my fair share of food out of it in just the few moments I'd begun eating.

I ignored the thing, stuffing another piece of cod in my mouth—no, it wasn't my preference, but my reluctant stomach had grown accustomed to a diet of fish over the past few weeks; still, what I wouldn't give to sink my teeth into something with a little more substance. I was about to swallow it anyway when a familiar figure stood in the doorway.

Prince Clark was finally awake! I nearly choked with relief at seeing him standing on his own two legs, though he leaned heavily on a cane, his form more emaciated. His blond hair laid limp across his forehead, but his amber eyes shone brightly in spite of it all.

Willa stood by his side and did a double take when she saw me. Had she not expected to find me here? It *was* early. When her gaze finally met mine, her cheeks reddened as if embarrassed for being caught staring. Before I could offer a smile, she focused her attention on Monty.

"*Nouvo maen*, Huxley," the old Brakan words rolled off the prince's tongue. It roughly translated to "morrows are for new beginnings." Hardly anyone used the language of old, but this was one of the few phrases that still stuck around.

"*Nouvo maen* to you, too, Your Highness." I stood and bowed. "Good to see you on your feet." In all honesty, it was strange. Seeing my charge as a fellow prisoner almost put us on equal footing. It felt wrong on so many levels.

"Good to be standing. Good to be alive." Prince Clark rubbed his temple, his wide grin looking even more prominent amidst the gaunt features of his face.

I nodded, glancing once more at the small woman by his side. If not for Willa's diligent aid and tenderness, I didn't know how the prince would have survived. "You have Miss Reid to thank for that. She worked tirelessly to bring you back to good health." I winked at her and watched as the blush on her freckled cheeks deepened.

She probably hated the attention, but she deserved every praise. All of Braka owed her a great deal, whether they knew it or not.

Prince Clark turned to her and tipped his head with a smile. "I'm forever in your debt, my lady." He then focused his attention once more on Monty and me. "Miss Reid mentioned I was out for quite some time. And by the looks of it"—he shook one of his atrophied legs—"it appears to have done a number on my body."

"Aye. It'd do a number to anyone in your same circumstances."

"What happened exactly? And, please, don't be kind about it." Prince Clark appeared eager to learn the truth despite the pain it might cause him.

Nodding, I cleared my throat. "In short, you've been proclaimed dead by poison, tossed out at sea, rescued, and recovered…all in the span of a little over a month."

"A true miracle if I've ever seen one," Monty chimed in.

Prince Clark slowly walked to where I stood and took a seat. I hesitated only slightly before doing the same. Again, I felt the strange sensation that this wasn't right. That we couldn't share the same table, not unless *he* was the one who had invited me to it.

But the *Neptucadis* was the breeding ground for oddities. Aside from Captain Aldo, we were all equals here, though given more time, I had a feeling the captain would tumble from his high seat and join the rest of us. This vessel had a way of doing that, I supposed. It was as if it hollered "Hang propriety. We are stranded at sea. Surely survival tactics trump social hierarchy."

I was inclined to disagree, but perhaps that was only the fighter in me. All my years of training didn't allow room for these rules to change, not when they were as integral as my blood and the veins which carried it.

"I'll be glad once all of this is over and I get my strength back,"

Prince Clark said, taking a sip of water from a cup Willa just poured him. "I wonder about my father, though. Was he devastated when he found out I was 'poisoned'?"

I swallowed. "More like irate."

"And the wildest part is that he blamed Hux for your death." Monty pointed a stick of dried seaweed in my direction.

The room went silent, Willa's expression unreadable and Prince Clark's stare one of daggers. "*You?* But that's impossible." He pinched his brow and looked me over, his gaze like a knife about to cut me open.

*Not impossible.* The notion was just too ridiculous to ponder for too long.

Would he seriously think me capable of such a thing? When I'd *loyally* served as his bodyguard for most of his life? He couldn't possibly pay heed to those lies…

Then again, I wasn't too sure.

Prince Clark pursed his lips and shook his head. "No." He clapped me on the shoulder. "I don't believe it. My father must have assumed wrongly. But why peg you of all people, I wonder."

I let out an inaudible sigh. This was just another reason why I always respected Clark; he was the most sensible of all the Barrington clan, one who didn't give much thought to stupidity.

"I'm still trying to figure that part out. Maybe when you see your father, you could ask him cordially for me." I fought to keep the snark from my tone but wasn't successful.

Monty guffawed in turn, downing his laughter in a long sip of water. He only emerged long enough to speak a singular word. "If."

"If?" Prince Clark turned his way. "What do you mean, *if?*"

I cleared my throat. "There's some truth to that word, Your Highness. You haven't met him yet, but the man who runs this vessel might as well be a jail keeper. Captain Aldo told us we can never leave here, but seeing as Braka's future is on board"—I motioned to him—"he might make an exception. If not, I have other plans."

Willa came around and refilled all of our water glasses, interrupting the flow of our conversation. I almost forgot she was there, standing quietly by like some meek servant. She hesitated slightly when she got to my cup, not meeting my eyes.

A yawn escaped her lips as she began pouring, sending water over the lip of my glass and splashing onto the table.

"I'm so sorry!" Her eyes were as round as saucers, her cheeks a bright red.

I didn't have the heart to tell her that the misplaced water was now sitting like a puddle in my lap.

"Wil—Miss Reid, would you care to join us?" I asked, hoping she'd put the pitcher down.

If possible, she blushed even further. "Oh no, I couldn't possibly—"

"You deserve a break."

"I'm perfectly fine."

No, she perfectly wasn't.

"Please." I touched her elbow, softening my voice. "Just for a moment."

Even she could tell that she needed to sit down. The poor woman only knew how to serve others and hardly took any breaks for herself. I had a feeling that the "shifts" she and Monty had taken consisted of her playing her harp or mixing more herbal remedies for His Highness. She hadn't tasted a good night's rest in weeks, by the looks of it.

She gave in and nodded, taking a seat on the opposite side of the table. A look of relief crossed her features as she leaned forward on her hands and massaged the space above her eyes.

"So, about these plans, Huxley," Prince Clark continued. "I'd like to hear them, especially if it means getting off this thing."

"That's right, Hux. You said you were scheming up something," Monty added.

I glanced at Willa and decided to keep my voice low. Though I felt like she could be trusted, I didn't want our conversation to worry her already exhausted mind.

I fixed my gaze on the men and proceeded to tell them about the armory door being unlocked and how it was only a matter of time before we could fight our way out of here. The only thing we needed was Captain Aldo's skeleton key to open the hatch and to wait for the right time—preferably when the *Neptucadis* stopped closer to shore.

What I failed to mention was the captain's looking glass and how its touch still plagued my memory. There *was* something curious about the instrument that I had yet to figure out, and part of me wanted to before we attempted a mass exodus out of this wooden trap carried by an unpredictable sea beast.

Only time would tell, and it seemed we had plenty of it until we could even attempt the plan at all.

"Sounds promising," Prince Clark said. "My fever may have broken just last night, but I can already tell I'll grow tired of this place rather quickly. You know I've never cared much for a cage."

I nodded. "I know it well."

Prince Clark may be the most rational of all Barrington's offspring and, in my opinion, the most suited to claim the throne, but that didn't mean he had to *like* always being indoors. In fact, that was one of the things I enjoyed most about guarding the prince. There had been plenty of weeks where we'd spent more time outdoors than in, especially when Albertus was being groomed for the throne.

Unfortunately, once his brother passed, Clark had to take over the role in his stead. Still, he would go outside any chance he got, befriending the villagers and hearing their plights, *listening* to them instead of making them trek to Farrador to beg an audience before his father.

"I wonder what's on today's agenda," Monty said, changing the subject. "It's been over a week since we last saw the captain. Do you think he'll ever show his face again?"

"He has to. There are only so many places one can hide in here," I said.

"I for one would like to meet this *illustrious* captain," Prince Clark added.

And Monty proceeded to fill him in on all the strange ways of Captain Aldo, the underwater excursions we'd gone on, and everything in between.

I chanced another glance at Willa, curious to see if she was trying to listen in on our conversation, but I had little to worry. Her head still rested in her hands but was slightly more drooped now, and her eyes were closed. Gads, the woman was sound asleep.

I couldn't help smiling.

She looked so fragile and innocent, a blonde little thing in need of a full day's rest. But to sleep here? At a table filled with men?

I stood, but not before Monty stopped me with a question.

"Where're you off to, mate?"

I motioned to Willa, her head leaning closer and closer to the table the further sleep claimed her. "The poor woman's been bored to death by our drivel. She's in need of her bed."

He lifted a brow and smirked. "And some pouring lessons, might I add. You look like you soiled yourself."

"Did I ask?" My stone-cold look threatened him should he mock me further.

"And to think you don't call this love." He chuckled, shaking his head. "All right, get on with it."

I excused myself before they could question me further. Or before I punched Monty in the jaw.

I gathered Willa in my arms and took to the hall; she hardly stirred with how deeply her sleep carried her. I didn't miss the way she felt against my chest, her thin frame a laughable contrast to my taller and bulkier one. But it was a strange comfort, and I found myself wishing I could hold her a little longer.

At her bedroom door, I shifted her weight in my arms before opening the door and stepping over the threshold. I'd only had a glimpse before, and now I was *inside* it.

The small room looked similar to mine, but instead of a bed made of fishing nets, hers was made of fabric and goose feathers. She had one porthole, a bedside table with a few books and a glass vase, and her harp rested in the corner. Various paintings hung about the walls, too, and on the bulkhead nearest her bed, hung a picture of a familiar couple with a little girl—a family portrait, I surmised.

I placed Willa onto her bed and pulled the blanket up to her chin, my thumb brushing a lock of hair off her forehead before I thought better of it. *Feather soft.* Heat climbed my neck; I took a few steps back, creating some needed distance, and focused instead on the quilt; it was embroidered in a nautical motif, waves and ships scattered throughout. *This* was soft. Much softer than Willa's hair.

Movement swam on my left, and I turned to find it was coming from within the glass vase on the nightstand. Peering closer, I saw white, iridescent scales and a red and light blue tail swimming around a stone castle; it was the smallest fish I'd ever seen.

A little piece of paper stood up like a tent before the glass with the word "Story" scrawled across it, and I could only guess it was the name Willa had given to the creature.

I smiled. She was the only person I knew who'd keep a fish as a pet whilst trapped at sea.

Turning to leave, I accidentally bumped into a stool I hadn't noticed, sending everything that was once on top, flying to the floor. I cringed as the contents clattered, but thankfully it wasn't enough to rouse her.

"Real smooth, Huxley." I chided my uncharacteristic clumsiness.

Chalk pastels and paint brushes filled my hands as I ushered them back into a tin can. Last to be picked up was a notebook; it had fallen open on a two-page spread of a castle, one that looked stunningly similar to Farrador. After peering closer, I realized it was.

Without thinking, I continued to flip through the pages, pouring over countless landscapes and drawings, some familiar, some not. My pulse sped up when I stumbled upon a drawing I had least expected to see: a portrait of myself, albeit, much scruffier than I was used to.

Slack-jawed, I peered closer at the details, struck dumb at the likeness. The arch of the brow. The curl of the ebony hair. The blue of the eyes. It was uncanny seeing myself in this way. But why on earth would she have a picture of…?

Then it struck me. The pictures on the walls, in this book—had Willa painted them? It seemed the most logical of explanations. How else would she have gotten that portrait of her family? It's not like the captain would have allowed her to waltz back to Farrador and grab it.

I was struck anew by how much I still didn't know about this woman, yet with everything I did learn, it was like solving an intricate puzzle I never wanted to end. And everything I did learn, I liked.

But why would she choose me as a subject of her art?

The idea did something strange inside my chest. I groaned, frustrated by my betraying heart.

If Monty were here, I was sure he would have waggled his eyebrows. He always had that knowing look, one that made me want to smack whatever thoughts he had out of him.

But despite what he might say, I wasn't some lovesick fool. I was wiser than that. I cared for Willa, sure. But until I figured out how to soften the calloused places of my heart, friendship was all I had to offer.

And I'd do well to remember that.

Back in the dining hall, I found Prince Clark conversing with Captain Aldo. The scene was jarring, to say the least. The once-proclaimed-dead-now-alive standing alongside the once-disappeared-now-present.

"Look who we found," Prince Clark said, his smile wide if not unsure. Monty looked ill at ease beside him.

"Mornin', Huxley." Captain Aldo acknowledged me as I entered the room. He looked like he always did with an air of dignified self-importance and not a trace of our last conversation having made a lasting impression. "Glad to see all is well aboard my ship."

I nodded. *As well as things can be.*

"Which brings me to my question: has anyone seen Cyril this morning? I thought he'd be here by now."

As if on cue, the man himself walked in, Ondru and Niam following closely behind.

"Good morning," Cyril said. He stopped in his tracks when he noticed everyone staring at him. "What's going on? Did I miss something?"

"You're right on time, my good man." Captain Aldo went over and slung an arm around the retired harpist's shoulders. "In fact, it's *that* time again."

Cyril stood straighter at the captain's words. It was another enigma, but Cyril seemed to know exactly what was being said.

"Already, Captain?"

"Aye. Within the hour, Neska will welcome you with open arms. You'll do fine." Captain Aldo shifted and pulled something out of his pocket before handing it to him. "Here's what's needed and the means of doing so." The small bundle in the captain's hand looked like a list of sorts and a burlap pouch I assumed was filled with coins if the *clinking* sound of metal was any indicator. "Ondru will go with you, and Niam will keep watch like usual." He snapped his fingers and Ondru took Cyril by the arm to lead him from the room, but not before Captain Aldo gave the man his skeleton key.

Once the three were out of earshot, I couldn't keep quiet. "What was that all about?"

Neska was a ways off from Braka; it lay to the northeast of Kethnar's mountainous border and leagues beyond the Wasteful Tides. I knew we were in foreign waters, but I couldn't place our exact location...until now. The realization was disheartening—I had hoped to be closer to Braka—for it surely complicated our escape.

The captain turned and faced the rest of us, a knowing gleam in his eyes. "Errands."

"What sort of errands?" Something told me they were different from the typical underwater excursions. There was no way he'd send aged Cyril to the depths. But why send the old man at all?

"Our stores are low. We need more food, clothes, bedding. The *Neptucadis* has never had this many occupants."

"A land excursion?" I looked at Monty and the prince, their brows raised in question. It was clear they were thinking what I was thinking: this could be the opportunity we were looking for!

"Don't get your hopes up, Huxley. The task is given to only one."

"Why Cyril? The man struggles to even do the most mundane of tasks."

Captain Aldo stepped closer and placed a hand on my shoulder, the gesture most unwelcome. I looked at his hand more than his face, hoping he'd take the hint.

"Because he won't go blabbing my secret. And I know he'll return." He leaned in, and my gaze latched onto his, stunned by the sudden, serious turn in his expression. "Besides, every loving father always comes back for their child if they can help it. *Always*." He nodded and squeezed my shoulder before stepping back to leave the room.

*The blasted...* His words left me reeling, souring the cod in my stomach.

Why did it seem like he was intentionally trying to strike a nerve?

Or worse yet...

Why did it feel like there might be something he was trying to tell me?

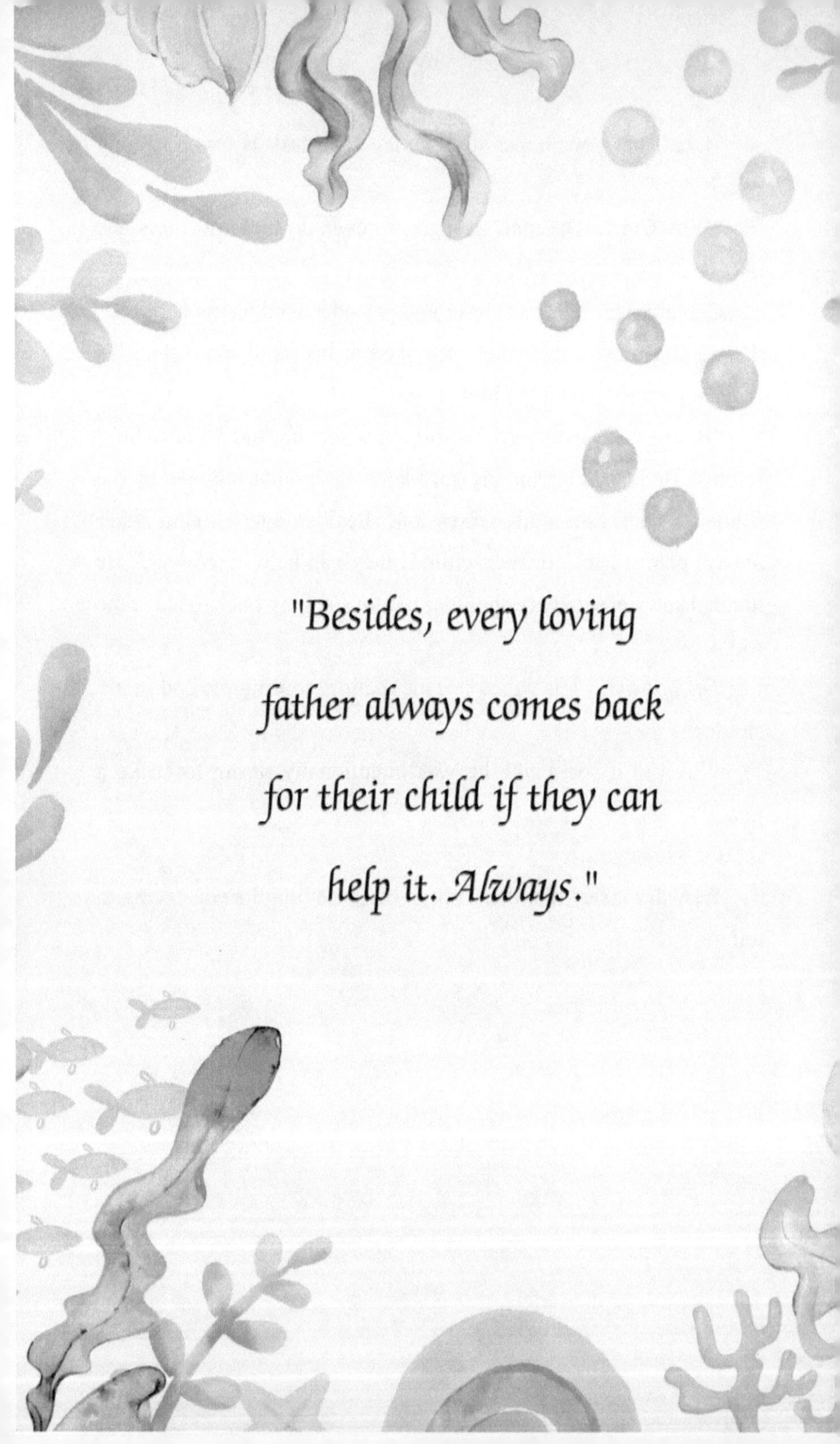
"Besides, every loving
father always comes back
for their child if they can
help it. Always."

# FIFTEEN

## A Seed on Neska's Shores

True to his word, the *Neptucadis* was docked at Neska's shores within the hour. Captain Aldo remained in his quarters, sitting in his chair which overlooked the sea. Ondru and Niam had already taken Cyril outside, leaving the rest of us—Monty, Prince Clark, and myself—to ponder our next move.

I didn't include Willa in that equation. Partly because she was still sleeping and mostly because she wasn't mine to worry about. Though a portion of my chest ached at the thought of leaving her behind, there wasn't anything I could do about it. How could I rightly take her away from her own father?

Once Prince Clark was settled, then maybe there was a chance…

"What's it to be, Huxley?" The very man clapped me on the back, the contact diffusing my erratic stream of consciousness.

The three of us stood in the hallway on the bottom floor just outside of our bedrooms, mulling over possible steps.

"How are we to get past the captain?" Monty asked. "He sits enthroned on his wooden seat like a king in his own right. He'd have to be pretty daft if he didn't hear us sneaking by."

"Which brings me to my plan." I moved aside the cloak I'd recently donned, revealing a baldric and the sword I'd stolen from the armory a few weeks prior. Sheathed, its golden hilt glinted in the torchlight.

"You don't intend to threaten the man, Huxley." Prince Clark quirked a brow.

"If it means our escape…"

The prince nodded, though it was clear he didn't fully grasp the direness of the situation. Yes, he wanted to leave, but *he* hadn't been locked away like some caged, good-for-nothing rat for over a month like the rest of us; in truth, his plight had been much worse. But threatening our jailor was the least of our worries and, in my opinion, was long overdue.

"So…are we going?" Monty looked like he was itching to move.

I nodded. "Follow my lead."

We climbed the first set of stairs and grew quiet when we reached the captain's quarters. Pressing a finger to my lips, we proceeded up the second set to the open trap door, everyone mimicking the lightness of my steps.

On the landing, the captain's back faced us as he gazed outside, his focus on the mainland stretching before him. Beyond the glass wall, Jollie's tentacles swayed this way and that with what looked to be clumps of purple herbs clutched in her grasp. More catmint, I guessed.

My shoulders relaxed; both the cuttlefish and the captain appeared to be distracted, which boasted well for our escape. And hope bloomed at the sight of blessed *land.* To touch it would be most welcome indeed.

This was it. Our time had finally come.

I motioned for Monty and Prince Clark to go to the set of stairs on the opposite side of the room. There, the hatch stood open and poured in the briny wind.

They moved quietly while I lingered behind, one eye on the captain and another on their progress.

We were so close…

"Getting some fresh air?" Captain Aldo's words stayed my retreat, turning my blood cold.

I unsheathed my sword, this particular blade not sullied by the salt of the sea, and took a few steps in his direction. I pointed the tip near the back of his head, waving Monty and the prince onward with my free hand, hoping they'd get the blazes out of here. Captain Aldo wouldn't deter us in our course. We would go home, and this would be our last goodbye.

But if he was as formidable as I supposed him to be, he'd be unsheathing a sword in turn, trying to impede our departure. Except I'd be the only one standing in his way. The others would be long gone, and from my glance toward the hatch, it appeared they already were.

"Put it away, son. There's no need for that." Captain Aldo didn't bother turning around. In fact, I detected a note of humor in his tone that he didn't seem troubled to learn I'd procured a sword at all.

His nonchalance unnerved me, but even more so his next words. "You're free to go if you so choose."

I didn't lower my weapon. Surely, the man was bluffing, a mere jokester he was.

Captain Aldo turned, scoffing when he saw me. *Apparently not.* He took his pointer and middle finger and lowered the tip of my blade. "Are you a cad? Go. Your friends are waiting."

Everything in me wanted to protest. To ask a million questions and demand a fair fight. One did not simply walk out of a prison without first winning the key, and yet here I was. But the rational part of me didn't want to question it. He was giving us all a chance at escape—without a duel no less.

Hesitantly, I sheathed my sword and stepped back, jogging— no, more like sprinting—to catch up with the others. The captain's subtle laughter resounded behind me, and it felt like sharp icicles trailing down my spine.

I tried ignoring him but kept mulling over his sudden change of heart. Something felt off about it, but I wasn't sure what.

On the deck of the *Neptucadis*, the wind whipped around the vessel, tousling my unruly mop of curls and my cloak. I could see Monty and Prince Clark on the shoreline, waving up at me, their expressions ones of relief even from so great a distance.

I climbed down the side of the ship, dodging Jollie's tentacles and waded to land. The cool water came up to my chest, but that mattered little when it meant freedom. It had never felt so good.

"I was almost ready to turn back. Thought he had you in there for good, mate," Monty said as I climbed onto the sandy beach, my sword banging against my drenched pants.

"How'd you leave it? Was he begging for mercy?" Prince Clark chuckled, still leaning on his cane.

I shook my head. "You won't believe it. He just let me go. All of us." It didn't make sense. *"Don't get your hopes up, Huxley. The task is given to only one."* Captain Aldo's words were like the nails inside my proverbial coffin, and yet here I was, a free man. "Come. Let's get away from this place before the captain changes his mind."

We walked across the sandy beach into a cluster of dense pines, oaks, and scattered tropical-looking trees. I didn't know much about Neska, but I didn't recall palm trees growing this far north. We entered the shade of the canopy and pressed on, trudging over sand and rocks. I thought we'd be stuck inside the trees for a solid half hour at least and was surprised at how quickly the foliage began thinning.

I was still coming to grips with the reality that Captain Aldo had let us walk away without a fight, but when I stepped outside the line of palms and conifers, only then did I realize why.

Endless blue stretched for miles before us with the barest sliver of land visible on the horizon. It all made sense now. We were on an island, and there'd be no going home after all.

"You've got to be bloody kidding me." Monty swore under his breath.

I said a few choice words of my own.

"Doesn't look like it." Prince Clark walked a few paces before dropping his cane on the ground. The rest of his body followed suit as he sat down and dug his feet into the sand.

I wanted to rip my hair out.

Niam stood along the shoreline, a spyglass lifted to one eye as he squinted out to the horizon. His accent came out thick. "Should be on the mainland any minute now."

"Where's Ondru?" I walked toward him, gritting the words through my teeth. It would take a while to get over this blow.

"Rowing Cyril. He's to help the poor man carry everything."

How I envied both of them. I grabbed the spyglass from Niam and took a look myself. Sure enough, two distant figures were in a small fishing boat, Ondru rowing and Cyril looking green in the gills.

"How'd you come by a boat in this place?" *And where might I get my hands on one?*

Niam smiled, taking back his navigational instrument. "We built it, Ondru and I. Made from driftwood and shipwrecks. Works out well for the capt'n. Figured that since he helps us, we can pass on the favor."

Had everyone on the blasted *Neptucadis* sworn allegiance to the scoundrel known as Captain Aldo?

"Where's that boat kept when it's not being used?" *Please say on board.*

"Why, here of course!"

*Blast.* I clenched my teeth so hard I wouldn't be surprised if they ground themselves into a powder. "I can't imagine the captain allows these sorts of excursions to happen often." It was a fishing sort of question, and I hoped he'd take the bait.

Niam shrugged. "True. He calls for the utmost discrepancy. Though I'm not sure coming here every third month would be considered infrequent either." He turned his spyglass out to sea once more and hollered. "Aye, land-ho!"

*Every third month.* That meant we'd be doing this again at the turn of the next season. Could I hold out that long, though? Especially when knowing that all that laid before me were endless leagues? What of Prince Clark and the fate of Braka?

I looked out to the sea once more, watching the waves lap against the shore before being pulled back out with the tide. It would be risky to swim such great lengths with no more than a sliver of land in sight. Folly. Madness. But perhaps when Prince Clark regained his strength, the feat could be attempted by the three of us.

Without a vessel of one's own, desperation would drive even the sanest of men to such odds. Crossing the wide bay into Neska by the skin of our backs might prove our only means of escape.

But even *that* would require waiting.

Sucking in a sigh, I turned around and trudged back through the forest. It was my aim to walk off some of my frustration, apparently made evident for even Monty knew better than to pepper me with questions.

Tall timbers pressed in around me the deeper I went, the fresh air filtering through the boughs—a blessed relief after being cooped up for so long. But even so, it carried with it the taste of bitterness, for I knew it wouldn't last.

I yelled, kicking the pine tree nearest my foot. Bark flew off and littered the ground, a shrapnel of false hope. I kicked the shrapnel, too, sending leaves and twigs scattering all around me.

As the debris settled, I placed my arm against the tree's trunk and laid my head down in turn, breathing in the salt of the sea and the sap of the assaulted conifer.

Anger wasn't an emotion I liked to categorize myself by, and yet I'd felt its burning presence ever since Captain Aldo's "capture." In truth, I'd felt it on and off ever since my mother died and my father left. Since Laurel broke my heart. Since King Barrington's false accusation…

My palms clenched tightly into fists. Who was I kidding? Confound it, I was more prone to it than I wanted to admit.

I desperately wished I was back at Farrador, taking out my aggression in a pseudo-match; that's what I'd done countless times before. But seeing as that wasn't an option, the reality struck me hard—its own truth a punch to my gut. Taking it out with sparring and swords would never attack the root. It would only prolong the turmoil.

I groaned into the tree as guilt threatened to swallow me whole at the realization. How long had I chosen to live like this? How long had my heart gone unchecked, only to be hardened by years of calloused thinking?

*"Nothing ever happens overnight, Huxley,"* my mother used to say. And she'd always follow it up with, *"It's a slow kind of fading when you allow your heart to be bought in by the world's whims. So be careful what voices you heed lest they become yours, too."*

She'd been right, of course. I'd listened to the voice of anger for years and let it consume me.

Was all hope lost for me, then? Was there to be no freedom from this blasted prison and from my own self-pity?

As remorse pooled in my middle, the sun broke through the canopy, casting its rays upon my lamenting ground. I looked up, and its touch warmed my face, assuaging the creases in my brow.

And it was then that I recalled another memory from my childhood.

I was only eight, but my bruised knuckles and bloodied lip were proof that perhaps I'd made a stupid mistake. I had yet to learn the consequences of my actions, that an unkind word didn't warrant a fistfight in the village.

But after the event, it was my mother's words, spoken gently and with conviction in our little cottage, that registered to my weary spirit even now.

*"Sweet Huxley, your loyal heart is virtuous, but you must learn its limitations. Not all is meant to be a battle. And when your mistakes fill you with guilt, remember this: look up."* She tilted my chin upwards, her expression kind and warm. *"It's never too late to ask for forgiveness. We have a Maker who's already made a way."*

She turned to a passage from the Great Book, leather-bound in all its glory. She cleared her throat and continued. *"It says here, 'My grace is sufficient for you, for my power is made perfect in weakness.' You see, Huxley, when you've done some wrong, there's still time to make it right. Our Maker's grace is enough. Let it be enough for you."*

Only, it had never seemed enough. Not then, when the flame of anger was just a spark. Not now, when my entire being felt consumed by it. Though I desperately wanted to believe it was. *Grace.* It was nigh impossible to give or receive when I'd been so wrongly abandoned, used, imprisoned… How could grace possibly help me when all I'd ever been dealt was the absence of it?

I shook my head.

No. That wasn't entirely true.

I still had Monty. He'd stuck by me through the good and the bad, having the guts to call me out on all my blunders. He was more brother than my own family.

And then there was Willa. Though I'd only known her for a short time, I felt relaxed just thinking about her. The way her cyan eyes lit up when she was excited, her gentleness and surprising turn of wit, her genuine friendship. She was a breath of fresh air in the prison I'd been subjected to, and I couldn't take that gift lightly, especially when I hadn't deserved it.

If these things weren't mercy, then I didn't know what was.

The sun illuminated the trees around me, dappling their green leaves in gold. It seemed to wink at me from above before darting once more behind a cloud.

*It's never too late to ask for forgiveness.* And perhaps I wasn't as far from grace as I'd thought.

"Absolve me, for the wretched man I am," I whispered skyward, hoping my words fell where they mattered most.

Forgiveness still seemed a foreign concept, but maybe one day it wouldn't be. Maybe there still was a chance for me after all.

And in that moment, something softened. I wouldn't call it a transformation, but it was more like a seed, the tiniest thread of possibility waiting to push up from the surface. And I was given a choice. I could explore it—tend to it—or I could ignore it and let it waste away in my internal fire.

But what would I choose?

It struck me how the choice wasn't always so easy, the task as daunting as it was insurmountable, but hadn't my mother said the Maker's grace was sufficient for even this? Maybe I didn't have to do it on my own.

Even if I wasn't enough, maybe *He* could be.

I pushed off from the tree, feeling more unsettled than I had in years. But it was of the good sort, a right sort of unsettling born from the realization that I couldn't rely solely on myself anymore. It was freeing and terrifying, but with it came a lightness.

And for once, the telltale fire burning in my middle was only a smoldering wick.

I wanted to do something about it. But what?

Monty and Willa. I felt as if I should thank them—show them I thought about more than just my sorry lot in life. I'd let Monty eat a portion of my next meal—that would be enough for him, and I'd deal with the sacrifice on my end. But Willa… No, she deserved something more suited to a lady.

A flash of goldenrod-yellow captured my attention as I scanned the forest floor, the last traces of sunlight dancing through the trees and illuminating my path. Walking closer, I bent at the knees to inspect further. It was a feather, a beautiful one at that, streaked with iridescent white and cobalt blue throughout. I glanced up and didn't see any birds in the trees, but I figured this must have fallen from one in passing.

It reminded me of her fish, Story. I had an inkling that she appreciated beautiful things, and I had the sudden urge to give it to her. Maybe it would even be enough to make her blush.

And for reasons I couldn't put into words, I knew that would be as much a gift to me as this feather would be for her.

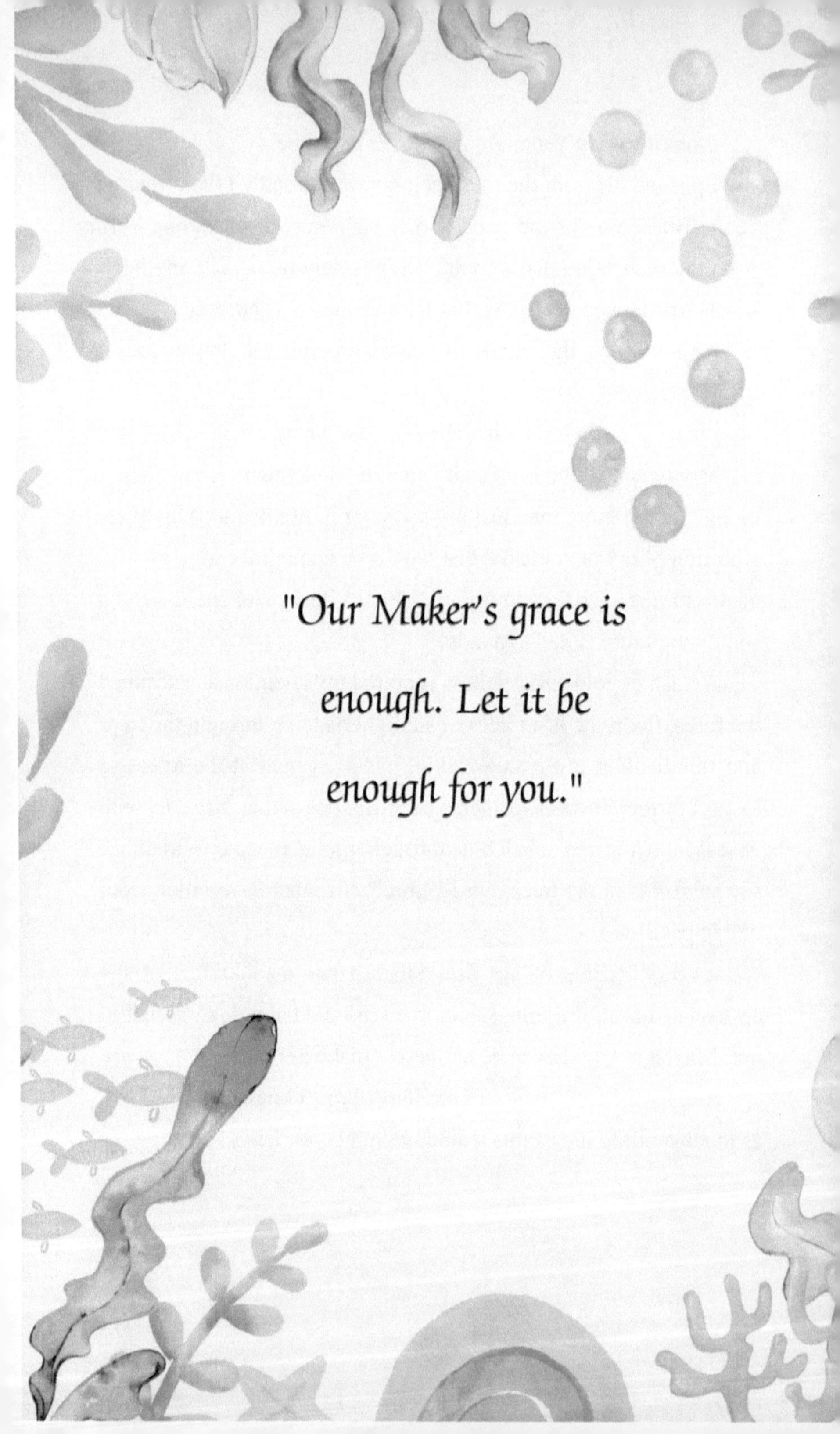
"Our Maker's grace is
enough. Let it be
enough for you."

# Sixteen

## Hidden Treasures

Hours passed with the light of the morning fading into the dusky gray of a day gone by. And with the dusk came Cyril and Ondru, their fishing boat packed to overflowing.

They'd brought back bed linens and washcloths; articles of clothing—shirts, trousers, and what looked like a new dress for Willa; another set of silverware, a skein of flour, a cask of oil, plenty of yeast, a sack of potatoes, some seeds, sprigs of herbs, and an assortment of fruits and vegetables meant for seasoning a meal. Not least of all were six chicken thighs and five large flank steaks, which I tried my darndest not to salivate over.

Monty, Prince Clark, and I reluctantly went back inside the *Neptucadis* to help haul in the large catch. By the time I thought about retreating to the outdoors once again, the hatch had already been sealed shut. Through the whole endeavor, Captain Aldo remained inconspicuous; the door to his bedchamber was closed, and I could only surmise he secluded himself behind it.

All the better for me.

I didn't revel in the idea of seeing him just now; it didn't matter what sort of revelation I'd had earlier. I still didn't like the man nor his trickery.

After everything was put away, it neared dinnertime, and I hadn't seen any sign of Willa. Was she sleeping in her chambers even now?

With everyone retreating to their rooms, I decided to find the answer to my question instead. Besides, there was a certain pocket in my trousers itching to be relieved of a golden feather.

As I neared her door, gentle sounds of a lilting harp filled the once-silence with song. I stepped closer, a floorboard creaking beneath my weight; I ignored it, pressing my ear against the door. The notes wound their way into my chest and squeezed it; there was something about this particular melody that felt like a graceful dance, making me long to do just that, the way my own father and mother had done plenty of times around the kitchen.

I'd been young then, but the joy they'd had in each other's embrace was memory enough to affect me even now.

I raised my hand to knock, second-guessing the action; I shouldn't interrupt her playing. If she was anything like me, I didn't relish having my training on the practice field cut short. I always thought that when one found something that gave them solace, it was borderline criminal to interrupt it. Or at best, inconsiderate.

But before I could walk away, the door suddenly opened inward, and Willa herself stood in the doorway, staring up into my face with a look of utter surprise. "Mr. Gannon!"

Heat climbed my neck, burning my skin. I must have looked ridiculous for standing this close. Like I was caught snooping. I hadn't meant… I swallowed. "This isn't what it looks like—"

"I thought I heard a noise—" Willa and I spoke at the same time.

I pulled at my collar. "I was just walking by."

She glanced at my proximity to the doorframe. "Do you typically walk this close to people's doors, Mr. Gannon?"

No. Not unless you were a prince or a threat to him. "I'd dropped something, and it rolled this way. I'd just retrieved the item when you opened your door."

She scrunched her freckled nose at my bold-faced lie. I had a feeling she could see right through me. "What did you drop?"

"I, uh…" I fumbled with my pockets, my hands growing slick with perspiration. What was it about this woman that made me lose all sense of myself? I was a bodyguard—a soldier—and I needed to remember that.

But a quick glance at Willa's face, noting the slight lift at the corner of her mouth, just about did me in. She was on to me. I was caught most thoroughly, trapped like a bass in a fisherman's net.

But perhaps there was still a way out.

My hand seemed to recall my purpose for coming when my words could not. Something yellow and most assuredly riddled with salmonella if Monty had a word to say about it. But he'd be happy to know I'd cleaned it with some water and a bar of soap.

I pulled out the offending thing, the purpose for my humiliation, and held it out to her. "It was this."

She eyed it carefully. "Why, Mr. Gannon, I'm surprised at you." Her smile now broke wide and free. "You said it rolled."

I blinked. Had I said that? *Blast.*

"I, uh…never mind that." I shifted on my feet. "It's for your fish…" No, that didn't come out right either.

Her brows drew nearer together. "My fish? How did you…"

"I carried you to your room."

Understanding seemed to dawn as her eyes widened and cheeks reddened. She glanced behind her, and I could tell she was embarrassed. Was it her paintings she was worried about or the idea that I'd *carried* her without her knowing?

There was the telltale blush I'd been waiting for…only, it wasn't happening at the right moment. I took half a step back, suddenly aware of the closeness of our proximity.

"I was hardly there for more than five minutes, I can assure you."

Her alarm faded into a soft laugh as she returned her attention to the object in my hand. "So, you're giving this feather to…my fish?"

This was all a disaster.

"No. I'm giving this feather to *you.* As a gift."

"A gift?"

I nodded.

She looked at me like she didn't understand.

I heaved a sigh and racked my brain for the words. I thought about saying, "Being stuck inside a wooden cage all day doesn't necessarily lend itself to elegance," but that sounded gratuitous. Then, "When I saw your fish…" but enough about the fish! That scaly creature had already derailed this conversation more than I'd hoped. Why were words so difficult?

I settled on, "I figured you appreciate beautiful things." Short and concise.

She took the golden object and twirled it in her fingers, smiling. Then she glanced up and tilted her head. "And you, Mr. Gannon?"

"Me what?"

"Do *you* appreciate beautiful things?" If Laurel or any other woman had asked me that question, I would have detected an ulterior motive beneath the battering of eyelashes. But Willa, the way she looked at me as if she was trying to decipher some hidden part, bore no sign of pretense.

And I knew she wouldn't let her question go unanswered.

I opened my mouth only to close it again. My mind wandered back to Castle Farrador and the top of the old keep. The way the sun crested the treetops and warmed the patch of grass at my back. It was my sanctuary, a place where true beauty remained untainted by the demands and disappointments life had continuously thrown my way.

Then I looked at Willa, seeing some of that same, untainted beauty in her smile. So much like Laurel and yet so unlike her in all the ways that mattered. And I choked on my words. "Aye. I appreciate beauty."

She nodded, and silence seemed to envelop us both with fragile arms, Willa stroking the feather and my gaze unwilling to meet hers.

I should have left then, turned to prepare for dinner, but I wasn't quite ready to go.

"So, why name a fish Story?" The question left my mouth before I had a chance at biting it back.

Willa looked up, scratching that space behind her ear—a telltale sign that she was nervous. She shook her head. "You'll laugh."

Forget my earlier thought; it seemed like the fish would be the savior of our conversation after all.

"Why would I laugh?"

"I tend to find meaning in everything, if you haven't noticed."

"You say that like it's a bad thing." I had noticed, but it intrigued me—challenged me to see the world through her eyes. "I promise I won't even crack a smile." I leaned against the doorframe. "Why Story?"

After a moment she sighed. "Fine." A hint of amusement lifted a corner of her mouth. "I guess it's because even the smallest of things are accounted for by our Maker. Didn't he make the land as well as the sea? With a name like Story, it reminds me that even the least of these are under his care. We all have our own stories to live and tell, do we not?"

Her words captivated me. They were laced with the same conviction she'd displayed earlier when tending to the prince. And I had no words of my own to meet them.

"You're smiling!" She tugged on my sleeve, drawing my attention to her hand.

"Am not." I schooled my features into a purposeful frown. "I'm merely ruminating over the wisdom."

Someone cleared their throat behind me, and I vice-gripped the door frame so as not to jump.

"When you two are done flirting, dinner should be ready in five. Apparently the Kethnarians cooked up a feast." Monty chuckled. He clapped me on the shoulder as he walked by, *winking* of all things.

Embarrassment filtered through my veins, and I could only imagine how Willa felt. Confound Bates. I'd slug the man later.

"I should freshen up." It wasn't until I stepped away from her door that I realized the truth of those words; I smelt distinctly of brine and fish. *Brilliant.*

"Oh, me too." She colored, backing into her room, slowly closing the door. Her face was the only thing visible now, peeking through the wood slats. She held up the feather as a last goodbye and beamed. "This is my favorite color you know."

I tipped my head, unable to contain my mirth. "See you at dinner, Miss Reid."

And she closed her door.

Dinner was both hot and filling, a welcome change after the scant fare we'd been given the past month and a half. Tonight's meal boasted of the steak, chicken, and potatoes we'd hauled in from earlier, and it was almost enough to make me forget Farrador's banquets.

However, I silently chided my earlier notion of giving Monty part of my next meal. Had I known we'd be eating like kings tonight, I would have thought of something else to give him instead.

Such was life.

The table was almost full with Cyril, Willa, Ondru, and Niam taking up one side and Monty, Prince Clark, and me directly across from them. Only one seat remained untouched, and that spot belonged to the enigmatic Captain Aldo. The man still hadn't shown himself since earlier this morning. Since he deflated all our hopes of freedom.

Part of me didn't blame him; if I was responsible for letting down half the crew, I'd hide away, too. Though, I had a feeling he was hiding away for different reasons.

Because of his absence, conversation flowed merrily around the table. We were an odd grouping, though; two men from Kethnar and most of us from Braka; a retired harpist and his daughter; a sailor and a royal guard; and a *prince* of all things, who, mind you, was supposed to be dead. For all intents and purposes, we didn't fit together. We were all as different as the land was to the sea, like commoners pitted up against royalty.

Which was partly the case as it was. However, Prince Clark wasn't one to stand on ceremony and preferred a natural way of things, though I never found it in me to abscond my role.

And for the second time, I realized it was all the *Neptucadis'* doing; this confounded vessel had brought us together—as equals— in ways that being on land never would have allowed.

What was it about the ocean that borne people in tandem, the current stripping away titles and politics as if we were all fellow journeyers to the final resting place, reminding us that one's humanity was indeed more important than one's station?

If Willa could read my thoughts, I'm sure she would have found a lesson in this chaos somewhere. She had a knack for that sort of thing.

After the plates were all cleared and the table washed, a blanket of sleep seemed to fall on the company. Even Willa, who'd rested all afternoon, looked like she was on the verge of going asunder.

Monty caught the direction of my gaze and leaned over, whispering near my ear, "What's your next move, Hux?"

His question could only mean one of two things: *"What happens now since we're still stuck here?"* since he'd seen my irritation on the island and knew I'd most likely conjured up a plan, or *"What's going on between you and Willa?"* if the slight wiggling of his brows was any indicator.

I didn't feel like answering either, especially the last one. I didn't even know how to.

"We wait." I was purposely vague, hoping it would be enough to cure his curiosity while still holding to the truth. There wasn't much we could do *except* wait.

Seeming to take the hint, Monty clapped me on the back and made to exit the dining room. "All right, then. Come dawn, perhaps you'll tell me what's *really* on your mind."

I shifted uncomfortably on my feet. I should have known Monty wouldn't let much slide; he usually saw right through me anyway.

"You need rest. You're rivaling Willa's sleepless streak by this point, Hux. And the Maker knows we don't need another loon-crazed codswaddle aboard this thing."

"Look who's talking, Bates." I rolled my eyes.

Everyone filtered out of the room like fish to a stream, going their separate ways for the night. Monty and I trudged downstairs, our steps heavy on the wooden boards while the *Neptucadis* swayed ever so gently atop the surface of the water.

The vessel had yet to move from off the coast of Neska's island, and I silently hoped we'd be docked here for the next three weeks or so, providing a more opportune escape.

"See you on the morrow, brother." Monty entered his room and casually flung himself on his bed before shutting the door in my face with his foot.

In a matter of minutes, he'd be out like a light. Sleep came easily to the Bates family, whereas I had to work for it.

I proceeded down the hall, ready to throw myself into my own chambers for a night of fitful slumber, when something caught my eye.

The door to the armory stood open, albeit only a crack. This wasn't news to me; I'd made sure the door remained unlocked ever since I'd stuffed part of my tunic in the door jamb a month ago. However, because of my little trick, I was doubly careful to always close it. To make it *appear* as if it was locked, when in fact it was quite the opposite.

The hairs on the back of my neck rose when my hand strayed to the sword strapped and concealed by my hip. A premonition of sorts crept over me.

*Captain Aldo.*

Because of my little stunt from earlier, the man had learned I'd procured a weapon. He probably made quick work of it, too, putting all the pieces together and conjuring up some sort of scheme because of it.

Was it he who'd left the door ajar?

Not wanting to take the bait, if indeed it was a trap, I pushed open the door the rest of the way and scanned the small space with hackles raised. I paused when my gaze settled on something curious.

Unease rose higher, accompanied by a pounding against my skull. When I saw what rested on the table, I knew for a fact that I hadn't been the last one in this room.

I looked over my shoulder, suddenly feeling as if someone was in the doorway, watching my every move, but it was only the stillness that answered. The only noise was the gentle lapping of waves against the *Neptucadis'* hull.

Steadying my nerves, I turned back to the object which originally drew my attention, noticing the familiar gilded handle sticking out beneath a worn cloth. Removing the fabric, I sucked in a breath at what lay beneath.

It was the looking glass, but this time, it was whole. No shattered edges. No broken glass ready to prick supple skin. If anything, it looked clearer and more beautiful than before.

With little hesitation, I picked up the object and rotated it gently between my fingers. It was heavy, but only just, and the weight of it felt comfortable in my hand as if it belonged there as much as my sword.

"What sort of trinket is this?" Awe laced the words that my lips whispered.

I didn't know much, but I felt as if I'd soon find out the answer.

"We all have our own

stories to live and tell,

do we not?"

# SEVENTEEN

## Secrets in the Looking Glass

As I peered into the mirror, I first noticed the haggard face of a man staring back at me, looking far older than twenty-eight, or at least, more unkempt than when he'd first left Braka. The beard was full and ungroomed, the skin of my face the palest it had ever been.

I was never one to pride myself on appearances, but even I could tell I'd looked better.

Pulling at the skin beneath one of my eyes, I brought my face closer to the looking glass only to find I couldn't see as clearly as before. I held the mirror back and squinted, my image spinning and blurring on its clear surface.

The memory of shattered glass made my hand clutch tighter to its gilded frame. This time, I wouldn't let go.

A tingling started at the fingers and spread through my hand before it climbed the entirety of my arm. It settled someplace in my chest before snaking out to the rest of my body. It was the strangest sensation, and yet something compelled me to hold on.

I looked deeper into the mirror and noticed colors blurring together before they leveled out and revealed a scene. At first, I thought it was a picture, but then the images began to move, and my breath lodged in my throat as I recognized myself, albeit a much younger version.

I remembered this moment. It was the same day my father had left on the MFB *Glad Tidings*.

*"Huxley, my boy,"* King Barrington said. *"With your father gone, I'll need you to keep a closer guard on Clark and an ear out for Tristan."*

I knew his request would try my patience, at least when it came to Tristan. The youngest prince was virtually a shadow, a mouthpiece of the king, never giving voice to his own thoughts except those which suited the Crown, which sometimes meant he didn't listen to me. And being only a year or two older than him certainly didn't help. Thankfully, I wasn't his personal guard, and at least Prince Clark was kind, though he was a few years my senior.

*"What about Albertus, Your Majesty?"* I knew the eldest prince was the prize jewel of Braka, that my father had been his personal bodyguard since his birth.

*"You're young, Huxley. One of my more trained men has that covered."*

I should have felt slighted, but being only sixteen, the idea of guarding three princes was a bit much. Two were still difficult, but nothing I couldn't handle. I was a Gannon after all.

Suddenly, the image in the mirror blurred once more, spinning wildly in an array of colors before it steadied into a new one. I saw myself again, but now, I was older.

I swallowed hard as I recognized the scene playing out before me. It was my eighteenth birthday. How could I forget such a cruel, ill-fated day?

*"Huxley, quickly."* My father's replacement, Morton, motioned me over from the doorway of Prince Albertus' bedchamber. *"Fetch Waldric, would you?"* I could tell from the unsteadiness of his voice that something was wrong. Horribly, horribly wrong.

*"Is everything—"*

*"Just go. Now!"* he barked at seeing me still standing there. I didn't waste any more time. This was urgent, and I didn't have to be a grown adult to read between the lines.

It was nighttime, and I should've continued my patrol, standing guard outside Prince Clark's bedchamber, but Morton was in earnest. I trusted he'd have everything under control in my absence.

I snaked through the corridors of Farrador, guided by the faint glow of the wall sconces. Torchlight flicked their fiery tongues, but I didn't linger to watch their dances. Not this night. I exited the corbel and descended a set of stairs that led to the lower bailey. A few more paces and I was at the door to the apothecary's hut, my fist pounding against the wood grains.

Chickens squawked angrily behind me as if I'd just disturbed their brooding rest. The moon cast an eerie glow from beyond thick clouds, a foreboding feeling creeping up my neck.

With the locals dropping like flies, I had little to wonder what ailed our crown prince. A plague was spreading through Braka, and its impact was often lethal. I silently prayed it would be anything but that.

Footsteps could be heard from the other side of the door. A flicker of light flashed from inside the nearby window, and a middle-aged face appeared beyond the glass, both eyes and hair a muddy brown. In a few seconds, the door was yanked open, and an exhausted-looking man stood in the doorway.

*"This better be important, Huxley,"* he said, rubbing his eyes.

*"It is, sir. It's the prince."* I saw his demeanor shift. *"Albertus."*

Immediately, Waldric grabbed his things, and the two of us sprinted back to the royal bedchambers. It took us no time at all to climb the stairs and run the length of the winding hallways. We arrived with no breath left to spare.

Waldric entered Albertus' chambers, relieving the much-anxious Morton. I resumed my post outside Prince Clark's room, left with my wandering thoughts on how the jewel of Braka would fare.

Again, the mirror in my hand swirled with a host of colors and blurred images before it settled on something new, a scene I was unfamiliar with.

*"How much longer will this take?"* King Barrington paced the length of a heavily draped room, his pinched brow as deep as the ocean.

*"I'm trying my best, Your Majesty. But the Crimson Death isn't easily won,"* Waldric said, his tone uneven as he bent over the prince.

*"Then try harder! This is my son you're saving. My son! Does that mean nothing to you?"* King Barrington fumed.

*"It means everything to me, your Majesty. He's Braka's*

*future."*

*"Then you'd do well to make sure he sees it."*

King Barrington crossed to the window at the same time the mirror switched again. This time, I heard the new scene before I saw it, a wailing and piercing cry shattering the silence.

It was the king's wife, Queen Gertrude, who two weeks later was kneeling at her son's casket, a wet handkerchief crumpled in her grasp. King Barrington stood beside her, silent tears cascading down his stoic face.

Then the scene panned to me, standing guard beside Prince Clark and Prince Tristan, two grieving and inconsolable brothers. Heartache splintered the walls of Castle Farrador, filling it instead with crippling devastation.

A cry lodged itself in my own throat, but I never shed a tear, for to do so would have been to give in. Instead, a brooding fire ignited in my soul, the kindling already made ready by the death of my own mother and the missing of my father. It was so bright and fierce I knew I'd just about explode should anything else add fodder to the flames. Thankfully, Laurel would be my consolation.

The mirror swirled once more, and this time, I was privy to something else. Something shocking.

King Barrington was by the docks with Waldric, holding him by the collar of his shirt, and I found I could understand the apothecary's emotions as if they were my own.

*"You're a dead man. A useless and poor excuse for a magician."* Suddenly, he thrust Waldric backward, the man's feet stumbling upon the landing.

*"I tried my best, Your Majesty. I did everything I could,"*

Waldric pleaded, his round eyes large. From his neck hung a familiar key, a destrier with ruby eyes.

King Barrington scoffed. *"Everything? If you had done everything, my son would still be alive. But thanks to you, Braka's going to fall into the hands of Clark, the most ill-suited of them all. And you say you did everything!"* The king unsheathed his sword and stalked forward, a look of menace in his bloodshot eyes.

Waldric scooted back on his hands, looking up in bewilderment. *"Please, Your Majesty. Is there any way I can earn back your favor? I'll do anything!"*

King Barrington paused, a look of insidious wrath crossing his features. *"Anything, you say?"*

Waldric nodded, swallowing as he stared at the metal tip of the sword. He only hoped for a truce, or some understanding, unaware of the darkness of the depths to which the king would stoop.

*"Then you won't mind if I rid Braka of all Norlocks, starting with your wife and kids."*

The words were throwing knives, cutting Waldric in all his main arteries. *"You wouldn't..."*

*"Oh, but I would. Seeing as you robbed me of my one joy, I'll rob you of yours. You're a sad excuse for a magician."*

Waldric shot to his feet, clenching his jaw as his pulse sped. *"How can you be so cruel? No man can bring back another from the dead, with magic or not. I've only known of One who can—who gives us life and takes it in his time. And you'd see it fit to take the lives of those who've done nothing against you? All because I failed to heal your son?"*

*"How dare you! Albertus was Braka's future!"*

*"And my children are mine! Not all of life is fair, though sickness or blight strike us down."* Waldric's nostrils flared, adrenaline pumping through his veins at standing his ground before Barrington.

The king curled his lip. *"I'm not changing my mind."*

*"Then take my life. It's mine you want, isn't it? Spare my family and take me instead!"* Waldric pleaded. He'd do anything to keep them safe, even if it meant giving his own life.

*"And let them walk freely, reminding me of your failure? No, I'd rather eradicate the filth of the Norlock name entirely. And how much sweeter knowing you're alive to feel the same pain of loss that I feel in my own chest. Yes."* King Barrington smirked. *"I've made up my mind. Your only choice now is to flee Braka by water. If you step foot on this land again, my men will strike you down."*

The scene ended in a swirl of desperation and struggle, as I could only assume was Waldric's way of fighting back.

But then the mirror revealed one last picture, this time of Waldric out at sea, the waves lapping over the lip of his boat. He lay sprawled as if half alive, out beneath the blazing sun. His defeated moans mixed with the howling of the sea winds.

When something suddenly knocked against his vessel, only then did he stir, peering over the edge. It was a cuttlefish, the smallest of its kind he'd ever seen, and it was in dire straits by the looks of it. With a torn tentacle, it struggled to swim.

*"Hold on, little one."* Waldric scooped up the small creature and rowed his boat to the closest shoreline he could find, not daring to step foot on land. He gathered native plants, herbs, and fruits and busied himself by mixing a tincture.

With hatred in his heart and a never-ending string of unassuaged guilt, he had an idea.

*"You'll grow big and strong, little one. Bigger and stronger than anything these waters have ever seen. Then you'll* really *give Braka something to worry about. That, I'll make sure of."*

The mirror sputtered and all the images blurred, swirling in a frantic color wheel until they all faded away. In its place was a smooth pane of glass, its reflection showing once more the lines of my face.

But this time, my eyes were bulging, and my heart hammered against my ribs. Was that sweat? My breaths came in short and ragged bursts. What had I just seen?

By all intents and purposes, this mirror was magicked, as magicked as the apothecary who wielded his herbs like some strange, oceanic magician.

I knew who the captain was now. Captain Aldo was actually Waldric Norlock, Castle Farrador's apothecary. All the pieces to this tremendous puzzle were falling into place. He *was* from Braka after all. But that still didn't explain why he looked so different; he was borderline unrecognizable below the Tides.

His hatred for King Barrington wasn't unfounded, either, much like my own.

A throat cleared behind me, and I felt my hands tighten around the handle of the looking glass. My heart pounded in its cage of bone, but I ignored it, turning around.

Standing in the doorway was the man himself, Captain Aldo—Waldric Norlock.

"I see you've found my mirror again," he said, a knowing look in his eyes. Something in his gaze almost made me think he had planned it all along. The door *had* been opened after all. "What did it show you?"

My mouth went dry. I was still trying to process everything. And besides, could I trust Waldric with what I saw? Could he trust *me*?

He seated himself on a nearby chair and ran his hands through his hair, sighing. "A man gets tired of all his secrets, Huxley. Of harboring it all himself. But I've looked in that same glass repeatedly to know the past can't change. The images are no less haunting now than they were back then."

"What are you saying? Why are you telling me all of this?"

"Because I've seen something else." He paused, hands forming a teepee as he leaned forward, forearms resting on his knees. "You see, in my travels beyond the Herring Sea, I came across that mirror in a sunken city; I knew it was special because the glass is actually a mermaid scale. Thankfully, I'd had the foresight to grab a replacement should the first scale break." He pointedly raised a brow at me, and the memory of shattered glass came flooding back. "It's magical, to say the least, and equally as stubborn. The mirror shows memories, old and new, including the thoughts and feelings to whom they belong. It reveals what it wants in its own time."

He leaned even closer. "It's no secret that we haven't gotten along since you stepped aboard, but recently, I've seen something that convinces me that you and I are not as different as we may think."

I swallowed the bile in my throat. After seeing how King Barrington treated Waldric in the past, it brought to light my own injustice with the same man. Waldric had been poorly mistreated, creating the nefarious Captain Aldo in turn. And what was Barrington's poor treatment creating in me?

"The king's wronged you like he's wronged me, son."

I flinched at his use of the word *son*. He had a lot of nerve to call me that when he was the one who probably had my father killed in the first place.

"What happened to the *Glad Tidings*?" I asked, needing to know the truth.

Waldric blanched at the change in conversation. "What does that have to do with the looking glass?"

"Everything."

Seeming to understand I wasn't backing down, Waldric shrugged. "I sunk it."

My gut heaved. I wanted to wretch. No matter how messed up this man's past was, it didn't give him the right to kill innocent men. "You killed my father. He was on that ship when it went down. Your own callousness against Barrington has turned you into a mindless killer."

It took everything within me to stay where I was and not wring the captain's neck. But if I did, I'd be no better off than the two men I hated most.

"Is that your opinion of me, then?" Waldric's voice suddenly hardened.

I stared him down, unblinking. "I see no reason to believe otherwise."

"Well then, I'm sorry to disappoint you." He stood, pacing the room.

196

Something rankled my nerves, growing disturbed inside my chest. What did he mean?

"I'm not adverse in telling you that I've done many things, some of which I still hold little remorse over, but mindless killing?" He shook his head. "I'm afraid you have me all wrong. There's only one man whose life I want, and he has yet to die by my hands."

"What about that ship? The crew? All these weapons? Surely they're articles of your plunder!"

"The *Glad Tidings* was listing when I came upon her. Jollie finished her off, but only after all the crew got off safely. What happened to them after, I know little of, but I figured a downed vessel or two would be just another slight to the king's name. Same goes for all the weapons; more in my care means less for him." He stopped pacing and looked me in the eyes. "Like I've said, I've done many things, but I've never killed an innocent soul. I'm not all wretched, Huxley, no matter how much my past deems I should be."

Then Waldric-turned-Captain-Aldo hadn't killed my father after all. A strange weight seemed to lift off my shoulders, but another one just as soon filled its place, this one pressing harder. Where did that leave my father now?

"Are you satisfied?" Waldric asked.

"Not yet." I figured if he was man enough to tell the truth, then I could continue asking the questions. "Why did you attack Monty and I at sea? Our boat was perfectly fine until you came upon us."

He rubbed his jaw. "I assumed you to be one of the king's men or the man himself. Braka hasn't released any vessels for years, and I finally thought I'd had my chance at justice." He shook his head. "Shameful, really."

It made sense, though it still didn't broker my forgiveness. The only redeeming quality was that Waldric had tended to Monty's and my wounds, some of which he'd inflicted upon us in the first place.

I stared at the elusive captain, seeing his façade slowly fading. Though, his outward appearance still didn't seem to match up with the Waldric I knew from my youth. Was this even the same man?

"None of this explains how you're unrecognizable. Why do you look so different from those memories in the looking glass?"

The man chuckled, cracking a genuine smile I hadn't seen in a long time. "I've been taking fogwort and orangeroot—appearance-altering herbs with the most bitter aftertaste. Makes you smell like a blasted patch of sod."

*Ah. That explains the grass.*

"It's something new I've been trying. Since you newcomers came aboard, none can be too careful. Figured I'd try hiding my identity for a while."

"Do Cyril and Willa know who you are?"

"Of course! That's why they're so nice to me."

I arched my brow, my lips twitching. *Right.* "Even when you keep them locked up here as prisoners."

The captain had the decency to look ashamed. "It started out that way; fear drives people to unreachable depths, I suppose. I worried they'd reveal my location and the king would make matters worse for not only me, but my family, if he had a change of heart to spare their lives." He expelled a long breath. "But over the years, the Reids and I have grown companionable, almost comfortable in such close quarters. I never told them this, but if they wanted to leave, I would have let them. They just never asked. I'd be lying if

I said I didn't covet their company."

"And Niam and Ondru?"

"Just some fishermen who were floundering off the coast of Kethnar. With no families of their own, I offered them a place to stay, to belong. They tolerate me on most days."

I was starting to feel the same way toward the captain myself. If only he'd let me off this blasted contraption, maybe we'd even be civil.

"Now, are you done with your questions?"

"Will you ever let us go?" I asked one more, voicing the only thing I wanted more than my old life back. He would allow the Reids to walk away freely, so why not us as well?

Waldric rubbed his chin. "Perhaps," he said. "But first, let me tell you what the mirror showed me. It could change some things." He grew serious. "Actually, it could change everything."

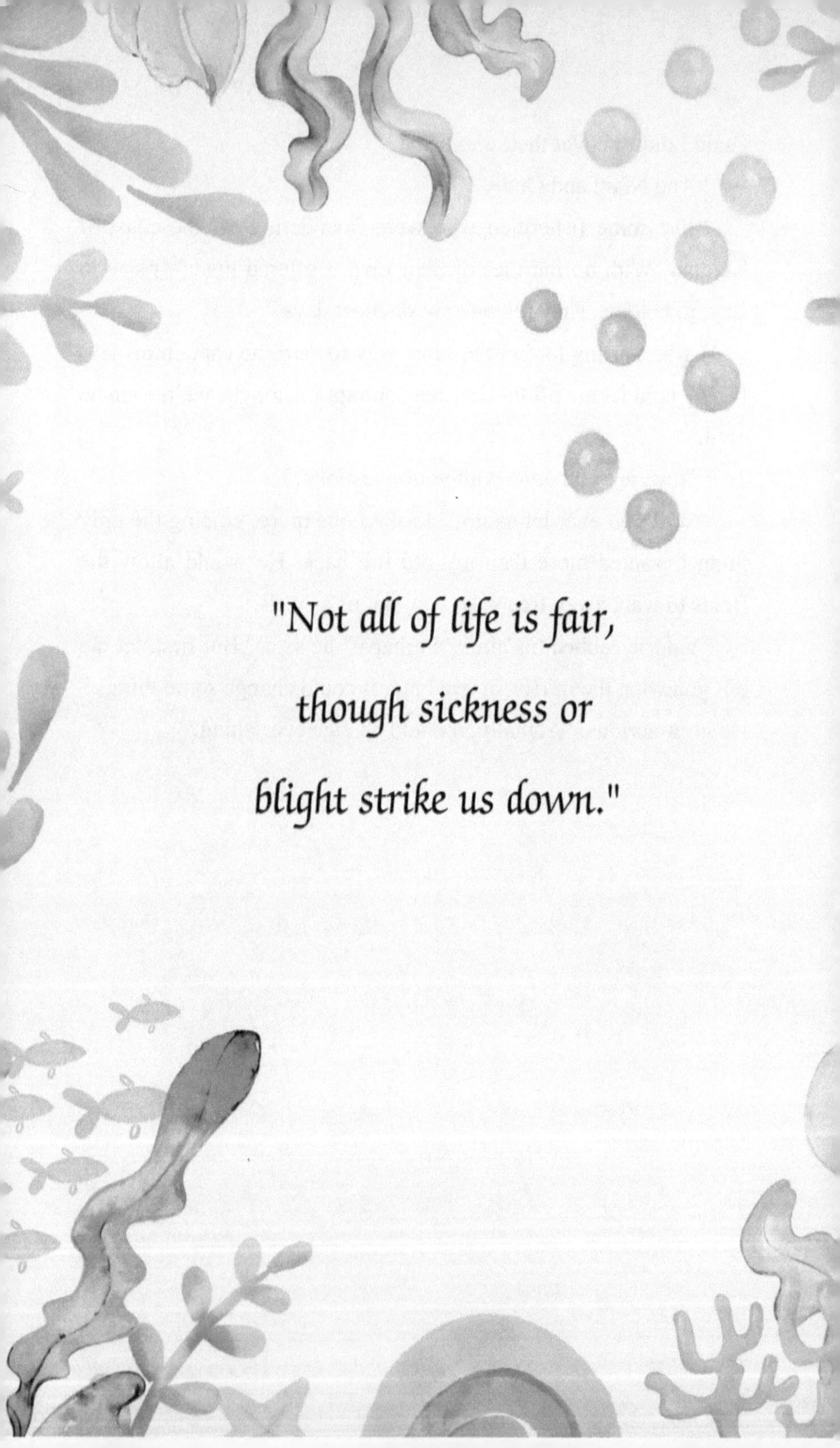

"Not all of life is fair,

though sickness or

blight strike us down."

# Eighteen

## A Rueful Liberation

Waldric took a deep breath and plunged right in. "The king poisoned his own son."

I felt my mouth drop open before the words completely registered. I couldn't have heard him right. "There must be some mistake. The mirror could be wrong!" What kind of man did that sort of thing with no remorse? And to their own child?

Waldric shook his head. "The looking glass tells no lies. As I stared into its depths, it finally revealed its mysteries. The first began with the king lacing Prince Clark's wine goblet with wolfsbane and skullcap; the coward had sent a messenger to forage for the plants, taking a foolish, though thankfully not lethal, dosage of each. And the second of you being dealt a nasty blow to the head and cast aside as carrion, fitted to be framed for the deed the king had administered by his own hands that same day.

"And his infantry followed suit, believing every word he said.

For who would deny their king? They chased you through the halls, as I can imagine you well remember, but the scene ended as soon as you tumbled from the castle window. Which explains much about the condition I found you in."

I didn't know what to say. If I had any doubts as to the truth of Waldric's words before, I didn't now. For how else would he have known about my freefall from Farrador if the mirror hadn't revealed it to him?

"I bear no semblance of dishonesty." Waldric must have misinterpreted my silence. "It wasn't until a few nights ago that I learned the rest of this confounded riddle. Which is why I've decided to speak to you, for your life seems to be uniquely tied to the fate of one prince like mine was to another. And like I said, the looking glass tells no lies."

The strange thing was, I believed him. It was starting to make sense, and those images I'd witnessed, some of them memories and others new, were too real to be mistaken as anything other than the truth.

Confound the blasted depths. I trusted this new version of Waldric. He wasn't my enemy after all. In fact, he'd been a trusted acquaintance before he was ruthlessly discarded from Castle Farrador.

Much like Prince Clark's recent dissolution.

Which reminded me… The prince didn't know the depths of his father's tyranny. The news would crush him. It would crush all of Braka.

"What about the prince?"

Waldric rubbed his chin. "He must learn the truth. In fact, that's all part of the plan I've been working on."

*Plan?* I'd been concocting a plan the entirety of my capture, and *now* the very man who'd imprisoned me was speaking of such things like we were on the same team. Which I supposed we were.

"But there's something else you should know before, Huxley."

A sudden coldness hit my core at the way he rubbed his hands together and sighed deeply. For some reason, I had a feeling I wouldn't like what followed.

I braced myself.

"Your father."

My stomach turned into knots.

The captain continued, "I only know a little, and as I said, the mirror reveals things in its own time..."

"Go on."

"He's alive."

I stood taller, the hairs bristling along the back of my neck. Something electric seemed to course through my entire being. "Alive?" Doubt crossed my mind in that same instant. "Are you in earnest?"

He nodded, and that same somber look remained plastered across his face. I knew he was telling the truth.

My father was actually alive! I'd lived a good portion of my life missing the man or thinking he was dead. To hear the opposite confirmed was jarring to say the least.

My thoughts suddenly turned sour. "Then why didn't he assume his position? Go back to Braka?" To *me*? It was a sucker punch to the gut to entertain the thought that came next: maybe he didn't want to.

"Now here's the finicky thing. The mirror—"

"Reveals things in its own time. I know." I filled in the blanks, quite tired of the mysterious adage.

"Just so. I only saw the truth in part. You see, your father is locked up somewhere, Huxley. Where, I couldn't discern. But it's enough to know that he *can't* go back home even if he wished to."

*Every loving father always comes back for their child if they can help it. Always.*

Suddenly it all clicked. Waldric's words from earlier came flooding back like a tidal wave crashing against my human vessel, threatening to sink me whole. It had been his way of assuring me that after all this time, my father hadn't abandoned me.

Waldric had known. Only part of the truth, but he'd condescended his throne of false pretenses to share it.

It was all so much to take in. My father was alive but imprisoned somewhere. This explained so much and yet nothing at all. Who would imprison my father? The man was as virtuous as they came.

"Do you think…" I had to keep from biting my tongue at the audacity of my next question. "Do you think Barrington has my father imprisoned in Farrador?"

Waldric rubbed his chin. "The thought had crossed my mind. I wouldn't put it past the old coot to devise such a scheme, and right under your own nose no less."

There it was again, that telltale flame, that fire burning in my core. But this time, there was a subtle tempering to the emotion. I still wanted to wield my sword, but it wasn't so much anger as it was conviction which prompted me forward.

"We have to go back." I rushed to the door, impassioned by this growing need to seek justice. Escaping was no longer a matter of wishful thinking. It was a matter of urgency, and if Waldric couldn't see that, then he was denser than a mound of earth. I turned to see if he followed, frowning when I noticed his gaze was distant, locked somewhere on the floor, and his hand continued stroking his chin. "Captain?"

"Prince Clark's life depends on him reclaiming his kingly seat. That snake he calls 'Father' will be retiring soon as per Brakan custom, if I remember correctly."

I nodded, though he didn't see it. But what was he getting at? It was true. Every king, no matter their aptitude, had to step down and give the reign to their first born once they reached the age of seventy; this was to ensure stability to the throne. It had happened to all the kings before, and it would happen to all the kings thereafter.

"And in order for the prince to claim his seat, and to potentially rescue my father, we have to leave here…" I held my breath, hoping against all odds that he might just acquiesce.

"Which brings me to my plan."

"Which is…?" I silently prayed his plan included us getting off the blasted *Neptucadis*.

"Well, it's one that will require a lot of orangeroot and fogwort. More than I have, unfortunately."

I felt my brows draw together. What sort of answer was that? "I'm not sure I follow."

He finally looked my way, and I was taken back by his expression. Was that a smirk on his face? "I'm saying we're going undercover, Huxley. Once we acquire more of the plants, Castle

Farrador will either celebrate their liberation or rue the day we impeached their traitorous king."

My heart rate picked up speed, the muscle pounding so loudly I could hear the blood rushing to my ears. Had Waldric finally succumbed?

"So, we're leaving?"

"Aye. Pack your things. We set out at dawn."

Morning came after another sleepless night.

Peering out of my window, it was evident the *Neptucadis* still bobbed along the ocean's surface like a resting gull, the telltale sign of a rising sun dappling the blue water with crimson and gold.

I was still in shock over Captain Aldo's change in demeanor, but it was bound to be expected. He was Waldric now, and the Waldric I knew back in Farrador hadn't been as callous as this apothecary-turned-sea-captain version; it was only a matter of time before his true nature showed through.

Hadn't Willa and Cyril said as much?

Waldric had told me to pack. The trouble was, I hadn't anything *to* pack. In fact, I had so little I couldn't even rightfully claim the sword I'd stolen as my own either. But it made quick work of things, for I knew filling in Monty and Prince Clark would be another hurdle to cross before we set out.

Before the sun had a chance to climb any higher in the sky, I left my room to tell them the plan, bracing myself for the impact the truth would have on both of them, especially the prince.

"There's no easy way of going about this, so here it goes." I ran a hand through my overgrown locks, watching a nervous Monty exchange an even more nervous look with Prince Clark. I knew the latter had been dealt a tremendous blow, both to his pride and his physical body; it was a lot to process, but the prince had always been of the resilient sort. That alone gave me hope that he'd bear this burden, too.

The three of us sat once more in the dining parlor, but this time, I was the one holding all the secrets. Taking a deep breath, I plunged right in. "King Barrington isn't who we think he is."

Prince Clark furrowed his brow and leaned forward; he didn't say anything, but his gaze was pensive.

"What are you saying?" Monty filled in the prince's silence.

I took a sip of water to buy myself a moment and continued. I told them about Captain Aldo—now Waldric—and his magicked mirror, my father's imprisonment, and ended with the hard-hitting truth about King Barrington.

Prince Clark's shoulders slumped forward, and his eyes looked pained, but I didn't detect an ounce of surprise. Rather, it was resignation, or acceptance, of what he seemed to already know.

"Are you certain?" was his only reply.

I nodded.

"Then what's done is done. Or what's done…*wasn't*, in his case."

"But your own father? How could he?" Monty looked scandalized, the news just about as hard for him to digest as it had been for me to share it.

The only one who didn't seem as affected was the prince.

"I only blame myself." Prince Clark stood and paced about the room. This time, he only slightly leaned on his cane, his every step seeming surer than the last.

"Begging your pardon, Your Highness, but that's the stupidest thing I've ever heard!" Monty added.

"I have to agree with Bates. The only one to blame is your father." How was any of this his fault?

Prince Clark stopped pacing and faced us both. "You don't get it. I should have seen this coming. My father…" He paused, ticking his jaw to the side. "We haven't always seen eye to eye, he and I. And ever since Albertus' death, he hasn't been the same. His love has blinded him, wounded him. I'm afraid Braka's current king has developed a blackened heart.

"If I had kept my guard up, sought the royal wine taster, ensured my wits were about me, I could have prevented his gaining the upper hand. I just never thought…" His voice hitched, straining with sudden emotion, but he swallowed and steeled his features. "I never thought he was capable of bringing about the demise of his own son."

A somber mood descended upon us all, the weight as heavy as it was disturbing. Silence lingered in its wake, allowing my thoughts room to tumble.

Had it been evident that King Barrington's heart had grown cold? Prince Clark was privier to insider information than I had been, to his father's plans and hopes for Braka's future. True, I was Clark's bodyguard, but I wasn't with the man every minute of every day, especially not during the mundane routines of Farrador. My station mostly consisted of trailing the prince when he visited the locals and standing guard outside his bedchamber should a conniving maid seek to boost her fortune.

In most cases, I always thought threats would come from outside Castle Farrador, not from *within*. But all along I'd been led astray. When my gaze was cast outward, I had failed to see the true beast roaming the halls beside me.

Only Prince Clark seemed to have an idea.

The very man continued his pacing. "I can only assume naive Tristan's been outfitted to take over the throne in my stead. My father always thought of him as his puppet. 'Someone more suited to run the throne than you,' he'd often say to me. Which translates to 'someone more suited to manipulate and get what I want.' Seems he wasn't mincing his words.

"He never respected my opinions. I always thought keeping our own people happy was a priority—our first wall of defense. A strong country within allows for stronger borders. But my father doesn't think like that. He wants alliances first, good political standing with our neighbors, and all the while our people are suffering. At this rate, Braka's ready for a revolt.

"And Tristan won't make matters any better. My father's seventieth approaches this October; the sixth to be exact. Which means his reign is almost up. It's customary to crown the new king the very next day, the seventh in our case. But I'm afraid I don't know how long it's been, how much time we have until then."

It struck me that *I* did. I knew exactly how much time had passed since being stranded on this vessel. I'd counted all the tally marks just this morning. "Five and forty days," I said, watching their confused expressions deepen. "Monty and I left Braka's shores on the nineteenth of August. Five and forty days have passed since, which brings us to…" I quickly did the math in my head. "The third of October."

"Blimey, it's been that long already?" Monty said.

"That only gives us four days. Three, more likely." Prince Clark grimaced. "But it has to be enough. It's more than I'd bargained for, anyway. When did you say the captain wanted to leave?"

"At dawn." I glanced out of the porthole. "And by the looks of it, it appears the time has come."

On cue, Waldric waltzed into the dining parlor, his coattails billowing behind him. He threw a sack of what smelled like boiled potatoes on the table and smiled. "Dig in, gentlemen. You need your strength. We have many leagues to travel yet."

"Captain, how long will it take for us to get to Braka?" Though now Waldric, he was still captain of this ship, and old habits died hard.

"About five days. We need to make a pit-stop to Kethnar's shores to retrieve the herbs, and once the tincture is made and applied, we'll be ready."

*Five days?* My heart sank. That was time we didn't have. "But the coronation is in four…"

Waldric pursed his lips, rubbing his chin. "We're hard-pressed, but we'll make it. Jollie here knows how to move; she'll turn five days into three, mark my words." He gave an easy nod. "It's high time we unearthed the truth. Unearthed the Tides and all its secret-keeping." He looked at Prince Clark with a mixture of sorrow. "Sorry, Your Highness, but it looks like your double-crossing father is due for a taste of his own medicine."

# Nineteen

## Back to Braka

We departed soon after Niam and Ondru hauled in the fishing boat from off the island. Waldric assured everyone that the small vessel would be necessary for our return on land if we didn't want to enter Castle Farrador resembling drowned rats.

The captain's plan only required the three of us—he, Prince Clark, and myself—to go undercover, but Monty insisted that he join, too. Waldric eventually acquiesced with, "More bodies, more mayhem. But there's greater success in numbers," before carrying on with the rest of his scheme. "We'll take the herbs, gather our wits, and Niam will row the four of us to shore before heading back for the others. In four days' time, Braka will be liberated." He went about navigating Jollie through the ocean, seeming so sure of his plan, though I could tell doubt pricked his nerves.

But where there was doubt, there was still the promise of

freedom. Willa and her father, along with Niam and Ondru, would be coming to Braka as well. They wouldn't be going with us to overthrow Castle Farrador, but they'd be free to walk the land and remain in Edgefold if they chose. And after many years of remaining stuck inside, it was about time, especially for Willa who hadn't tasted the sun in far too long.

But if I was honest with myself, as much as I wished to be rid of the cage that was the *Neptucadis,* I'd miss the ease of seeing Willa every day. Funny how a prison could grow comfortable depending on the company.

So much was still to be figured out when we went ashore, but Waldric assured everyone that if his plan succeeded, everything would be made right again.

Though I didn't quite know where that put Willa and me. And I wondered why that even mattered.

Two days had transpired when Waldric finally stopped Jollie along Kethnar's southern coast. I stood above deck, watching him in his blubberdud and oxygen tube swim to the shore with a knife and burlap sack in tow. He moved deftly, creeping along the bank and cutting the long, leafy stalks with precision at the base of each plant.

He stuffed the greenery into his bag before he suddenly dove beneath the water's surface. Fifteen…twenty minutes went by, and I was starting to wonder what had become of the captain. Had he suffered a shark attack like my near encounter with the great white?

But the beasts usually didn't come this close to shore.

As if proving my fears to be irrational, Waldric resurfaced and made his way back to the *Neptucadis*. Instead of using the rope along its side, Jollie lifted him with one of her tentacles and placed him on the deck beside me.

"Right, let's get to work." Waldric tipped his head and walked past me as if he'd just been out for a morning stroll and not a rigorous swim. The burlap bag was slung over his shoulder like a limp fish.

I couldn't help finding the scene humorous. Even after all I'd learned, the man was still an enigma.

Once inside, the captain pulled over a table and took out his plunder. Plants and flowers were scattered over its surface along with three jars of something blackish-green. Monty, Prince Clark, and I gathered around, watching him organize and mumble to himself.

"What's this stuff?" Monty held up one of the jars.

"Kelpknot. Only found along Kethnar's coast. When harvested, it produces what I call seapaste."

Waldric plucked off the grayish, fuzzy leaves of what I assumed to be fogwort and mixed them together with the orange-yellow sap of what I guessed was the orangeroot. The scent was unlike anything I'd ever smelled before—like earth and rain intermingling, not wholly unpleasant, though not something I imagined would taste good when swallowed. But then another smell cut through everything else, reminding me once again of my coveted place atop Farrador's keep: fresh cut grass.

Once finished, the captain poured the brownish mixture into

four separate cups, handing them to each of us in turn.

"Drink up. Takes about two hours for the full effects to kick in," Waldric said. "And this is only batch one."

Monty sniffed the concoction, eyeing it cautiously. "Out of how many?" He moved away from the table to drink it in private.

"Two."

Prince Clark downed his glass without a second thought, and I steeled myself for the worst with a sharp intake of breath before doing the same.

I cringed as the slimy liquid coated my throat, tasting as if I'd just submerged my taste buds in a bitter bed of sod. It was clumpy like grass, too. And we had to drink this *again*?

Waldric finished his portion and licked his lips clean, seeming quite satisfied. "Tastes ghastly, I know, but it grows on you after a while. Now for the minksblot."

He grabbed the same ingredients and made a second batch, but this time, he added a drop of fuchsia-colored oil. It didn't alter the smell, but the consistency changed noticeably.

"Is this the second batch?" I asked.

The captain shook his head. "Every disguise needs an antidote. Wouldn't serve us too well if we showed up undercover and remained unrecognizable for its entirety. No point in trying to take back what's yours when you don't look the part." He took the concoction and poured it into four separate vials. "Thankfully, this one is fast-acting, which will come in handy."

The man was brilliant. Or insane. Perhaps a bit of both.

He now grabbed something else—a purple flower and a jar of seapaste that smelled strongly of seaweed and sulfur when opened.

He ground the flower in a pestle, adding a drop of that same fuchsia-colored oil, the minksblot, a spoonful of goop, and chamomile extract. It reeked.

"What in the blasted depths… Isn't one horrid smell enough?" Monty asked from across the room. He looked exceptionally green as he held up the half-empty cup of grassy-liquid, plugging his nose so as not to gag.

Waldric chuckled. "The potency should wear off shortly."

"Another remedy, I assume." I motioned to his new experiment.

He looked up, smirking, before settling his gaze back on his task. "You could say that. A lying tongue is its own kind of malady."

I felt my brow narrow. What did that have to do with anything?

As if sensing my confusion, Waldric continued. "It's an apothecary's job to provide healing, and a mouth riddled with deceit is just as much in need of a remedy as any broken bone. Some herbs provoke looser lips than others."

I swallowed, wondering if I heard him correctly. "A truth-potion?"

"Potion, tincture, syrup. Call it what you want." He shrugged. "How else do you think we'll get the king to play along? Plants have many properties, Huxley, and they're not all strictly used for healing. Some are merely used to get what you want."

I nodded, the orangeroot and fogwort coming to mind; I could feel their effects beginning even now. And then there was Jollie of the Tides. The cuttlefish had done the captain's bidding with little resistance; how much more so would the king once his tongue was under Waldric's command.

But something still didn't make sense. "If you've had the ability to make the king tell the truth all this time, not to mention disguising yourself in the process, why wait until now? You could have exposed Barrington years ago!"

Waldric grew pensive, his hand slowing on the pestle. "I suppose that after a while, a man begins to question the truth of things when there's none but him to ruminate over the past. But there's strength in numbers—enough to remind you a call to action is necessary when so much wrong has been carried out." He paused. "And with the king's birthday approaching, there's no wisdom in waiting any longer."

I nodded my understanding. There *was* strength in numbers; that was why we had an army in Farrador, a built-in brotherhood to shoulder the weight of responsibility. To uphold integrity. Though if they were still my brothers after all this time was yet to be determined.

The captain finished his concoction and poured the liquid, which was now miraculously the consistency and color of water, into an empty jar. And like he promised, the potency of the smell had all but disappeared.

Prince Clark picked up the jar and slowly turned the glass in his hands, studying it. "Do you think it'll work?"

There was a pinch between his brows, and I could tell his thoughts were churning. Like he was trying to reconcile the father of his youth to the monster he'd grown to be. It was one thing to hear the rumors, but it was another entirely when they came from the very mouth of someone you'd once trusted. Especially when that someone was your father.

"Aye. Tried and true. Herblore never fails, Your Highness." Waldric nodded, a solemn look in his gaze. If it was socially appropriate, I would have expected the man to clap the prince on the shoulder like he'd done to me on numerous occasions. The apothecary was more father to us than our own fathers had been.

Instead, he cleared his throat and pulled out his compass before glancing out the window. "Right. Should take Jollie a day and a half to get us to Braka. Then we can carry out the rest of the plan."

Prince Clark nodded. "Let's be on our way, then." He turned on his heel and left the room, a heaviness to his step that wasn't there before.

It was evident he knew what needed to be done, had even anticipated the hard truth coming all along, but that didn't make it any easier. Just because one knew a storm was rolling in didn't mean they could keep the rain from falling. He needed time to process, and I couldn't blame him.

"The prince has got it right, I think. Everyone to their own chambers. I'm instituting emergency rest before this grand adventure. Round two begins tomorrow."

Monty groaned, and I had to bite my tongue to keep from laughing. He had just finished the last of the grassy drink, and his complexion resembled that of a sick child.

Emergency rest would be wise, especially in his case.

We both made to follow after Prince Clark but paused when Waldric's voice stopped us again.

"One more thing." He had a knowing gleam in his eye. "When you awake, don't be alarmed when you don't recognize one another. You won't even recognize yourself."

After Monty and I parted ways, I grabbed a beach plum from the second-floor storeroom. Proceeding to Willa's bedchamber, I only stopped when I noticed the very woman sitting by herself in the dining parlor.

There was still some time before the herbs kicked in and altered my appearance, and I wanted to be sure Willa saw me, the real me, before saying goodbye.

I paused in the doorway, my heart doing something strange beneath my ribs as I watched her twirl a blue chalk pastel between her fingers and stare out the porthole. She chewed on her bottom lip, one elbow propped on the table and her knees gathered up close to her chest. Her notebook was opened to a blank, white page, and a pinch rested between her brows.

She looked almost…sad.

I knocked on the doorframe to alert her of my presence, but I couldn't find it in me to cross over the threshold. "Wil—Miss Reid?"

She glanced my way, and a blush climbed her cheeks. "Mr. Gannon!" She stood at once, a small smile splitting her features. "I was hoping you'd walk by," she said quietly, and the blush only deepened.

*Did she really?* My traitorous heart jumped.

"I was just coming to find you. To say…" I couldn't bring myself to actually utter the word *goodbye.* I didn't want to. Instead, I took a step over the threshold and held her gaze.

It was as if she could read my thoughts, for her smile faltered a touch, and she averted her eyes to study the floor. "Yes. Everything's about to change soon, isn't it?" She rubbed the space behind her ear, and uncertainty lingered in her voice.

I could feel her words slosh around in my stomach as much as I'd heard them. And I couldn't help myself anymore. I bridged the space between us, standing only inches apart from her petite form. "All for the good, I imagine," I said, not quite believing my words. When she didn't look up, I took a half step closer, tucking a finger beneath her chin and lifting it ever so gently. "Willa?"

When she looked up at me, her cyan eyes were large and glossy. Full of emotion like the waters that carried her. "Even the good can hurt sometimes, Huxley," she said, and I felt my breath catch at hearing my name on her lips. "Especially when one's grown comfortable or used to life on the seas."

I nodded, my mouth suddenly dry. "You'll finally be free. And with your father, no less."

She smiled wryly, glancing outside. "Free." It was like she was trying the word out on her tongue, tasting something new. "Yes. I suppose we shall be." She grew quieter. "All that's left is to figure out everything in between." She looked at me again.

Her words implied much, and I felt them to my very core. *Everything that involves living life apart from the ocean. Moving back to Braka. Us?*

She swallowed and studied me further. "And you? What will you do now that you're on the cusp of freedom?"

I glanced out the porthole like she had, seeing my uncertain future unfold before my eyes, then settled my focus back on her.

Out there was freedom, yes, but in here… I'd somehow found something I'd least expected. I'd gained more within this prison of wood than I'd ever achieved on my own. And all at once, leaving this vessel didn't feel as compelling. My heart belonged within these wooden walls more than it did in my own body.

I reached a hand up and tucked a blonde lock of hair behind her ear, brushing the space by her jaw ever so lightly. My words came out quiet, my throat tight. "I suppose all that's left is to figure out everything in between."

Her eyes held understanding. "Everything in between," she repeated softly.

I nodded, lingering a moment longer before dropping my hand and taking a step back.

Something like hurt flickered across her face, making me regret pulling away, but I couldn't bring myself to bridge the gap any closer. Not until I knew the certainty of my future and what sort of life I'd be inviting her into. There was still a chance the plans would fall through, that the herbs wouldn't work.

She deserved more than that.

She deserved more than *me*.

And this was as close to a goodbye as we would come.

There was nothing like going home. It was dark—being in the early hours of the morning—and yet with the water reflecting the warmth of the moon, the world was alight in soft hues. The wharfs and stone walls that proved a barrier between the Tides and Braka finally came into view the closer we rowed toward them. The waves lapped against the masonry, splashing against the wooden docks, while the *Neptucadis* bobbed in the water behind us. A slight mist fell upon our heads and kissed our cheeks.

Waldric had been right. We all looked drastically different, and after struggling to down the second batch of grassy-drink, it was made evidently clear just how changed we'd become. Even still, there were enough commonalities between our old selves and these newer versions to identify each other by. For example, Monty's locks had taken on a blondish hue and his features looked years older, and yet his hair still curled the same way and his eyes still beheld their telltale curiosity. Prince Clark and myself underwent similar alterations, our hair colors changing to lighter shades and our skin wrinkling in places it shouldn't until thirty years from now. And I even noticed the prince's voice climbed half an octave.

But there was something more—we all felt it regardless of our changed appearances—this premonition of despair. Would our mission succeed? Waldric seemed to think so. But plants could only do so much against a powerful ruler. Would the truth be enough?

Suddenly, something along the coast captured my attention, and my eyes were drawn upward.

Monty followed my gaze, his mouth growing slack. He blinked twice and rubbed his eyes before fixing them once again on the object of his surprise. "But that's impossible!" he whispered beside me.

Perhaps the impossible was what we needed right now.

The Edgefold beacon was lit! Though it was faint, none could deny the amber glow exuding from behind the rain-speckled glass of that tower.

"It hasn't been lit in years." Prince Clark's voice held the same reverence as Monty's. He had a special affinity for the beacon, seeing as he knew it and its sister tower in Greymist were a sign of hope and assurance for his people. Before the resurgence of the Crimson Death, it had been lit every day—to lead Brakans home and give courage to those on the mainland. But Barrington shut down the ports and forbade its glow. "How do we come by a miracle such as this? And at this hour where our need is greatest?"

If I wasn't mistaken, I could see a sheen coating the prince's eyes.

Niam rowed on, and the mood shifted amongst our company. Backs sat a little straighter, shoulders a little taller, and our eyes looked ever onward to the horizon.

A quiet reverence settled on all of us as we approached the shore. When our boat hit the wharf and everyone piled out, our task became more pressing.

We'd finally made it to Braka, and on the day of the coronation, no less. This meant King Barrington had already turned seventy and his son, Tristan, was set to be crowned the new king before the day was done. Which meant we had to get moving.

"What about that cloak, Bates?" I pressed Monty, remembering his promise to lend one of his to the prince. We all needed coverage to hide the swords Waldric outfitted us with, and the *Neptucadis* only carried so much clothing.

Monty nodded and ran to the boathouse along the shore, unlocking the door before stepping inside; that shack had been in his family for generations, as proper as a castle was to a king. And there was even a secret passageway that connected the boathouse to the beacon on the hill, a tunnel I'd happily traversed a time or two in my younger years.

After rummaging around for a few minutes, he returned with a crimson, albeit musty-smelling, cloak. He handed it to the prince. "Hope you don't mind smelling like mildew and brine, Your Highness."

Prince Clark chuckled. "I already smell like the confounded sea. What's a little more?"

Cloaks donned, swords strapped by our waists, and the heavens steadily brightening…we were ready, and our time was growing short. It was now or never.

I turned to find Waldric, eager to execute phase two of our plan, but paused when I saw his feet planted firmly on the dock and an unreadable look on his face.

"Captain?"

He ignored me, continuing to survey the land that stretched opposite the ocean and the wharfs. I followed his gaze. Though far away, the pinnacles of Farrador could be seen poking through the grayish morning, the familiar red flags fixed at the tops, but this time lying limp without a breeze to provoke them. And in that moment, I had a strong feeling about what had his mind in a knot.

"Waldric." Using his given name seemed to snap him out of whatever trance he was in.

He looked at me with dull eyes, then blinked slowly. "Excuse me." He shook his head. "Haven't been back…" He ran his tongue over his teeth. "It's been a long time." His eyes narrowed, and I wondered what he was thinking. Last he'd been to Braka, his wife and children had been alive. He'd had a life and future. And now...?

The once-Brakan apothecary balled his hands into fists and set his jaw. He took one step forward, then two, and before I knew it, he was running. Running up the hillside and onto the long cobblestone street that would eventually lead to the castle.

We followed him in silence, ready to put an end to the tyranny that had ruined all our lives. For Waldric, for Prince Clark, and for myself.

He didn't have to say a word.

# TWENTY

## Undercover Usurpation

By the time we reached Castle Farrador, the sky was bright enough to see color. The gray stonework of the castle looked the same as it always did, but Waldric's furrowed brow said otherwise. Since the apothecary had been excommunicated from Braka all those years ago, a lot had changed. Much had gotten worse within those diminishing years, and if we didn't stop Prince Tristan from taking the throne, much worse was still to come.

Prince Clark and I had only been gone from Farrador for a little over a month, but that didn't mean being back wasn't any stranger. Neither of us was welcome here, and at least one of us was supposed to be dead.

As we inched closer to the castle, we stopped at the exterior gates, the barrier intending to keep any and all unwelcome threats out. I used to think the added precaution was wise, like the outer curtain wall wasn't enough protection already. But hindsight's always a spar to the ribs. Now I scoffed at it. The real monster had always lain within, and no amount of gates or battlements would keep the evil out.

Through the iron gates, I noted the drawbridge leading to the lower bailey was drawn up, and soldiers were stationed at the ready should any disruption ensue.

My stomach clenched. There was my comrade, Hugh, standing guard by the barbican, the castle's fortified outpost. Instinctively, my hand jumped to my shoulder, thankfully healed now, but it was a type of wound I knew would linger. True, his actions had spared my life, but did he have any idea that he was working for the enemy?

"Don't suppose you have a fancy plan to get inside," Monty whispered beside me, his words mingling with the approaching dawn.

"As a matter of fact, I do." After Waldric had given his portion of the plan, he'd said we needed to break into Farrador. That's where I took over. "There's a secret entrance into the castle. Discovered the passageway as a child. Discovered all of them, actually."

Prince Clark gave me a look. "And you never told me? I don't know whether to be offended or impressed."

"Sorry, Your Highness. I've gotta keep *some* secrets."

"Speaking of…" Waldric interrupted. The man wasn't one for lingering.

*Right.* I nodded and started to move. I led everyone around the outskirts of the gate and into a wooded glen abutting the castle grounds. As we pressed deeper into the trees, we eventually came upon some boulders, and they grew in size the further we walked.

We stopped when a series of large stones towered all around us, creating a natural circle of caverns and caves. There was even a section where some smaller stones led upward into a spiraling stair, and at the top was a lookout where you could view the valley resting below the trees.

This was the spot. The trees were overgrown, and the shadows cast from the rocks were as recognizable as the birthmark on my ribs. I knew the hidden door was close by; it had just been some time since I last used it. My hands roved over brown and gray stone, searching, feeling along the rough crevices to find that telltale notch, the latch that would prove victory for our entrance into the castle.

"Can't say I haven't been here before," Prince Clark said behind me. He placed a hand on one of the boulders and marveled at its sheer size. "Are you telling me there's a secret door in one of these, and I haven't known it all these years?"

As if in response, my hand found the latch, and a door that looked unmistakably like a rock swung open. A gust of cool, musty air assaulted us in the process.

I glanced at the sky and noticed the sun hanging there amongst the clouds as it climbed, unaware of our urgency and our race against it. It was at least six in the morning now, which meant the villagers would be coming for the prince's coronation within two hours, if the customary time was kept.

I motioned for everyone to follow after me into the passage.

"But it's so dark," Monty muttered.

"Remember the beacon, son," Waldric said, pushing Monty

forward after Prince Clark stepped in behind me.

His words were more than mere comfort. They were truth itself.

*Remember the beacon.*

Aye. We'd do well to remember it even beyond the end of this tunnel.

The passage emptied us into a storage room on ground level. Thankfully, this was where the servants' quarters were, so there was no immediate fear of being caught by the guards.

Though we were in our disguises, we still had to proceed with caution around the castle. If caught by Barrington's men, there would be no telling what they'd do with four suspiciously cloaked individuals.

We could have waited until the coronation-bound villagers thronged the castle gates—blending in would have been no small issue—but after Waldric explained his plan to use the truth-telling potion, he said it was even more urgent for us to arrive early, staking out the royal goblets.

There were many customs within Farrador, and since coronation day only came every thirty to forty years, tradition was its own law—not to be changed or broken. It was customary for the royal family to drink two toasts, bookending the ceremony. To drink before, thanking the old king and acknowledging his years of service, followed by the ceremonial rights and the passing of the crown. And then to drink after, to the good health and just ruling of the new king.

It had been this way for generations, and it would be this way for generations hereafter. Which provided the perfect opportunity for Waldric's scheme to work.

"We're to head for the kitchen," he said.

The very man led the way, knowing every twist and turn by heart despite the years he'd been gone. It would have surprised me, but then again, Waldric had spent many a time in the servants' quarters, nursing the sick back to good health.

It made me think back to Willa. Had *she* walked these same corridors when her father was employed as the harpist? No doubt she had, but the idea of her doing so no longer sent a sharp pang to my heart. It actually ached.

Gads. It'd been less than four hours, and I already missed the woman.

Prince Clark, Monty, and I followed after Waldric. It didn't take us long to locate the double wooden doors leading into the scullery, the smell of fresh-baked loaves and herbed butter tickling the hairs of my nose.

Monty's stomach rumbled, drawing the attention of everyone. He shrugged. "Must not have eaten enough boiled potatoes."

Shifting around our small band, I peered through the slit between the doors and noted a tallow candle burning on the sill and Cook Greta bending over a steaming pot on the stove. She was singing, the song robust and carrying in her deeper voice. And there, on the butcher block, were the royal goblets: two golden chalices lined with rubies around the rims, a set fit for kings, and then subsequent smaller ones that lacked the same adornment, a host fit for the rest of the royal family and staff.

Aside from the glasses on the table, everything was just how I remembered it, the familiar scene a warm comfort to my middle. Cook Greta had always liked me, mayhap she wouldn't mind me taking a "peek" at the goblets.

I made to push through the doors when a hand gripped my shoulder, yanking me back. My eyes met the hard steel of Waldric's. "The blast do you think you're doing? Cook Greta will sound the alarm just as soon as you step foot through that door with you looking as you do now."

Horror washed over me. In my haste to execute the plan, I'd almost forgotten about my altered appearance. I was a simpkin. A fool.

"How do you suppose we get them, then?" Monty was always the one to ask the questions everyone was already thinking.

"We're to create a diversion. Then plant the bait," Waldric said. "Watch and see." He pushed back the folds of his cloak and extracted a small pouch from the pocket at his waist. Once he opened it, the corridor filled with the terrible stench of rotting meat, a smell so pungent it made my eyes water. "This isn't even the worst of it, I'm afraid." He brought a finger to his lips to signal quiet. Slowly, he opened one of the doors and threw the small pouch along the far side of the room, its contents scattering about the floor. It rolled and tumbled until it stopped beneath a low table, completely out of reach. "Give it a moment."

As expected, Cook Greta began fanning the air in front of her. She plugged her nose. When that didn't work, she walked about the room, first sniffing and then plugging her nose some more. "Merciful…of all things holy and good!" She exhaled, running to one of the windows and flinging it open. Then she opened the other one. And suddenly, she exited the kitchen altogether by the side door that led outside.

"Now, if you'll excuse me." Waldric slipped into the kitchen, completely unaffected by the noxious stink exuding from the small space, and laced the two ornamented goblets with the potion. Before two minutes were up, he was back by our sides, a smug look on his face.

"Talk about some diversion." Prince Clark chuckled, clapping Waldric on the back. "What was that ghastly thing?"

"Bandyhorn pear tree and skunk cabbage," he said, like we should already know the plants meshed into that gaseous concoction. "The easiest part's over. Now's the waiting game. You all remembered your antidotes, correct?"

Each of us nodded, tapping the spaces on our person where the vials were stowed.

A sudden thought struck me, and my hand gripped Waldric's shoulder in earnest. "The royal wine taster…"

"What about him?"

"Surely he'll drink the potion, too," I said.

"And all the better for him. What's another honest fool in a throne room of deceit?"

"So it won't matter?"

"*He's* not the one I'll be directing my questions toward," Waldric assured me.

Suddenly, voices sounded along the far end of the corridor, and they grew louder with each passing second. Most likely they belonged to servants, but there was no use being caught standing here.

"Now'd be a good time to show us those secret passageways, Huxley."

I nodded, once again leading our group through the castle and to the closest one I could find. We entered a blessedly empty room at the opposite end of the hall which housed a small cot and a chamber pot in one corner and a built-in closet in another. It was that closet that would be our means of liberation.

I'd accidentally stumbled upon its secret properties when shirking my duty as a young boy. Who would have thought running away from my task would prepare me for the greatest task of my life.

All that was left for us was to enter the passageway and find the one that led to the throne room.

The minutes ticked by soundlessly inside my head. There wasn't a watch or timepiece nearby, but I felt the passing of time keenly.

After navigating the twists and turns of Farrador's secret tunnels, we'd finally made it to the throne room where we waited like mice in the walls, peering out through the cracks in the stonework. The silence was deafening with our ears pressed against the wall of the great room beyond, straining to hear any inclination of sound.

Was it already eight o'clock? Had the ceremony been pushed back?

Suddenly, what sounded like scuffling feet and then, "A word, Your Majesty," echoed beyond the stone.

The muscles in my jaw clenched. I watched as King Barrington entered the room with his red robe billowing behind him, his cane an extra footstep clopping along the stone floor.

That villainous, deplorable…

"What is it now, Parvine?" he snapped at his royal advisor.

"If you'll excuse me, Your Majesty…"

"Get on with it, then!"

"Guests will be here within the hour. Is His Highness ready to take the throne?"

"Why wouldn't he be? My son doesn't cower under responsibility."

"No." Parvine's words were measured. "He does not. Prince Tristan is young, though. Much younger than most kings."

Barrington growled, and I could see the makings of fire in his eyes. "The last thing I need to be reminded of is all that I've lost, Parvine. We all know it should have been Albertus instead of Tristan who's crowned today."

"Don't forget about Prince Clark."

The hairs on the back of my neck rose, and I felt the very prince stiffen next to me. He looked like he was clenching his jaw.

"He would have made a great king, too," Parvine said.

Barrington was silent for a moment before he cleared his throat. "'Tis a pity," he said and walked away.

The remainder of the hour seemed to blur together as guests shuffled inside. I glimpsed bits of the activity through the cracks in the wall, the room filling up swiftly. The faces of the villagers ranged from joy and excitement to uncertainty and unease.

The latter had it right. If only they knew what was about to transpire.

I turned and found Prince Clark as stiff and rigid as before, and I could only surmise what was going through his head. I sincerely hoped Waldric's truth-potion would work. Though for the prince's sake, I half-feared for its success.

"Now's when we move, Huxley. The truth will only last so long, about ten minutes to be exact," Waldric whisper-shouted to me, and I took the hint. We needed to blend into the throng while it still moved; it wouldn't do us any good hiding in the walls forever. And we only had so much time until the potion's effects wore off once it was digested.

We moved about the passage, all the while listening to the whispered conversations from the inner room. Eventually, we came to a wall of solid stone that, when moved aside, allowed us to exit into the adjacent corridor. Looking back, a carved destrier marked the passageway's location, but the average onlooker would only see it as Farrador's symbol.

With little difficulty, we slunk into the throne room, Prince Clark and myself on one side and Monty and Waldric on the other. But before the apothecary left my side, he muttered the words, "Don't be hasty," into my ear, his eyes lingering on the prince.

I simply nodded, not sure what he meant.

Once situated in our respective posts, the atmosphere shifted. Trumpets blared their familiar fanfare, announcing the arrival of the royal family.

First entered King Barrington and his wife, Queen Gertrude,

dressed in their coronation robes of brilliant gold. Following shortly behind was Prince Tristan and Royal Advisor Parvine, dressed in a similar fashion. Relatives of the family entered thereafter, and members of the clergy followed suit. Everyone was flanked by guards.

They made their way to the dais where the king and queen claimed their seats; Prince Tristan and Parvine sat to the right of them, closer to the wall. Everyone else either stood at the forefront of the crowd or near the foot of the dais.

The archbishop of Lammersmith, the cathedral town within Braka's borders, rose from a seat hidden in the back and approached the front of the rostrum, his hands outstretched as a means to silence the excited onlookers.

"Welcome and *nouvo maen!*" the archbishop proclaimed, slipping into the language of old. The man was aged in years that far surpassed the king, a kindhearted individual with soft eyes. "Today is a morning of new beginnings, is it not? And what better way to usher in the start of a new day than with a new king!"

Cheers erupted from the crowd, and King Barrington clapped loudly.

The archbishop proceeded with his speech, providing the customary phrases that elicited claps and eye-rolls from everyone.

I stifled a yawn. The man was anything if not slow.

Eventually, he made it to the beginnings of the first toast, and my nerves jumped to attention. A glance across the room showed Waldric in a similar state, his eyes locked on the king. I heard Prince Clark's intake of breath beside me.

It was now or never.

"The first toast, customary for the retiring king." The archbishop reached for one of the kingly chalices and gave it to the royal wine taster to drink. After a few seconds had passed and nothing happened, he then handed it to Barrington, seated on his throne. Prince Tristan received its twin while the rest of the royal family beheld the lesser-ornamented goblets, all of their drinks tasted and claimed poison-free. Everyone else in attendance boasted no such luck and simply raised their drinks in anticipation.

"We thank you, Your Majesty," the archbishop droned, "for your excellent years of service. For your stalwart faith and commitment to Crown and Country. Braka releases you from your duty with the highest of honor and regard." He raised his own chalice. "To King Gerard Albertus Barrington II! May you retire honorably!"

Everyone raised their glasses and their voices, from King Barrington to the lowliest peasant. Drinks were consumed, applause was given, and suddenly a voice rang out clear and strong above it all.

"Who poisoned the prince?"

It was enough to make the room go silent.

# TWENTY-ONE

## The Returning of a King

It was Waldric, and he hadn't wasted time mincing any words. He stepped out from the crowd and stood in the center of the aisle, his face that of stone. "What really happened to your son?"

Guards flanked his sides immediately, each of them keeping a firm grip on his arms.

Out of the corner of my eye, I noticed Prince Clark's hand stray to his sword. He took one step, then two.

Sensing his urge to jump in amongst the throng, I gripped his shoulder, shaking my head as I held him back. It wouldn't be wise to fight now in a throne room full of people.

I turned my gaze back to Waldric. A muscle twitched in his jaw, but he didn't take his gaze from off the king. *Don't be hasty.* His parting words finally made sense. They weren't for me; they were meant for the prince. He knew this moment would be hard for Clark, and Waldric had wanted me to be alert.

"And who do you think you are? Disrupting the ceremony like a blackguard!" Barrington fumed from his throne.

Waldric narrowed his eyes. "Don't dodge the question, Your Majesty. It would do little good not to comply."

"Comply! To a mere peasant? Bah!" He laughed, looking out to the crowd. "Can you believe this fool? Telling *me* what to do!"

"What really happened to your son?" Waldric asked again, ignoring him.

"His Majesty doesn't have to answer to the likes of you." One of the guards slapped Waldric across the face.

"What does His Majesty have to lose if he answers truthfully? Surely he has nothing to hide." Prince Clark shouted beside me, his face shielded from the crowd. It was wiser to wield words than weapons.

Surprisingly, there were other voices that echoed his same sentiments, and I assumed one of them was Monty's.

Something like fear crossed the king's face, but he steadied it just the same. He shifted in his seat. "We all know the Crimson Death took dear Albertus."

"He's not the son in question. Did you attempt to poison Prince Clark?" Waldric said, ignoring the red mark now blossoming on his cheek.

The crowd moved their gazes from Waldric to the king, watching this curious scene unfold. Only the apothecary-turned-sea-captain would have the gall to stand up to Barrington.

"The notion is preposterous! This man's insane; send him to the dungeons at once, Your Majesty!" a guard shouted.

"You will answer," Waldric said over him.

The king seemed to be biting his tongue, the taste of fear palpable on his face. He held his breath, but that only made his eyes bulge all the more. It was as if he had no other choice but to comply with the truth-tonic after all. He exhaled, and the word was somehow forced between his teeth. "Yes," he whispered.

Gasps erupted from the crowd, for the admission was as clear as day amidst a silent group all holding their breath. The guards at Waldric's sides even loosened their hold a touch as if their limbs were shocked into reality. Queen Gertrude screamed and swooned to the floor, Royal Advisor Parvine attended to her, and Prince Tristan stood to attention at once.

"Your Majesty?" the archbishop said beside him, horror in his eyes.

"But his death wasn't an attempt! I made sure of it!" King Barrington exclaimed loudly, face red, his tongue now loosened with the tonic.

The room was in an uproar.

"Father, how could you?" Tristan's voice rang louder than the rest, shock and pain laced in every feature of his face.

Movement shifted on my right, and before I could stop him, Prince Clark emerged through the throng of overwhelmed people, pulling another round of gasps from everyone.

Even I could tell by the quick glimpse of his profile that he had downed the antidote.

"I'd like to counter your statement," he directed toward the king.

Tristan's eyes widened when he saw his brother. "Clark?"

Barrington paled and jumped to his feet. His face went as white as though he had seen a ghost—which, in fact, he probably thought that's what he was seeing. "But…but it can't be! Impossible!"

The guards stepped away from Waldric and gave both him and Prince Clark a wide berth, obviously uncertain of what was going on.

"Why'd you do it, Father?" Prince Clark's voice was surprisingly even, but his clenched jaw told of his pain.

"I…" King Barrington was aghast.

"It's useless to fight, Your Majesty," Waldric interjected. "The truth always wins in the end." And we only had about five minutes left before the potion ran out.

"You're supposed to be dead!" Barrington said, stepping closer to the edge of the dais, his gaze locked on his son.

"Thanks to your poor skill in herblore, I'm not," Prince Clark gritted through his teeth. "Why'd you do it?"

The king, seeing as it was useless now to rein in the truth, let the words spill vehemently from his mouth. "Because you were too free-spirited, too uninfluenced. You spent more time fraternizing with the common folk than strategizing in the name of politics and war. I knew early on that you'd never make a good king," he spat.

"So you sought to finish me off. Had it been your plan all along?" Prince Clark asked, hurt making his voice tremor. I could tell it took every ounce of his strength not to reach for his sword and brandish it before his father.

"Only after Albertus passed. I knew Tristan was more suited to the throne than you'd ever be."

When Barrington said "more suited," I could only guess that meant "more controllable." That he was able to be puppeteered.

Tristan looked completely offended as if he'd just realized the same thing.

I fished the antidote out of my pocket and moved closer to Waldric and the prince.

"And you framed my bodyguard for the act you so *skillfully* conducted." The derision in Prince Clark's tone was slight, yet anyone could tell he was making a mockery of the very man who had ruined his life.

"The Gannons had been a facet of Farrador for years. To blame the poisoning on him seemed the easiest of solutions. Huxley Senior had already been dealt with, so next came his son…"

*Dealt with.* My heart rate sped at the mention of my father. The contents of the antidote were already coating my throat by the time I pushed through the crowd and stood my ground beside the prince.

"What have you done with my father?" I asked.

King Barrington's eyes widened upon seeing my face, his complexion almost as red as his robe. "You!"

"My father. Where is he?" I needed answers. Now. "In your filthy dungeons beneath our feet?"

"No." He shook his head, his expression still one of disbelief. "In Vastia's prison. Along with the others from his crew."

*Vastia?* That was the next country over. Right between Braka and Kethnar. "What purpose does that serve the Crown?"

"Much. Planning Clark's death was far easier with one less Gannon around."

His words were like a dagger. Just how deep did Barrington's malice run?

As if reading my mind, the king filled in the remaining blanks.

"Your father and his crew came rowing to Braka's shores after the *Glad Tidings* failed; by that time, Albertus had already been gone three months. My men intercepted them at the border and sent them to Vastia for safekeeping. If any word got out of their survival, then families, especially yours, would demand to see them. A pity, really. I quite liked your father."

"You're mad." I already knew Barrington was capable of great evil, but this was another level entirely. "Next you're gonna tell me you staged the Crimson Death."

"You wouldn't be wrong."

"Excuse me?"

"The sea beast, that is. The age-old rumors of the creature are not contrived. Though with my council, the rumors have grown within the past few years and eased Braka to a standstill. Nothing prompts adoration for one's ruler like fear."

"So you've locked our borders, snuffed out the beacons, just to suit your own warped agenda," Prince Clark chimed in. "And our people have suffered greatly because of it! Just walk through Edgefold and Greymist, and you'll see for yourself."

The crowd began to clap in agreement, cheering the prince on.

Tristan took a step back, his face coloring red; he looked embarrassed. I could only surmise no amount of speeches rehearsed under Barrington's tutelage could incite such a reaction.

"I have no need to walk through. I know my people, and my people know me." Either the truth-potion addled his brain or King Barrington was deranged.

"*Your* people?" Waldric finally spoke again. "By what lens do you gauge such hypocrisy? You've had *your* people wrongly accused, inhumanly banished, the innocent slain, one of your own kin poisoned, and you sit here saying you know *your* people!" he sneered, his jaw clenched. "Tell that to my wife and kids."

Barrington's face contorted, his eyes alight with fire. "How dare you! Some lowly peasant chiding me in my throne room! No doubt your wife and kids deserved whatever befell them, if they're anything like you, whoever you are."

Waldric uncorked his vial and downed the antidote in one gulp. Within a few seconds, the change began to take place, erasing the appearance I'd come to accept, the dark brown hair and hazel eyes, for the one I'd recognized as a child, eyes and hair the color of mud. Captain Aldo was no more.

King Barrington reeled, stumbling backward into his throne. "Has everyone from the past come back to haunt me?" He shuddered.

"You've wronged many. Too many," Waldric said, stepping forward with his hand dangerously close to his sword. "Tell me what happened to my family."

Prince Clark and I had received our end of the story, though there was still much to digest. Now it was Waldric's turn to seek justice.

"I spared them."

That wasn't the confession I anticipated, nor Waldric apparently, for something like hope kindled in his demeanor.

"Spared them?" His voice grew hoarse. "Tell me. Where are they?"

"Your wife was sent to the local brothel like the light skirt she is and your wily children to the orphanage. Where they are now is beyond me."

The look on Waldric's face was beyond pained, and a fury burned in his eyes. Maybe death would have been a mercy.

"You lying, lowlife snake!" Forget Prince Clark, it was Waldric who needed watching; he drew his sword and made ready to attack. He would have if the prince and I hadn't held him back. Waldric ignored us, choosing to continue shouting at the king instead. "How long has your heart been blackened, darkened by shadows?"

King Barrington opened his mouth to respond, but it was as if a light had suddenly dawned in his mind. And just like that, I knew our time was up. The truth-telling potion only lasted so long, and it had run its course.

Realizing what he'd just done, and by the looks of all in attendance, not to mention Waldric's sword, King Barrington paled and began to shake. He cleared his throat and shifted uncomfortably on his feet. "Surely you don't heed the tales of an enraptured king filled with drink!" he said to the crowd. "This can all be explained."

"You've done all the explaining yourself!" someone from the crowd shouted.

"*You're* the blackguard!" came another.

"How could you?" Tristan said again, this time with tears in his eyes.

Panic shone on the king's face. He retreated behind his throne and gestured to his guards. "Don't just stand there; seize them!" He pointed to the three of us at the center of the room, his eyes widening upon seeing Waldric's blade still unsheathed. "Arrest these men!"

No one moved.

Sensing his authority was diminishing, the king made a run for it, as fast as one could with a cane, and tried to sneak out the back behind the dais. But Hugh, my old friend who had been guarding the barbican earlier this morning, seized him by his robe and dragged him forward to face the room like a man. Another guard grabbed his other side, flanking our king who had fallen from grace.

Hugh made eye contact with me and tipped his head. A silent understanding passed between us, an unspoken apology, as his gaze raked over my shoulder—the place where his sword had left its mark. I knew he could never take back what was done, but I understood why he had done it.

Barrington's reign had been its own kind of poison.

The archbishop cleared his throat and stepped forward. "Well, these are grievous times, indeed. Dark are the days that have befallen Farrador as of late, and darker still is the heart of one who should have considered all of yours." He looked at the king and shook his head, removing the crown from off his pate.

"I'd fear for Braka's future, but we've been spared. Some small grace amidst this tragic tale." He turned and looked at Prince Tristan, frowning slightly before dipping into a short bow. "I'm sorry, Your Highness."

He then turned to Prince Clark. "But there's hope with the return of our prince, our new king." He walked down the steps of the dais and met Prince Clark on the floor.

The archbishop nodded. "If you would, Your Highness." He gestured for the prince to kneel, right then and there in the center of the throne room, fish-smelling cloak and all. "I know this isn't the customary way, but seeing as the circumstances…"

"I wouldn't have it any other way." Prince Clark knelt.

The archbishop cleared his throat. "Your Highness, with a heavy heart in anticipation of a brighter future, I, by the power vested in me, given by the Maker above and by all earthly authority in Lammersmith, Edgefold, Greymist, and the regions beyond, crown you His Royal Majesty, Clark Guthrie Barrington, King of Braka."

Applause erupted from the crowd as the crown was placed upon the prince's head. And when he stood, all in attendance bowed.

"Your Majesty, what say you?" the archbishop said. "What shall we do with this treacherous king of old?"

King Clark cleared his throat, a sheen coating his eyes, much like how they'd looked gazing upon the beacon. But instead of the hope witnessed by that light, they were now covered in pain. A pain so deep that its roots ventured into pity. "His crimes deserve execution," he said.

The archbishop nodded. "Yes, Your Majesty."

King Clark held up his hand. "I said he deserves execution, but the punishment he receives will be less than acquitting." The room held their breath as they awaited the new king's verdict. A single tear streamed down his cheek as he locked eyes with his father. "Mercy. He'll receive mercy in execution's stead."

"Mercy?" Waldric sounded offended.

"In Vastia's prison. Where he can spend all his remaining days thinking about everything he's lost, with the hope that his failings bring him to repentance. Or else rot away for all eternity in his own self-imposed misery."

Though still frail from his bedridden weeks, King Clark looked stronger and fuller in that moment than his father had ever been.

And when the sun streaming in through the window from outside shone upon his countenance, no man had ever looked kinglier nor more worthy of the crown he now bore.

"It shall be done." The archbishop nodded to Parvine, who had the deranged Barrington dragged out of the room and prepared for his imprisonment. Then he turned to face Clark, kneeling and raising a cry high in the air. "Long live the king!"

As the crowd took up the cheer, King Clark's verdict weighed heavily in my chest. *Mercy.* Did Barrington deserve it? No. The man was vile. But something inside me burned anew, and this time it wasn't fire. It was emotion. Hot tears stung the corners of my eyes.

How could a son so willingly pardon his father for such heinous crimes against him? Barrington deserved death, and yet Clark didn't think it was his position to grant it.

*Forgiveness.* Hadn't I just received my own? But it was another matter to give it. The word churned my stomach, but maybe this was just another aspect of the Maker's grace. If Clark could forgive his father, then maybe I could forgive mine. Forgive Laurel and all the times I'd been wronged. Forgive Barrington.

I looked at King Clark again, and a deeper respect for him burgeoned inside my chest. He was always meant to wear that crown regardless of his order of birth.

And it was in that moment that I knew I wanted to be more like him. I was ready to let that seed take root.

I opened my mouth, eager to join in with the rest of the attendees. With a battered heart filled with hope of restoration, I watched as Clark walked toward the throne and shouted, "Long live the king!"

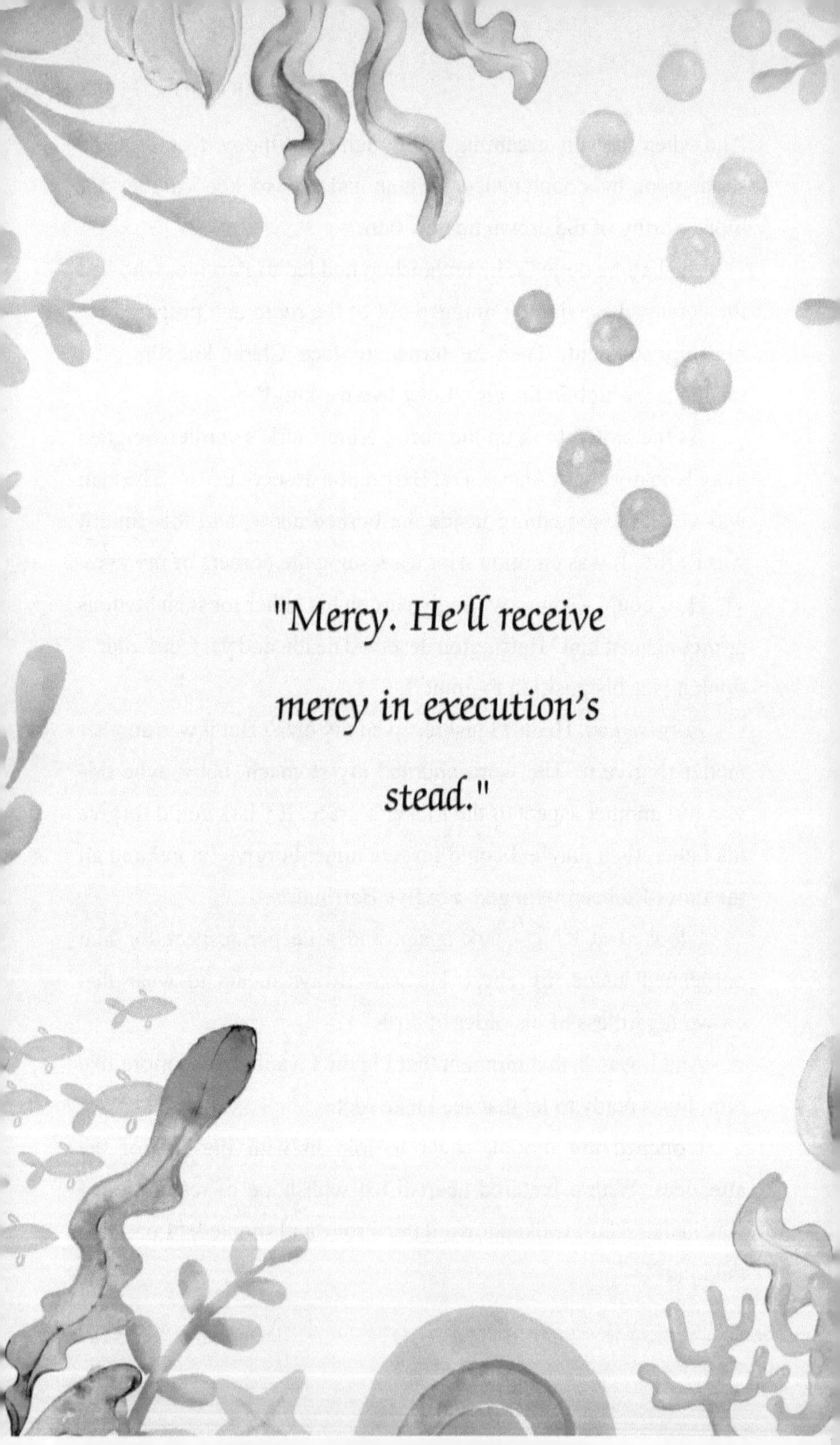
"Mercy. He'll receive mercy in execution's stead."

## Endings and Beginnings

The cool breeze tousled my hair, caressing my beardless chin before whisking off to nip someone else on the face. It was always this way atop the old keep, a windy haven under the sun. The days were growing colder, the heart of autumn revealing a wall of golden and red trees where only green had been a few short months ago.

It had been three weeks since Clark was crowned king, and in that time, the fishing ports were back open, the poverty amongst Edgefold's lower class was slowly being remedied, and Monty had found purpose in his job again. The beacon, which his brother had taken a chance at lighting upon our boat nearing Braka's shores, was always shining; that was something King Clark said was a priority.

Speaking of Monty, he and Gloria Silke were due to ring in their nuptials by the coming of the new year. The man had finally found his tongue at long last. Monty would never admit it, but I had a feeling Waldric may have helped in that department; he was an apothecary whose herbs provoked loose lips, after all.

Niam and Ondru were given jobs as boatswains and shipbuilders per request of the king, and they resided under Monty's management. Being from Kethnar, their hearts were always at ease by the water, where they could look upon the unchanging moon and sail at their leisure.

Jollie was released from Waldric's care, seeing as she was no longer needed to do a captain's bidding. And the *Neptucadis* was detached from her tentacled form, slipping to the bottom of the Tides where the MFB *Glad Tidings* rested, marking the beginnings of a graveyard of ships.

But even so, that didn't stop the visits. Once a week, Waldric would depart from Farrador with some catmint, the minty smell lingering in his wake, and I had little to wonder who he was seeing; that creature had grown attached to him after all those years, and a bond like that wasn't easily broken. Part of me wondered who needed whom more.

Waldric ended up finding his wife and children. The stories were too sad to repeat, but after scouring the brothels and the local orphanages, he paid for their releases and took them home—to Farrador where he was reinstated as the castle's apothecary. I'd never seen the man so happy. He still loathed Barrington and never brought himself to utter the man's name, but he was learning to forgive.

Something we all seemed to be learning these days.

My father... He, and what remained of his crew, was finally

released after being stuck in prison for the past ten years. Vastia's king didn't realize he was keeping hostages of a heedless war, thinking instead he was harboring criminals. And all because of King Barrington's malice. Huxley Senior ended up coming home the same day Barrington left to take his place, to atone for his actions in Vastia's prison like the criminal he was. I heard my father had some words with the old king, but mostly, I heard the journey was rough on his weakened body.

We'd spent a little over two weeks getting reacquainted, assuaging hurts and easing guilts we'd been carrying for years.

*"It was never supposed to be like this, son."*

*"I know, Pa."*

*"I'm so sorry."*

Misty-eyed and with a lump in my throat, I nodded. *"Me too."*

We'd hugged, we'd shed some tears, and we'd been learning how to exist in each other's company ever since. And slowly, gradually, the fire in my middle eased into a warm ember. It was strange getting a second chance at living the life you'd always dreamed of having; the impossible became possible overnight.

The same went for Queen Gertrude. She thought she'd lost Clark forever, and now he was the king. How joy mixed with grief. She and Tristan quietly resided in Farrador, Gertrude learning to live her days without her husband and Tristan learning to take ownership of his own life. It was a low blow to realize he'd been his father's puppet all along, but his brother's homecoming was easing the sting a little; he hadn't wanted to be king after all.

Their family was mending, much like my own.

And what about me? Well, there wasn't much to add. I'd

reunited with Verdun, our rides through the nearby meadows invigorating for the both of us. King Clark reassigned me as his personal guard, and we'd spent more time outside the castle grounds than I'd thought suitable for a new king.

Life was returning to normal, and yet....

Not quite so. There was this funny feeling inside my chest, a space once vacant and hollow, now grown so large it needed filling. Preferably with burnt sweet rolls, late night conversations, and everything in between.

Suddenly, the wind rushed past me again, but this time, it brought words. And in it was a voice as angelic as the starry host at night.

> *Hearts are mended under the brilliant sun*
> *Words tender when spoken, not won.*
> *And beneath the moon, two souls find rest*
> *For in the midnight the light shines best.*

I knew that voice. The words were clearer and stronger the closer they came, and when I turned, there was Willa standing at the top of the stairs, looking utterly enchanting in a dress of palest green.

I found myself staring unabashedly, forgetting to blink.

"King Clark said I might find you up here." She smiled, walking over to where I stood, leaning her arms against the battlement beside me. Her gaze raked over the grass by our feet and then out toward the changing trees. "So this is where you come? It's beautiful."

I was rendered speechless. I'd never thought Willa would be in my sanctuary, but with the fading light of the sun caressing her golden locks, she looked like she was right where she belonged. A facet of Farrador, much like the crimson flags on the highest pinnacles.

"Father said I need to report back at eight. There's a ball tonight in the king's honor, and I'm to play the harp." She sighed.

I knew that sigh. Willa was a gifted musician, but I knew where her heart truly lay: in the artistry of a paint brush or a set of pastels.

King Clark had been kind enough to reinstate Cyril as Farrador's harpist, but with the aging man's shaky hands, he declined. Thus, the job was offered to his daughter, Willa, who took the opportunity in his stead. Both of them lived in the castle, and as far as I could recall, so did her fish, Story. The Reid clan dwelled permanently in Farrador's guest wing on the third floor just above my own.

I cleared my throat. "Surely the minstrel and fiddler can take up the tune should you need time to recover." *All that's left is to figure out everything in between.* I swallowed, pressing my luck and taking a step nearer. "And maybe even allow time for a dance or two with a smitten, lowly soldier."

She didn't have to look up for me to know a slow blush climbed her freckled cheeks. But when she did, she seemed to be searching my gaze for something, and appearing to have found it, smiled knowingly. "Yes. There might be time for that."

We grew quiet, the gentle tug of the wind drawing us closer. The familiar barred owl called into the approaching night, and the beacon, though a pinprick from this distance, could be seen down by the shore, glowing amidst the gathering darkness.

It was a crisp but perfectly autumnal evening. And when my hand found Willa's resting along the cool stone of the castle, fingers intertwining with hers, we stayed like that until the sun set and the ball began, the owl's song a prelude for the encroaching night and the rest that was to come.

*The End*

"There was an end to our voyage under the sea."

— Jules Verne, *20,000 Under the Sea*

# Glossary of Captain Aldo's Medicinal Herbs:



Amla - small, green fruit; treats fevers, prevents heartburn, and deters aging

Bacopa - white-flowering, creeping herb; helps with positive brain function

Bandyhorn Pear Tree* - medium-tall tree that resembles an oak; produces nuts shaped like a pear; when crushed into a powder, it smells like rotting fish

Bearberry - dwarf shrub with red berries; treats inflammation of the urinary tract; the whole plant, especially the leaves, is toxic in high doses

Bee Pollen - increases energy, relieves inflammation, and serves as an antioxidant

Calendula - orange-flowering plant in the marigold family; treats various skin ailments such as eczema, allergies, and rashes

Catmint - purple-flowering plant; can be used as a sedative and as pest repellent with its minty odor; cats (and occasionally cuttlefish) love it

Chamomile - white-flowering plant; relieves anxiety, relieves mild pain, and fights mild skin irritants; when used in the truth-telling serum, it aids in the loosening of the tongue

Chicory - bright-blue woody plant; aids in digestion and protects against diseases to the liver and spleen

Comfrey - purple-flowering plant; used as a poultice to stop bleeding and heal broken bones; may cause severe liver damage if used too much

Echinacea - purple coneflower; treats sore throat and is used as a supplement for the common cold and other infections/viruses

Fogwort* - grayish, fuzzy plant located along the shores of Kethnar; smells like grass and is used to alter the appearance

Hawthorn - small shrub with red berries; treats heart failure and promotes a healthy heart

Kelpknot* - dark green plant located along the shores of Kethnar; when harvested, it produces blackish-green goop called *seapaste*

Lion's Mane - type of mushroom; used to improve the memory; speeds recovery of nervous system injuries

Maca Root - green, medicinal root plant; the root is harvested and used to increase energy and balance hormones; smells of butterscotch

Minksblot* - fuchsia-colored oil from the *minkweed* plant; helps diffuse strong scents

Motherwort - small, pink-flowering herb with large green leaves; calms anxiety and lowers blood pressure

Mullein - common weed; soothes the respiratory tract and aids in breathing

Orangeroot* - like its name, it has orange roots and sap; located along the shores of Kethnar; smells like grass and is used to alter the appearance

Plantain - common weed; reduces inflammation and heals

wounds

**Poppy Flower** - flowering plant (comes in a variety of colors); a narcotic; typically used to treat pain or induce anesthesia

**Rue** - evergreen herb with yellow flowers; sets the body free of a variety of diseases and poisons

**Sage** - green herb; strong, earthy-mint odor; a cleaning agent, pesticide, and generally known as the "cure-all" for all infections

**Skullcap** - blue-purple flowering herb; known as "mad dog" in the common tongue; eases muscle tension and aids in sleep; has the ability to slow the heart rate

**Skunk Cabbage** - maroon-flowering plant; smells like rotting meat

**Valerian Root** - pink or white-flowering herb; helps promote healthy sleep due to insomnia

**Wolfsbane** - blue/purple ornamental flower; the entire plant contains toxins and is extremely poisonous; should only be used on rare occasions

**Willow Bark** - grayish bark from a willow tree; reduces pains and fevers; best used in tea

**Yarrow** - yellow-flowering plant; reduces inflammation and aids in wound care

*Note: Many of these herbs/remedies have side effects. Be careful should you choose to ingest any of them.*

# Acknowledgements

I write this portion of *Unearth the Tides'* tale with a full heart. Like the crew on the *Neptucadis*, so many hands go into making a story what it is, into making it come alive. And in some way or another, you've all helped breathe life into Huxley's story, giving me the encouragement to keep going.

Firstly, I want to thank the *A Classic Retold* team, for Allison Tebo, who reached out and asked me if I'd like to join. What an honor! It has been nothing short of an adventure, and getting to work with you all—Emily Hayse, Jenelle Leanne, Emily Golus, Nina Clare, Allison Tebo, Hannah Tindle, Penny Kearney, Rosie Grymm, and Tor Thibeaux—has been a great delight; I feel spoiled to be thrown into a mix of such talented writers. I can't wait for the world to read all of our books.

A special thank you also to Mike Golus, Emily's husband, for creating our *A Classic Retold* website. It looks awesome!

Also, I want to thank Jules Verne himself. Without his *20,000 Leagues Under the Sea,* my retelling would have been impossible to write. Though he is no longer with us, his stories still carry on. What a legacy!

A huge thank you to all my alpha readers: Renae Powers, Robin Degan, Jennie Ryan, Kayla Jones, and Emma Dryden, who all read *Unearth the Tides* at its literal worst and gave me helpful critiques and encouragement despite its rough shape.

And to my beta readers, my second and crucial line of defense:

Alexus Weibe, Ella Meyer, Tara Koch, and Valerie Cotnoir, thank you for all your helpful feedback, giving me the push to go a step further and really dig into the emotions of my characters, especially Huxley.

To all my Earth-Treaders—my street team—thank you for your continual support in helping to launch this story. I couldn't have done any of this without your help. You're all amazing!

Thank you to my wonderful endorsers—Nova McBee, Chelsea Bobulski, Erin Phillips, Erica Dansereau, Caitlin Miller, Jane Maree, and Jordan Taylor Nilan—your words of encouragement mean so much to me. As someone who is inspired by your stories, I feel so blessed you've taken a chance on reading one of mine.

A special thank you to Nova McBee for being an awesome critique partner and mentor for this story. Your help and encouragement have been invaluable. I appreciate you so much.

For my dear friend and editor, Caitlin Miller, it was a pleasure working with you professionally! You're always one of the first people to read any of my writing, and it was such a gift having you edit my words for publication. I am so blessed to know you!

For my cheerleader and proofreader, Micaiah Keough, working with you is always a joy! Seeing your little icon pop up in the Google Doc is something I'll never tire of, and I'm so thankful for your keen eye and attention to detail. You're the best!

For my writing friends, sisters in Christ, kindred hearts, and so much more, Jordan Taylor Nilan and Erin Phillips, you both are huge blessings in my life. As the writing ebbs and flows, you two remain constant buoys amidst the churning and tumbling waves, encouraging me to keep going and always pointing me back to

Christ. I love you both more than you know!

For my family, who oftentimes doesn't know what number story I'm working on, thank you so much for all your love and support. I'm so thankful for parents, brothers, and sisters-in-laws like you. Love you all!

For my dear husband, Zac, thank you for believing in me and encouraging me in my creative pursuits. I adore you from head to toe, and I'm so blessed that you're mine. And we can't forget about Moo, our cat. Thank you, little floof, for sleeping on my toes and warming my lap all those late nights of writing.

Thank You, God—my Maker—without Your gift of story, I wouldn't be able to write at all. Thank You for Your grace that we so often reject and try to achieve by our own doing. Like Huxley, may we all come to a point where we realize You are more than enough, reminded that our penalty of sin has already been paid.

And for you, dear reader, thank you for picking up *Unearth the Tides* and taking a chance on this little story. I hope you enjoyed it and that it brought you some encouragement!

Alissa J. Zavalianos grew up in New Hampshire and currently lives there with her wonderful husband and their adorable cat Moo. As a child, she always had a love for nature, books, and fairy tales, and as she grew older, that love bloomed all the more. Alissa loves Jesus and is inspired by birds, mountains, castles, Tolkien, Lewis, and the way a cold breath of wind feels on her bare toes.

Feel free to follow Alissa on her website https://alissazav.wixsite.com/website and on Instagram @authoralissajzavalianos.